OF THREE FAMILIES

Denis Dwyer

High Play Publishing

CONTENTS

To Dale, as always

FROM FORGE
TO FARM

The horse plunged in its traces as the shrill whistle of the steam merry-go-round in the paddock opposite pierced the air. And then with a terrified snort and explosive surge, the ride from hell began for the short, elderly lady in its gig. The horse bolted down busy Gloucester Street and with a great clattering of hooves and screech of wheels, careered round into Colombo Street, scattering people in its path. The lady barely clung on, knuckles white. Moments before, she had been quietly waiting for her daughter to return from shopping. Now she was in deadly peril of the gig capsizing or smashing into one of the shop verandas or one of the vehicles along the way. Even worse, God forbid, into one of the huge tramcars trundling down the street for Christchurch in 1892 was a busy, burgeoning town. The animal was beside itself with terror, eyes wide, nostrils flaring, ears pinned back. People along the way rushed screaming and shouting onto the footpaths and into shop doorways. The gig swayed left and glanced off the veranda post of a confectioner's before crashing back onto the street. The lady's large hat stayed on thanks to the four-inch steel pin securing it, but by now it had slipped over her eyes and she couldn't spare a hand to raise it. The ride had become a hurtling, blind nightmare. By toughness and great fortune, she remained with the gig, clinging on with all her strength and will. She knew only too well that to tumble out could bring the gig with its great iron wheels crashing on top of her, crushing her chest or limbs, maiming or killing. She was old but she was robust. She had been a pioneer, helping break in the land with her husband, and she was not ready to go yet. She hung on, praying for the fearful passage to end.

Then, as if by a miracle, the horse began to slow and then stopped, the suddenness almost jerking her out the front of the gig. A long, high empty wood cart had been pushed directly into its path, leaving it nowhere to go. The cart was too big and solid to go through and too high to jump. In moments the young man who had watched the wild progress down the street and pushed the wood cart into place, was at the horse's side, restraining and calming it. The lady, Mrs Eliza Goodwin, sat back recovering her breath, calming her heart.

'You were lucky m' lady. Another moment or two and the gig could have been over and you with it.'

The speaker was solidly built, of average height with merely the suggestion of a moustache, with closely cropped dark hair, in a working man's clothes. He was surprisingly composed, considering the circumstance. He had hazel eyes full of kindness and a solicitous manner about him, focusing on her and seemingly oblivious of the plaudits of the crowd that had gathered. He had emerged from The Red Dart Livery Stables and Smithy across the way. Then an older man appeared, bearded, large and loud, in work shirt, moleskin trousers and hat.

''Well done Toby my boy,' he said. 'I see you saved the day.' He went to the horse and ran his hand as big as a plate gently down its face while it stood quietly, breathing heavily.

'I was in the right place boss,' said the young man. 'I heard the hullabaloo in the street and saw I could safely stop the horse in its tracks.'

The lady had by now recovered some of her breath and stepped from the gig to comfort the horse.

'Mrs Stanley Goodwin, I believe,' said the older man. 'You must have had a nasty fright there, m' lady. That damn steam whistle set the horse off no doubt. The same thing happened yesterday. That place needs closing. Horses and modern contraptions don't mix.'

'Mr Wallis, isn't it?' she said, turning towards him. 'Mr Goodwin has spoken of you. I believe some of our horses have been in your care. Your young man came in the nick of time.' She extended her hand to Mr Wallis. She then turned to the young man Toby.

'Eliza Goodwin.'

'Toby Page.'

'Thank you for your help. I believe I owe you a great deal. You showed extraordinary pluck. I was beginning to think I was a goner.'

'Pleased to have helped,' he said and turned again to the horse which now stood drooped and shivering.

'You'll be needing another horse to get home,' said Mr Wallis. 'This one's done its dash. You can rest it here and pick it up later in the week. Meantime m' lady, you've had enough of a shock. Let Toby here drive you home.'

Mrs Goodwin protested she did not want to be any trouble and that she had a daughter with her, but Wallis insisted Toby take her home in one of the firm's buggies. By the time the two-horse buggy was ready, Mrs Goodwin's daughter, Priscilla, had appeared with a large shopping bag in each hand. Bystanders had pointed the way and she had run the best part of two streets. She was much taller than her mother and her long legs had carried her swiftly but she was quite out of breath and gasping, her face creased in concern. Eliza Goodwin assured her she was fine, thanks to the intervention of Toby Page. Introductions complete, Toby took the reins and headed straight north to the Riverside Station of Stanley Goodwin.

They talked all the way. Toby could never get enough information about farms and farming. He was a town boy but his heart was in the country and with animals. He had worked constantly with horses since age 12 and was acknowledged to have a way with them. He had, too, an artless charm about him that enabled him to mix equally well with lady or commoner. His mother Minnie mixed with all sorts and she and his nan took pleasure in speaking well. Toby had always loved language himself. There were no 'aves' or 'ads' in his conversation and sometimes he used words that would have his workmates scratching their heads and asking such as, 'What the 'ell is 'affinity' when it's at home?' By the time they neared the station, he had drained Mrs Goodwin of an immense amount of information. She had explained that her husband had been an early emigrant and had entered the service of the State as a surveyor. How, when he acquired Riverside, he was one of the first to turn a furrow in Canterbury. She and Priscilla spoke of their nine miles of country on the Waimakariri River with sheep and cattle as well as crops, their other property which ran to the foothills of the Alps and their 52 station hands, besides the household staff. Talk shifted to the seasonal rhythm of life on the estate. Finally, she called a stop to it though Toby was keen to hear more.

'We've been talking nonstop about us,' she said. 'What about you and your family?'

'There's just my mother, my nan and me,' he said. 'You might have heard of my mother. Minnie Page.'

'Not the Minnie Page?' she said. 'The suffragist and painter?'

'Minnie Page is your mother?' echoed Priscilla.

'The one and the same,' Toby said, unsure what their next response would be.

'We are great admirers of your mother, though some are so bloody-minded they will not have a bar of her thinking,' said Priscilla. 'What was it the member for Ashley said when Sir John Hall's amendment about the women's franchise was discussed? "You might as well give the vote to dogs and children".'

'Where does your mother get the courage to speak as she does?' said Mrs Goodwin. After a moment's reflection she added,

'From the same place, perhaps, her son gets the gumption to stop a bolting horse.'

'What became of your father, may I ask?' said Priscilla. She was never one to hedge her conversation and besides, he was such an open young man, she was sure he would not take offence at the question.

He paused before he answered. 'I know only that he died soon after I was born. A fall from a horse. I never knew him. It has been just my mother, my nan and me at home. And Mr Wallis at work. He took me on direct from school and I have been with the stable and smithy since, learning the trade. Mr Wallis is a good man, demanding but fair, and I have much to thank him for.'

They drove on to the homestead, a splendid manor house at the end of a splendid drive of poplar trees. There, Mr Goodwin emerged, short and squat with a friar's ring of white hair. He looked expectantly at them with keen, intelligent eyes as they neared.

'Good business practice,' he said. 'Leave with one horse and come back with two.'

'Bessie had had enough for the day,' said Mrs Goodwin.

'So had mother,' said Priscilla and recounted the day's adventures.

They invited Toby in for a cup of tea and buttered scones before his return to town. Toby ensured the horses were watered before he stepped inside the massive doorway. He gazed in wonder at the luxurious furnishings and at the ornate staircase winding up out of sight. Priscilla drew his attention to a painting in the hallway. It was a landscape by Minnie Page, 'Summer, Governors Bay'. Toby gazed in pride at his mother's work. Minnie had studied at the Canterbury College School of Art, eventually excelling in studies of people which was how she made most of her living now, along with a little teaching. She did portraits by commission and he had heard her extolled for showing the essence of her subject without tricks. Toby remembered when that landscape was painted. He would have been no more than eight. They had stayed with a friend at Lyttelton and driven out to the bay at the weekend. The bay had been just like that, with the light playing on the water and boats bobbing. The design drew the eye in and the colours were fresh and sparkling and a little dreamlike. He was proud his mother painted what she saw and felt without keeping to dull convention, and that she said what she thought without looking for favours.

While Priscilla chattered on with him at afternoon tea, Eliza Goodwin withdrew and Toby saw her speaking earnestly with her husband. Before he returned to the buggy, Stanley Goodwin was at his side.

'My wife tells me you want a life at farming.'

'Yes, I want that more than anything,' he said.

'It's not an easy life,' said Stanley Goodwin. 'It's not all this,' he said, sweeping an arm to indicate the comforts. 'We came here with nothing and slept in the bush until we could build a rough whare. But you get back what you put in and it's been a good life.' He put a hand on Toby's shoulder. 'I'm very grateful for your help to Eliza. From what she tells me that could have ended much worse. Will you come and work for me as a groom and as a cadet? Twenty shillings a week with board. I could use another good man and you will discover what this farming's all about.' He withdrew the hand and added, 'It'll be up at four though and out on the frosty plain.'

Toby's mind raced. Working in the livery and smithy had been the only job he had known. Mr Wallis had been the only boss he'd ever had and he couldn't have had a better. Mr Wallis had been like a father to him. There were other things to consider. Separation from his mother for the first time in his life and separation from his nan, his mother's mother, small, opinionated, and feisty like her daughter but loving too. Separation, as well, from his sweetheart Josephine. Still, they would all be only a ride from town away. With Josephine it was never any more than a kiss and a cuddle for Mr Wallis had drilled into him that when a baby came, it was more times than not the woman who had to bear the consequences. He was so hot on the subject that Toby had begun to wonder if there was something personal to it.

Goodwin gave him time to reflect. Goodwin had had a lifetime of working with men and he liked the stamp of this young man. Toby Page did not look the type to be work-shy and he could certainly use a good, all-round man on the farm. Goodwin did not say so and might not even have been conscious of it, but with five daughters and no son, Toby Page would fill a niche. There were the four sons-in-law of course but they were far away doing their own thing on farm or in office.

'Yes, all right I will,' said Toby and in one stroke changed his job and his home. 'Thank you very kindly. I will have to discuss it though with Mr Wallis and give him ample time to find another.'

Mrs Goodwin appeared and was very pleased as was Priscilla Goodwin. Priscilla was now in her 40s and content with life as a loved maiden aunt, but she had enjoyed the company of the open young man and the connection with the redoubtable Minnie Page.

As Toby drove the buggy back to town, his mind was swirling. The offer was a good one when you considered a general labourer was lucky to get seven shillings and board. It would be more money than he was making at the livery stable and smithy and with board thrown in besides. Best of all, he would be learning hands on about farming. He would miss the smithy but Mr Goodwin would have need of blacksmithing too and he could keep advancing his skills. As the horses trotted on at an easy pace, sending up small clouds of dust at each step, Toby thought of something else he would have to forgo – his regular sparring with mates in the boxing hall. Puts the sand in a man, the trainer said. Toby was not a 'bruiser' – more a devotee of the 'sweet science' of pugilism, taking as much satisfaction at blocking, ducking, slipping, and feinting as landing a blow. His interest had been sparked by the sight of the great Bob Fitzsimmons some years before in Timaru, before 'Ruby Red' went to America to make his name and that of New Zealand famous. Fitzsimmons was a blacksmith too, with a mighty torso and arms above his lanky legs. But the farm work, Toby thought, should be good for his fitness and he could still punch ball, shadow box, and skip and might even persuade some of his work mates to spar with him.

It wasn't easy to tell Mr Wallis who had taught him and mentored him since he was a schoolboy in short pants, and come to his defence once when a workplace bully had played a dangerous and nasty prank on him before he was able to look after himself. That had cemented a bond between him and Mr Wallis and seen the bully go down the road.

'You want to leave me,' Frank Wallis said. 'Are you sure now boy? Jobs are not to be squandered. There will be a dozen lined up for yours.'

Toby struggled to find words but Frank Wallis could see the sincerity and gratitude in him and shook his hand firmly.

'Well, I hope you'll not forget us and drop by from time to time. Mr Goodwin's a good man and you'll do well with him. He's got some fine horses, too, you might get your hands on.'

And so it was that Toby Page became a groom to the owner of a fine Canterbury estate, and a farm cadet to boot, ready to turn his hand to whatever was needed. There was more to come, both good and bad, than he or his mother could ever have guessed.

A PRICE ON HIS HEAD

Minnie Page and her equally diminutive mother Peggy lived in a pretty cottage on Oxford Terrace by the Avon River. The front garden was full of lavender and the back garden had been carefully planted so that it was a brilliant splash of pink, yellow and red in spring and summer but also had colour the whole year round. Just down the road was the venerable Canterbury Club where the well-heeled gentlemen of town and country expounded on the issues of the day. Each time Minnie Page walked down Cambridge Terrace, she glanced at the Canterbury Club and imagined the trumpeting within. Since the election of the Liberal Party in 1890, the hallowed walls must have echoed to many lightning bolts of anger and outrage, and its waiters must have observed many bold gestures and considerable flushing of the skin.

'But there is an excellent reason why less than one percent of the landowners in this country control sixty-four percent of the freehold land,' one gentleman would be saying. 'It is economy of scale. Break up an estate into fifty smaller units and what have you got – fifty tinpot outfits that can barely make a profit amongst them. My estate, on the other hand, provides work for one hundred and twenty farmhands and their families not to mention the dozen or so domestic servants in the house.'

He might well have added, 'It is also deuced better for the Hunt to have long paddocks than paddocks so short you're no sooner over one fence than there's another one to jump.'

Minnie Page imagined a group in a corner discussing the female franchise. 'Most women do not want the vote.' This from a dapper man of the city. 'They would rather leave it to us and get on with their household duties. Their brains do not work like ours. They do not have the logic, do not see the whole picture.' She had heard any number of the pillars of the community expound in this manner. Heads would be nodding in that communion of souls desperate to bond, each sip of whisky and gin confirming them as jolly good fellows all. And indeed, most of them were, by any score, sound and decent citizens. And she had to concede that many men, including some in that club, were now putting their weight behind the cause of female suffrage, recognising their mothers, their wives, their sisters, and daughters had a brain as good as theirs.

Prohibition was another issue that could get them going and Minnie Page herself was in two minds about that one. Many of her suffragist friends were members of the Temperance Association or other such bodies and she could well understand why. Alcohol was cheap and readily available and had been the ruin of many families. On the other hand, a drink could relax mind and body for those who could control it. That very day she was on her way to meet Toby at Warner's Hotel and she intended to have a small brandy and ginger ale. He had said he wanted to talk about something with her and she had suggested Warner's. At such times she found it best to get away from familiar surroundings to see things more clearly; home walls could cramp the spirit and confine the thinking. She sensed huge change was in the wind for the country and now, perhaps, for her family as well.

He was waiting for her, standing foursquare, surveying the passing traffic, occasionally greeting friends. They hugged and found a quiet corner of the bar. He had told her the night before of the incident with the frightened horse and of driving Mrs Goodwin and her daughter home but he had not told her of his decision to leave his home and work. He had at least saved her from the upheaval for one more day. That morning, he had left the house early, having arranged to meet her at 5pm at Warner's.

He came directly to the point and told her of Goodwin's offer and his decision. 'So, I'll be leaving the city for the country. But I'll still be seeing a lot of you and Nan. I'll be in and out all the time with one thing and another. It's not as if I'm over the Alps or away down south.'

It was a shock to her right enough for she, her mother and Toby had never been without one another.

Minnie looked at her son and saw his father in him and realised the decision was for the best. Toby was made for the land. When he was outdoors amidst animals and nature, he came truly alive, just as she came alive when she picked up a brush and created something new on the canvas. Toby began to talk nonstop of the estate and its livestock and crops and the string of racehorses Mr Goodwin owned and about everything he could learn in his new job and about his 20 shillings a week and board. He was sorry to be leaving Mr Wallis and she was sorry in that regard too for Mr Wallis had taken the father's role in raising him – firm but kind and steering him away from a young man's perils. She gave him his blessing and they walked home with his arm around her shoulders.

'There's Josephine to tell too,' he said. He had to acknowledge he had grown very fond of Josephine. She was a good sort and they'd had many laughs together.

'If it's meant to be, it will last,' said Minnie.

Toby's workday on the farm started at 4am, as promised. He rose in the dark from his bunk in the station hands' quarters, dressed, relieved himself, splashed some water on his face and helped to feed and groom the horses. At 6.15am there was the boom of the cook striking a large circular saw with an iron bar and breakfast at 6.30. At seven the station manager Barney Halligan was there with orders of the day for the hundred and one jobs. Barney Halligan told him of an incident that ensured he paid attention to his work – the man-in-charge went for a cup of tea, an ill-trained dog got into the yard and in minutes 108 sheep were smothered to death. Over the weeks and months, he learnt to turn his hand to any station task. He worked Monday to Saturday with few 'smokos' and rest on the Sabbath. Sometimes on the Sabbath he would come to town to see his mother and nan and they would marvel at the tan on him and the whiplash body and the self-assured air of the man close to the land.

Soon a particular task was put Toby's way – placating an angry neighbour after the Christchurch Hunt had gone through. This most recent of Goodwin's annual hostings of the Hunt had generally gone well. Members of the Brackenfield Hunt to the north took part as well as some guests from the Rangitikei and when the hounds got the scent of the hare, the 'music' poured out of them and a great body of riders in scarlet or green streamed across the countryside. What a sight it was for Toby himself, taking part on Prince as a groom of Goodwin. Most of it was over ideal, flat-jumping country with good gorse hedges. Prince flew high and far, relishing the challenge. Though there was a sense of all in it together, Toby was keenly aware of a pecking order. He ensured he waited his turn at the fences, never pushing in and above all, never ahead of the Master. It was a fine pack, free running and deep-chested and no sooner had one hare been run down than another would start up and away the pack went again. The hunting continued until dusk.

But Toby knew there was trouble even before Goodwin approached him back at the house. A team of draught horses of a neighbour, Tom McKay, had become hysterical at the commotion of the Hunt streaming through, and had charged through a fence, taking Tom McKay with them.

'Toby, very bad form from the Hunt I'm afraid. Would you kindly do me a favour this evening. Apologise to McKay for me, inquire after his health, and tell him I'm sending two station hands tomorrow to repair his fence.' Goodwin retired back into the house with a 'Humph' and a clearing of the throat, looking decidedly embarrassed. After all, without the co-operation of the neighbouring farmers, there would be no Hunt.

It was a badly bruised and battered Tom McKay who gave Toby a fusillade of ripe language that evening, much of which Toby had never heard before and marvelled at.

'I should bloody well think so,' Mr McKay said on hearing fencers would be arriving the next day.

When McKay stroked his beard and came away with a twig from the hedge, he delivered a particularly vile curse. Finally, he seemed to realise that Toby was merely the messenger and instructed him to pass the remarks on to his lordship. Discretion would rule that out but Toby made a mental note to suggest to Mr Goodwin a crate of beer and a couple of bottles of whisky might help the Hunt get access to the McKay property in future.

Toby also assisted Goodwin with the most passionate of his sporting interests, horse racing. New Zealand was as passionate about horse racing as Home and with horses and people needing to be close to the tracks, clubs abounded – more than 70 south of the Waimakariri River alone at one time. This thriving recreation in the young colony drew people of all classes, from the toffs who donated the plates and cups to the touts who tried to make a quid by one dubious means or another. Goodwin had once trained two of his horses himself, on a roughly finished track on his estate. But he had soon realised he could not do them justice and put them and soon others with a public trainer, Eddie Hare at Yaldhurst, near Christchurch. Toby helped with the horses' grooming and shoeing and Eddie Hare soon respected his eye, ear, and touch. It was Toby who looked at one owner's coaching mare and heard the owner write her off as broken-winded. But Toby saw something special. 'She's worth a go,' he said. The mare was relieved of her coaching job, put into training, and won some good races.

When November Cup Week approached, Toby was more often at the stables than the estate, taking a bed in the trainer's house. Goodwin's main hope on the first day of the Spring Meeting at Riccarton was Criterion in the Jockey Club Handicap of one mile. First prize was a handsome 300 sovereigns. An owner could sometimes win as much again through bets with other owners in the paddock. The 300 sovereigns and a winning bet were a good reward, to be sure, but for most of the patrician owners, the greatest joy was to hold aloft the silver cup or plate in front of their peers.

The day dawned with a light frost and a chill that straightened the backbone and put a spring in the step. Toby sucked in the warm, earthy aroma of the stables as he helped see to the horses. The great week was here at last and who knew what it might bring? Racing was a journey into the unknown but Toby could see that Eddie Hare had the horses as fit as hands could make them and all they needed was a good passage and an ounce of luck. There was nothing hurried, nothing loud and raucous, on that or any other morning at the stables but the horses that would be racing knew it was their day. They sensed it in countless ways. Then, quite suddenly, it was time to take the three horses the short distance to their stalls at Riccarton racecourse.

The wattle trees were in full bloom on the approach to the course. The racecourse was a showpiece of the city and Cup Week was a long-established tradition – there had been racing at Riccarton Park since 1855. When Toby had seen the horses settled, he strolled to the paddock to catch the atmosphere. Five-horse brakes and bullock drays were discharging passengers and already there were thousands on the course and thousands more coming through the gates, most dressed in their finery. It was a sea of hats and caps, from the occasional broad creation with feathers to bowlers and Tam O'Shanters. The country people left their gigs, buggies, and other conveyances in the paddock, sometimes taking the horse out of the shafts, sometimes leaving it in, and putting a hitching rope round the horse's neck and to the fence. Some were already dispensing champagne and food from large wicker baskets. Toby saw Mr and Mrs Goodwin and Priscilla leaving their carriage.

On the lawn, Toby recognised Henry Redwood, dubbed 'Father of the New Zealand Turf', unmistakeable with clean-shaven face and great white beard under his chin, chatting with hunting men Toby had met. The bookmakers had been busy in the city and now, on the course, were doing brisk and noisy business, shrieking the odds. Some could see only harm in gambling but Toby believed people should have the right, though for the good of their pockets they should be informed and disciplined.

'Thirty-three to one!' shouted one, drawing several instantly to him, like gnats to the flame. Meanwhile his tic-tac man was relaying a message to him by semaphore on the other side of the paddock.

The totalisator was attracting custom as well and Mrs Freeman's Tea Pavilion was already a great centre of attraction. Toby knew his mother would be amongst the heaving masses, probably today with some of her more bohemian friends, enjoying the zest and colour of it all. Soon, on the lawn nearby, he could see Mr and Mrs Goodwin and Priscilla mingling with others he recognised as Goodwin daughters and their husbands and children. As Toby watched, Goodwin was talking to a distinguished-looking man in a long, grey overcoat, black silk scarf and dark felt hat. Sir Robert Drake was president of the Rangitikei Hunt Club and had been a guest with his eldest son Paul at the recent combined meeting of the Brackenfield and Christchurch Hunts. Then Paul Drake appeared and gave Goodwin a carry bag from which Goodwin withdrew a bottle of whisky. A gift, no doubt, for their participation in the Hunt. Goodwin had seen Toby nearby and now he called him over.

'Toby, you know Sir Robert and his son Paul.' They nodded their acquaintance. 'Would you be so kind as to take this bag and place it out of sight in the box in our carriage. I'll be over to see the horses soon.'

Toby took the bag, threaded his way through the crowds to the paddock and soon identified Goodwin's carriage and the two horses which pulled it. Bearing in mind the recent warning of Mr Inspector Pender that the town this week would be full of thieves and vagabonds, he slipped the bag with its bottle into the carriage's box under the driver's seat as surreptitiously as possible.

But Toby's action had not gone unobserved. Simon Drake, 21, the second son of Sir Robert, had seen his brother Paul give Goodwin the bottle and the subsequent transfer to Toby Page. He had followed Toby at a distance and seen him go to the carriage and come away without the bag. It was simple enough, after Toby left, to transfer the bag discreetly to the buggy he had hired in town, and tuck it safely out of sight. He turned away with a smirk of satisfaction. It was his due. Paul had more than enough as the eldest son and heir to his father, and enough success already too– head boy of his boarding school, head of cadets, captain now of the Rangitikei Royal Rifles and at just 26 a member of the Rangitikei County Council. Even Paul's name – Paul Robert Drake – festered with Simon, reminding him that Paul was the favoured son. A more generous soul than Simon's would have been content to be a Drake and content as well with his considerable success with the ladies for Simon's lithe body, charm and dazzling blue eyes drew the eyes of women wherever he went.

Simon Drake had travelled to Cup Week with two of his usual

roistering companions, Eddie Shaw and Henry Thompson. The third, Arthur Wilson, couldn't come – he had been busy waging war against poachers on his property. The four, known as the 'Hellfire Boys', were said to like the sound of breaking glass. Simon wasn't even sure his father and brother knew he was there. Shaw, Thompson, and he had had a riotous trip to date, drinking and cavorting most nights and now drying out and looking to make money on the horses.

But the bag and its bottle of whisky had not ceased its travels at the racecourse. Toby Page witnessed the transfer of the bag to the thief's own buggy and when the well-dressed thief was gone, he hurried over and transferred it back to Goodwin's carriage. Better to put things right on the quiet. Toby then swiftly returned to the horses to assist Eddie Hare. His work done, he proceeded to the shilling stand which was far from the finishing post but was little used and provided a view unobstructed by hats. As he watched the stable's entrant in a six-furlong race cantering to the start, he thought of the tall, dark man who had stolen the whisky. Unusual for a man dressed like a toff to stoop to such a thing. Was he a common thief who dressed up for race days as his modus operandi and had fluked the sight of the whisky bottle? Or was he indeed a toff and was there more to it?

Toby banished the thoughts as the race began. Their two-year-old was buffeted at the start, stumbled, and for a fearful moment looked like she might fall. To Toby's relief, the jockey stayed on but the leaders were stretching away in full stride before she got going. By the middle of the back stretch, she was in the pack and finished gamely for second. A meritorious effort. Their second runner finished a disappointing fourth but had also been unlucky, boxed in and getting out too late. The young jockey would learn from that. Soon it was time for Criterion and the pulsating crowd was treated to a thriller.

One horse, Buckmaster, went out like a mad thing and still held the lead coming round the final bend. Its supporters were starting to believe as it pounded into the straight still two lengths to the good. But the pack was closing in and sharing leadership of the pack with another was Criterion, making its run wide out. In a few mighty strides, the two leading chasers caught the tiring front runner and then it was a two-horse race for the glory and the 300 sovereigns. They tore to the finish line at a terrific pace, neck and neck, now one ahead, now the other, until, just short of the post, Criterion reached into himself, found something else and pushed clear to win by a head. Punters were going berserk in the main stand and even the shilling stand became noisy for a few seconds from Toby's cheers. He could picture the Goodwin family whooping and celebrating. It would be Goodwin's best win and he deserved it for the money he was putting into the sport. The Goodwins left soon afterwards to celebrate at home and Toby was pleased there was a bottle of whisky waiting for him in his carriage.

Simon Drake and his companions Eddie Shaw and Henry Thompson left just before the last race. They were looking for a good meal at their hotel and more drink and exploration of the town's night spots. To Drake's surprise and anger, when he reached for the bottle of whisky, it wasn't there.

'What the hell?' he said, and turned the air blue with profanities.

'What's wrong?' Shaw, large and bombastic with a walrus moustache, was sour himself from bad betting. He should have been a wealthy man from his mining interests but ill-judged gambling such as today's, had taken its toll.

'I had a bottle of whisky here. Tucked it away out of sight.

Damn thieves.'

'I did see someone at our buggy,' said Thompson. He was pipe-smoking and had mutton-chop whiskers and hair swept across to the right. 'Solidly built young cove in a jacket and tie. I couldn't see what he'd have to take so I forgot about him.'

Drake's eyes blazed with rage. 'Just a minute,' he said to Eddie. 'Henry, can you come with me?' As Drake stalked through the paddock, he unleashed a stream of abuse and instructed his companion, 'Tell me if you see him.'

The crowds were dramatically thinning by now, many leaving before trains or roads became too crowded, some penniless, some drunk from too much liquor, some weary from too much excitement, some elated from their winnings. The band was packing up as they went by. Betting slips, the detritus of crushed hope, lay everywhere. They passed all sorts, the rich in their fine carriages and, to the side, factory hands and servants trudging on foot. Two policemen had a man in their grip, probably a pickpocket. Drake and Thompson peered inside the beer tent, but not there. They combed the lawn and the paddock but it was not until they neared the stalls that Drake stiffened at the sight of the 'thief'. Drake's instinct was to rush up and smash him in the face, but he thought better of it.

'Come on, let's go and have a word to those larrikins over there.'

To Thompson's surprise, Drake walked straight over to a couple of hulking toughs standing nearby. Slouched against a fence, they each had a bottle of beer in the hand, breaking the rule of no drinking outside the beer tent. They looked the sort of roughnecks who would strut into a pub and challenge the bar to a fight. Drake drew the hated figure to their attention and shoved money into their hands.

'Make a good job of it now,' he said over his shoulder as he and Thompson departed.

The two of them came at Toby minutes later, when he had finished his work with the horses and was about to leave the course.

'Let's be having at you then,' shouted one, raising a beer bottle to crash it down on Toby Page's head.

But he had let his intentions be known too soon. As the man swung forward, Toby stepped nimbly to the side, pivoted on his right foot, and brought all the force from the twist of his body into his right fist. It landed square on the jaw of his assailant with a fearsome crack though it had travelled no further than a foot. It was a blow from the barbarous old bare-knuckle days. Toby loved boxing for its 'sweet science' but when it came to a crux, he could attack as well as defend. The ruffian staggered back in shock and pain, making a peculiar gurgling noise. His knees buckled, his feet went and he dropped to the ground. The bottle that could have seriously maimed or even killed Toby Page rolled away on the grass. The other cursed and came flailing in with mighty though wild punches. Toby knew that if he went down, he would get a fearsome kicking. To stay on his feet was the thing. He drew back, as if in fear, throwing the attacker off balance, and then rose out of his crouch and drove his left fist hard as he could into the other's liver, doubling him over. As the fellow straightened up, Toby hit with an explosive right hook. The blow landed flush on the chin and knocked the man right on his back. He was out to it when he hit the ground. The first assailant was by now on his knees and in an obvious hurry to get away. He looked fearfully up as Toby approached.

'What is this about?' Toby asked.

'Somebody doesn't like you,' the first man muttered, reaching into his pocket and showing a pound note.

Then Toby knew it was the bottle of whisky and that far away a toff would be gloating that Toby would be lying broken or worse. Next moment a stable-hand was by Toby's side with a pitchfork in his hand.

'Where did you learn to fight like that? You're no mug with the fists. I was ready to step in if you'd needed me but cripes, you handled those blokes all by yourself.'

Toby was pleased his fists had sorted it out rather than the prongs of a pitchfork.

To his relief, the second assailant was starting to stir and come round. He left them to it, bruised and battered; they might think twice before taking on such an assignment again. It was sobering, though, to know he had an enemy prepared to pay to have him beaten. He had a strong feeling that things were only going to get worse.

HOT AIR RISING

By the time 1893 wheeled around, Toby was attuned to the rhythm of life on the farm. The station hands' quarters were comfortable enough and the food tasty and ample. The only thing he quaked at was the flocculent horror of tripe, though the others wolved it down. He revelled in being close to nature and was learning all the time how to work with it. He saw and smelt rain before it arrived, he saw first-hand that thunder could cause a horse to bolt, rain could flood a field or bring down a bridge, a gale could flatten a crop, lightning could kill an animal or cause a fire and snow could make the job of the rabbiter harder. Some mornings the mountains to the west soared into the bluest of skies; others, they might not have been there, the mist was so dense and the cloud so low. He loved all of nature, even the summer winds from the north-west that left the land baked and blistering in monochrome brown. Some days he was too weary to appreciate the bleak magnificence of his surrounds. Sometimes, when he was working on the far reaches of the property, he camped out overnight under a twinkling ceiling that made all people of the world one and all concerns universal.

On the bracing spring day he drove Mr and Mrs Goodwin and Priscilla to a brunch at Opawa, he acquired valuable insights into social structures and lifestyles. In a loop of the Heathcote River as far as the Port Hills, they passed one opulent house after another several storeys high with spectacular entrance ways and driveways. As he sat at the servants' table adjoining the kitchen, he marvelled at the quantity and range of food and drink being prepared and taken through for breakfast. But he soon realised he had seen but the beginnings for as the day wore on, amidst the chatter and tennis and walks in the garden, processions of food continued to flow from the kitchen. The rewards of success, he thought, often from the efforts of someone in the past. He pondered, too, the enormity of work behind the scenes emanating from the invitation's two little words, 'At home'.

Toby grew fond of the Goodwins. He could see they were tough and hardy to have achieved what they had but they were 'gentle folk', considerate of others. Agitators were calling for more break-up of the big estates and once, a shot had whistled perilously near Mr Goodwin's head when he was riding. Goodwin was sympathetic to their demands and had already sold off part of his estate.

Priscilla was unusually quiet on the ride home; Toby gathered she had had a proposal of marriage from a wealthy widower. They were both content to ride in reflective silence.

Toby had by now become the son Goodwin never had and Goodwin had followed Wallis as the father Toby had never had. One day Goodwin's usual golf caddy was indisposed and when Toby stood in for him, it was a lesson in managing impatience. One of their opponents, a well-known surgeon of the city, studied each shot as though about to negotiate a scalpel past a vital organ. As they waited and waited and waited for the surgeon to play, Toby could feel himself becoming dangerously tetchy. He wanted to shout, 'For heaven's sake man, play your shot!' But then he got a grip on himself and discovered it helped greatly to look away at other life in the park: the riders cantering in the distance, the mothers with perambulators, the people out walking, the dog straining at the leash. Indeed, anything with life, and by the time he looked back, the game had usually moved on.

Goodwin maintained a team approach which was a worry to Toby. 'We struggled there,' Goodwin said after missing a putt of 18 inches.

But Toby gave him credit that despite vexations that could drive a testy man to madness, Goodwin never once swore at him, threw a club, or hacked a piece out of the ground in anger and was scrupulous in his counting of strokes, unlike one of the opponents, a notable city businessman, whose arithmetic had to be corrected more than once.

Other assignments were more physical and hazardous such as the time he had to deal to two feral dogs which had been worrying the stock and killing lambs at the upper station. He took Prince, his favourite hack, and one of the dogs Brutus, a bull mastiff, and rode off with provisions for a week. The next day they found the remains of the kill and Brutus got onto the scent. Far in the distance the sky was in tumult and a flash of lightning nearly proved fatal for it drew Toby's attention from the horror charging at him from bracken to the side. He barely had time to get his shotgun up and levelled before the blast dropped the renegade dog dead at his feet. To his relief, Brutus dealt with the other. Barney Halligan was pleased with the result, especially when it had taken just a day and not a week, and Toby got word that Goodwin was as well.

Then, in September 1893, came the great day for Minnie Page and her friends when the women's suffrage bill passed both Houses of Parliament. There was little extravagant language on the front pages. Simply 'Womanhood Suffrage' in bold headline. But New Zealand had become the first sovereign state in the world where women had the vote. Contrary to what the more virulent doomsayers had suggested, the sun came up the next morning and life carried on as usual.

Toby visited town regularly to see his mum and nan. One Saturday afternoon he attended a public meeting to support her. Within minutes the hall was in an uproar. Minnie Page was on the stage with three others: the Rev Chatterton, of grim, clean-shaven face, austerely impressive, the prohibitionist the Rev Leonard Isitt of solid build with a heavy moustache, and Mr Prendergast, chairman, a tall, sallow man with a trim, military moustache. Prendergast struggled to maintain order. The air was so full of vitriol Toby feared a wrong comment could see people rush the stage. Perched at the end of a row on a bench near the front, he was poised to hurry to his mother's side if necessary. License or no license brought out great passion on both sides. He himself enjoyed a drink but luckily remained benign and could control it. So far here, to his relief, it was just noise in the hall, most of it from a group of agitators at the back. Toby turned to see who they were. Three he recognised straightaway as publicans of the city and one other as a brewer's representative who had been a frequent visitor to the livery stables and smithy. With them were men who might be described as seasoned drinkers, some well-known in sporting circles.

The Rev Chatterton of the Baptist Total Abstinence Association had just sat down to cheers and boos having 'warmed up the audience'. The licensed supporters had taken umbrage at being called the devil's henchmen and were still simmering as the chairman introduced the Rev Isitt and hurried back to the sanctuary of his seat. As the Reverend Isitt rose, a further chorus of boos drew the bevy of policemen nearer.

'Ladies and gentlemen,' the Rev Isitt began, 'I am grateful for your welcome (ironic cheers from the rear) and honoured to be on the same platform as Minnie Page. I fought, along with her and others, for the women's franchise and how pleased we are to have it at last (strong applause). I am pleased to be in a country where women are no longer classed amongst criminals, paupers, and lunatics. You married men should be aware you are infinitely better thanks to your wives – in fact, women are proving themselves to be the best men in the family. But I don't want to talk on the broad question of women's rights. I will leave that to Minnie Page. After all, she knows it better than me. I will talk instead of women's responsibility in the one great evil of our day – the drink traffic (boos from the back).'

He lay forth then, with great style and flair, on how women must not see liquor as a stimulant as it was nothing of the sort. Rather, it dulled the senses and led to bad judgment, ill health and ultimately gloom, despondency, and penury. Toby could see his mother shifting uneasily. He knew very well she was not a total abstainer. She enjoyed the odd tipple but seldom in public. She was, though, happy to be on the same platform because the temperance movement was a great supporter of more rights for women. Their members had favoured the women's franchise, in part because they believed it would help their own cause.

The Rev Isitt was well into his stride now, his statements thudding home like the blows of a sledgehammer, and most of the audience were loving it while the agitators at the rear appeared to have fallen into a soporific malaise.

'Five years ago there was no Prohibition Party,' he thundered. 'Prohibition was a name and nothing more. Today there are Prohibition Leagues in nearly every part of the colony. They may call us fanatics but we are getting stronger every day and we shall show at the next election we are a determined and united party. We are glad the temperance movement has become a political question. What does it mean for families? Gaoler Garvey of Wellington has stated that 85 percent of the inmates of the prison are there through the effects of drink and Gaoler Phillips of Dunedin has testified to an even bigger percentage. Investigate here in Christchurch and you will find two-thirds of the cases of charitable aid are caused by drink. Tradesmen's bad debts as well can usually be laid at the door of the public house.'

'Bloody rubbish! Cock a doodle doo!' shouted someone from the rear. 'We should buy up all the teetotallers and ship them out of the country!'

'Harping on about it!' shouted another. 'I'll 'ave another one. Your turn to shout!'

The nearest policeman moved across and tapped the protesters on the shoulder, gesturing they keep their mouths shut or else.

The Rev Isitt had noticed the action of the policeman and threw out a statement to torment the liquor interests. 'I challenge any man here to prove there is as much nourishment in a quart of beer as there is in the oatmeal that would cover a half-crown piece.' He went on to quote a host of statistics from Britain and America proving the efficacy of prohibition and rounded off his address by stepping right to the front until Toby feared he would step right off the stage.

'I beseech you to declare once and for all, No License! It would be the greatest reform the world has ever seen!'

He stepped down to boisterous applause and a volley of boos.

'What about the sly groggers it would bring in its wake!' The raucous shout boomed over the dying claps and boos, so loud the lungs that produced it would have done credit to the bellows of a forge. Toby recognised that voice and turned to confirm it. Yes, a man accustomed to shouting 'Time gentlemen please!' Zac Morrison, around 50, large, with heavy jowls and a red face.

It was a challenge the Rev Isitt could not ignore. With a nod to the chairman, he rose once more.

'Mr Morrison, publican, I see.'

'Excuse me, hotel keeper,' said Morrison.

'Whatever,' said Isitt. 'The sly groggers are a concern, I grant you, with the troubles they bring. But worse by far are those who peddle the poison right in front of our eyes.'

Amidst a fresh storm of abuse from the back and others

scattered throughout the hall, he muttered to the chairman, 'I've said my piece,' and sat down.

But the 'peddle the poison' had tipped one of the publican agitators over the edge. He stood, shook a fist, shouted, 'You've got it coming Isitt!' and added several other epithets which sent a shudder through those who had led a more sheltered existence. At a nod from their sergeant, two policemen grabbed him and bundled him out the door.

It was now the turn of Minnie Page. As she stepped forward in her tailored jacket and dress reaching to the ankles, she looked fashionable but at the same time, thought Toby, so tiny and vulnerable. What conviction and doggedness it took to mount a rostrum when as many faces scowl as smile at you! He was awestruck at her commitment to the cause of women, children, and the family. He knew she was not against marriage as some had claimed but did wonder if she remained single in respect of the memory of his father or wish to be independent, or was it just circumstance? He knew some men would have needed little encouragement to put a ring on her finger. But again, he was grateful his mother was not afraid to express her thoughts and feelings unlike the many 'buttoned-up' others. The audience gazed up at her expectantly as she waited, defiant, for the noise to subside. When there was silence, she began.

'Girls must be prepared to depend on themselves, not on a man,' she said. 'To this end, they must receive a good education, an education as good as that a boy receives. Why should a daughter be less privileged than a son? We must acknowledge our daughters have brains as well as bodies. Their choice must not be limited to domestic servant or factory hand in a garment establishment. We must open our professional occupations to women. If we don't, we are stifling the ability of half our young.'

She went on to argue that when women did achieve a professional occupation, they must be treated as the equals of men. 'Why should the woman teacher receive half the pay of the man, as at present?'

With each issue she raised, Toby knew she would be picturing the faces of women she knew who were striving to better themselves. She spoke of the young domestic servant deserted by her betrayer and called for her not to be shunned but provided with support to help her back on her feet. There were constant patters of applause as she spoke but occasional dissenting voices raised as well.

The three vocal dissenters were seated near the front, in the middle and at the back, as if working in unison, thought Toby, to engage the whole hall. Toby had a good view of the heckler near the front, a spare, acidic-looking man with a moustache, in a tawdry brown jacket. When he stood during the most virulent of his out-bursts, claiming Minnie Page was disturbing the natural order of things, his spittle flew far and wide, causing those in front to raise their collars. As he fulminated against her, his eyes were pinpricks of hatred and his features were twisted as if he were wearing a grotesque mask. Toby winced at each of his objections but considered him harmless enough. He was one of those, Toby guessed, without any real authority of himself and depending for his self-esteem on the greater status of the male. He pondered what a grisly witch-hunter the man would have made. The bulbous-nosed man in the middle, bald on top and heavily bearded, was the more nastily personal. 'Where's your old man?' he shouted at one point. 'Oh, that's right, you drove him away.' The great bull of a man at the back drew on sarcasm. 'You'll never be satisfied Minnie Page will you!' he bellowed. 'Next a female member of the House of Representatives, then Premier, then Governor!'

The trio of hecklers were not enough to put Minnie Page off her stride and Toby sensed the vast majority in the hall were with her. She aired legal matters regarding family. 'Why should the father have sole legal rights regarding his children? The married woman must have independent legal status to give her shared legal guardianship.' She had told him of a house stripped to the floorboards by bailiffs after the husband's drinking and gambling had put him and the family in hopeless debt. 'The woman must have control, as well as her husband, over property.' She urged, as well, that women of the unfortunate class, the prisoners and prostitutes, receive practical rehabilitation to better themselves. To finish, she used the ploy of Mr Isitt, advancing right to the front, and picking up the words of the heckler at the back and throwing them back at him. 'Why, indeed, might a woman not be a decision-maker for the nation? Why should our nation have chambers filled only with men? Why might a woman not be a Member of Parliament?'

This was a clarion call that surprised even many of her supporters in the audience who had been thrilled enough with the gaining of the female franchise the year before. Most had not been so bold as to think beyond that. There was a moment's silence before an eruption of clapping and cheering. But now, as Minnie Page finished, the heckler near the front shot to his feet and shouted in fury, 'Haven't you done enough damage already woman with your damned female franchise? You would set wife against husband and break up families! It is for the man to lead the family and it is for the man to put bread on the table and the woman to tend to her home duties.' His eyes were tiny beads of hatred as he continued to rant and he stopped and sat down only when a policeman came to the front, caught his eye, and thumped his truncheon into the palm of a hand. Toby exhaled with relief. All was well. His mother had fronted both friends and enemies and spoken as well as ever. Now she was safely back in her seat and the chairman was proposing a hearty vote of thanks to the speakers and drawing attention to a collection being taken up to defray the travelling expenses of Mr Isitt.

Minnie Page farewelled the others on the stage and well-wishers from the audience and made ready to leave. She would not need travelling expenses – she had arrived at the hall in Riccarton by bicycle and would return to Oxford Terrace by bicycle. She was deeply grateful for it. The bicycle had so greatly advanced people's independence, enabling travel to be much further than before. Some of the more hoity toity looked askance at women on bicycles but Minnie considered those people quite out of touch with the times. When the Atalanta Cycling Club, the first women's cycling club in Australasia, had been formed in 1892 she had been a foundation member. She had a bag with her knickerbockers and plimsolls and it took but a moment to use the ablutions room and change into them for the road. The hundreds of people had now mostly dispersed, mainly by foot and buggy, and a few, like Minnie, by bicycle.

'Are you sure I can't give you a lift home in the buggy?' said Toby. 'It's no trouble at all. There's room for your bicycle.'

'No that's fine son,' said Minnie. 'The ride through the park will do me good and I'll be home in no time.' It was now later afternoon and the light was beginning to fade but she would have a good path all the way. 'Thank you for coming in. Take care on your ride back to the estate. Love you son.'

Toby gave her a mighty hug full of love, relief, and pride all in one, and then she mounted her Raleigh safety bicycle and was soon out of sight down the road heading towards Hagley Park.

◆ ◆ ◆

Minnie breathed in deeply and exhaled slowly. Another meeting done, another battle fought for the cause. The meetings were stressful but better at least than being a street-corner evangelist. There was scarcely anyone else around and soon she was passing by the Riccarton Cemetery. But a noise brought her to a stop. What was it and where was it coming from? From her left. She wheeled her bicycle off the path and into the cemetery itself.

'Help!' came the piteous cry. 'Please someone help me!'

Twilight was thickening to darkness but there was just enough light to see that the noise was coming from the ground, amid the tombstones and slabs of granite. Minnie Page entered the cemetery, laid down her bicycle and peered into an open grave. A woman was standing there, distraught and shaking, a bag at her feet.

'Oh, thank the Lord,' she said. 'I was cutting through the cemetery on my way home and fell into this hole and can't get out. The earth just comes away. It's like a living death.'

One glance and Minnie Page knew the sides of the grave were too deep and sheer for her to pull the woman out. Shouting she would be straight back, she dashed to the nearest house and in minutes, two men were there with a rope. The woman passed up her purse and shopping bag and then, following the men's instructions, turned her back to them and put the rope round her back and under her arms, passing them the other ends of it. In moments she was out from six feet under. It had been a terrific shock when she tumbled headlong into the grave and she might have broken her neck. She still felt groggy when she reached the surface but had enough of her senses to thank her rescuers and to realise that one of them was the woman whose face had stared at her from the newspaper – the famous Minnie Page.

The police were grateful when the woman came forward the next day to report the incident, embarrassing though it was. For she and the two men were the last people to see Minnie Page before she disappeared.

ALARM BELLS RINGING

I t was not until dark that Toby's nan grew concerned. Minnie scarcely ever rode her bicycle after dark. As one hour became two and she heard nothing, she mentioned her fears to a neighbour and he very kindly went to the police station in the centre of the city and reported Minnie missing. The police suspected Minnie was staying the night with one of her many friends but they sent out a patrol to check the route from the hall at Riccarton through the park to Oxford Terrace. When they found Minnie's bicycle, abandoned, at the corner of the park and Rolleston Avenue, the investigation took on a whole new urgency.

Minnie Page had been a constant worry to the police, and a constant annoyance to many of them too. They were, as a group, bastions of the status quo, vying with the Methodists as about the least radical group around. Mrs Page's demands for change set the teeth of many of them on edge and brought forth comments from, 'Look here, that's going a bit far,' to 'Utter poppycock. She's quite cracked, you know.' But even the most hidebound recognised there were many times when women needed protection from their husbands (and occasionally the reverse). The policemen also took their role as upholders of the law very seriously and when word got out that Minnie Page was missing, there were visits to homes and workplaces all over the province of known opponents of her and her cause.

Toby was working in the stable when he got word from Barney Halligan that Goodwin wanted to see him. One look at Goodwin's drawn features and Toby thought a valuable thoroughbred was dead through misadventure, or that he had neglected to do a vital duty. It was worse than he could have imagined.

'Your mother is missing.'

'What's that? When?'

'The police want to speak to you. They have sent a message. They are on the way here now. Your mother did not arrive home after her public meeting yesterday and there is concern.' Goodwin saw Toby grimace in agony and his body slump. Goodwin was himself dismayed and worried. He had thought at first the explanation could be as simple as staying overnight with a friend, but the detective's mention of the abandoned bicycle scotched that one.

'When did you last see her yourself?'

'I saw her ride away on her bicycle after the meeting, heading for the park and home.' His mind was frantically whirling. If only she'd taken up his offer of a lift. And then he had thought of her small stature and how easy it would be for someone to overpower her. He had offered to teach her self-defence but all she had said with a laugh was, 'My tongue is my sword boy and that's all I need.' There had been those men at the meeting, spitting out their venom. And not only them, others like them all over the province who wanted to keep the missus in her place, bolstering themselves by making sure they ruled the household. Did rage get to one of them when opportunity presented and the woman stirring up the trouble rode into their very path? Or could it have been something more primal than that? A man forgoing the brothel, throwing himself on her and carrying her off somewhere secluded?

Goodwin took in the haunted eyes, the collapsed body. 'You need time off my boy. You can't work like this.'

Soon the police buggy was there with Bernie Frost, detective first class, and Ron Sangster, sergeant first class. Goodwin invited them into the house where they interviewed Toby at length and got a detailed account of Minnie Page's movements the day before as well as a description of the meeting and, especially of the three men there who had caused Toby concern. The detective believed he knew the man at the centre of the hall and the man at the rear, and would investigate that. The man at the front was not known to him. Had there been any earlier worrying incidents? Toby gave them enough to fill the sergeant's notebook: the meetings that had erupted in chaos, the eggs that had once been thrown at her in the street, the snarls and looks of hatred and disdain she sometimes drew when shopping, the nasty, anonymous letters leading up to the Act of Parliament giving women the vote, the offensive objects in their letter box and dumped in the front garden. There was so much to go on that the police must have scarcely known where to start.

'Why didn't she tell us these things before?' Frost asked.

'She wanted to cause least trouble,' said Toby. 'I did believe the vote would be the end of it but there was always more for mother to do, more girls and women and families that needed her help and she was never going to be quiet.'

Frost had been one of the policemen irked by Minnie Page. He had said more than once to a constable at the rallies for women's suffrage, 'Why doesn't she give it a rest? By jingo, she's always drumming on about it.' But, as time went on, and the issues broadened, he had developed a grudging admiration for her. There was no denying she had had a huge impact and that she had some valid points. He wanted opportunities for his own daughters. Now, he, his sergeant and Toby sat in silence. Through the open window they could hear a wind had got up and was rustling the leaves of the poplar trees lining the driveway. The trees led down to the highway stretching north to the river and south to the city, and from the highway other roads and tracks led east to the ocean and west to the mountains. Somewhere, in all that immensity of fields and houses and beach and bush, Minnie Page was waiting to be rescued. Unless – and the thought had already crossed their minds – she already lay dead and buried.

Toby knew he must be at the centre of the search, and with his nan. Goodwin allowed him to take a horse and trap and take leave until his mother was found. Frost confirmed Toby's address in the city and promised to keep him appraised of any developments. Mrs Goodwin and Priscilla, fearful and shaken, joined their father in wishing him good luck and waved him away tearfully. He returned to the city with the policemen, keeping good distance behind their buggy to stay out of their dust. He realised he had to get a grip on himself if he was going to be any use to his mother.

The following day the newspapers had the story and it was on people's lips everywhere. Minnie Page had polarised people's opinions but now the vast majority were afraid for her and sympathetic. Many wishes of good luck and goodwill arrived at the house in Oxford Terrace and as Toby went the rounds of his friends and acquaintances, everybody was wondering who was behind it and where she had been taken. In the vacuum of information, the minds of the more imaginative, including that of Toby, ran rampant, conjuring up ghastly scenarios of abuse and beatings, rape and bondage. He dared not sit around and think too much. He had to keep busy and after he had been around his friends, he went to the corner of Hagley Park and Rolleston Avenue, where the bicycle had been found, and began a search of the park on foot from there. He was looking for anything of Minnie Page and anything that might indicate foul play. Hagley Park was huge, as were the adjoining Botanic Gardens that were his next place of search, and from time to time he stopped, gazed into the distance, and pondered the misery of it all.

The police were mounting their own exhaustive search and interviewing suspects. The two hecklers in the body of the hall were identified and brought in for a grilling. Both were highly indignant and convinced the police of their innocence, but not before getting a good shake-up and an instruction to be more temperate in expressing their opinions in future. The heckler towards the front of the meeting had not yet been identified. Certainly, he was not as well-known in the city as the other two. That evening Bernie Frost told Toby of their interviews and said they were still looking for the third man.

'I can assure you and your grandmother, Mr Page, we are leaving no stone unturned. There have been several possible sightings of Mrs Page we are looking into. The search is going on around the clock.'

Bernie Frost had good reason to pull out all stops. He was reporting directly to the police superintendent on this one and from what he gathered, the superintendent was fielding inquiries from the mayor and politicians. There had been the small consolation of resolving some other matters: locating two men they had been looking for regarding burglaries, identifying several illegal bookies and several receivers of stolen property, and discovering two illegal stills. The police were taken aback when one man came to them, insisting on being locked up. But it was nothing to do with Minnie Page – he said he had no means of subsistence and no home. The magistrate sentenced him to four months' imprisonment with hard labour.

The inquiry passed into the third day and Minnie Page's disappearance was as mysterious as ever. Toby was now starting to run on empty. He felt as though the life had been drained out of him. The kidnapping of a loved one is surely one of the hardest ordeals to bear. Not only is there the feeling of helplessness, but the mind is prey to whatever ghastly fears it conjures up. Toby was sleeping only fitfully, his slumbers shot through with frightening images of abuse and murder. Once, he woke up drenched and his nan told him at daybreak he had been shouting in the night. On his searches in the city, by foot, bicycle, or trap, he would peer at each dwelling, factory or warehouse and wonder if his mother was being held within. At times the anger would overwhelm him and he would go to his punching bag hanging from a rafter in the laundry and pummel it so hard the rafter itself would creak and groan. At other times the gloom of it all and his ruminations would put him in a deep funk and he would be close to despair. His nan was now an old lady of 66. It seemed to Toby she had been getting smaller by the year until, he surmised, she might shrink away altogether. But since her daughter had disappeared, he had seen a strength in her that astonished him. She had kept to her routines, ensured Toby had good food put in front of him and received with grace many of Minnie's friends, offering a cup of tea. She accepted the expressions of concern and deflected any comments that hinted at something worse. Toby could see up close the source of some at least of Minnie's own indomitable spirit.

On the third morning, when Toby was sitting slumped at the breakfast table, his nan put a consoling hand on his shoulder. 'We'll get through this boy. Minnie's out there somewhere. She's a strong one. She'll turn up.'

But as she moved away, her hollow eyes and sunken cheeks suggested her hopes were fading.

Day by day, the horror and mystery of the disappearance of Minnie Page gathered yet more column inches in newspapers up and down the country. Not that it was uncommon for people to go missing. Every week there were sorrowful pleas from family even in Great Britain and Ireland for information on relatives in New Zealand who had apparently been swallowed up. 'Last heard of in Auckland in 1891,' they might say. 'Aged father and sister want news.' And there were many people, the police could tell you, buried in unnamed graves because no one could identify them. The public were familiar with people going missing but the Minnie Page story had affected them profoundly. She was splashed on the front page of the dailies and was beginning to feature in the many small newspapers of the heartland that came out once or twice a week. After all, the story had everything the owner of a newspaper could want – a missing celebrity who polarised opinion like few others in the country, the likelihood of foul play and the enduring mystery of who had taken her and where she was. It was a story people could not dismiss. It lingered on the mind. The businessman in the office, the passenger on the tramcar, the farmhand in the top paddock, reflected with knitted brow on the sombre mystery of the disappearance of Minnie Page.

This was no time for the enemies of Minnie Page to propound their politics. They sunk out of sight except for expressions of sympathy by their leaders for Minnie Page's family. As for the city, Christchurch had never had such a scouring. Reported sightings of Minnie Page continued to stream in and each was assiduously investigated. There were hammerings at doors, households turned inside out, abandoned buildings combed and even a long stretch of the Avon riverbed dragged. Nothing. On the third evening and then the fourth, Detective Frost had no findings to report to Toby and his nan.

A breakthrough came on the fifth day. A traveller in a trap on the main road north of Christchurch in the Marshland area, sitting high above his horse, spotted a bag in long grass at the side of the road. Inside was a dress. He had followed the newspaper reports closely and been one of the many tormented by the mystery. He marked the spot with a stake he found nearby and hurried to the police station with his news. Detective Bernie Frost confirmed with Toby and his nan it was the dress of Minnie Page and within an hour there was a police road block there and any traveller north or south had to account for their presence. The kidnapper had snatched her bag as well as her person and Minnie, quick-thinking as ever, had turned it against him by leaving it along the way as a marker. The search for her switched north of the city to Marshland, Styx, Belfast and as far as Kaiapoi and Woodend. Straggling little places north of there were placed on alert as well.

In those small communities, scarcely anyone was now entirely above suspicion. After all, the offender or offenders could well be hidden in plain sight right in their midst. The ocean and rivers were not far distant. Could not the offender have done as he wished with Minnie Page, dumped her in a watery grave never to be found, and merged back into respectable life as a worker at the Kaiapoi Woollen Mill or whatever – farmer, military volunteer, cadet, footballer, member of the Kaiapoi Wesleyan Mutual Improvement Association or member of the Order of Oddfellows? Did anyone really know his neighbour? It was now the investigation had an unfortunate side-effect. Suspicious eyes turned on the eccentrics of the district. They were harried and hustled by self-appointed vigilantes and questioned at length by the police who were duty-bound to follow-up the denunciations. Dogmatists, with all their hatred, fears, and prejudices, turned on the most vulnerable of all – the harmless souls who had withdrawn into themselves to find their peace. In the cities, these casualties of life could drift anonymously from day to day but in the hamlets, they were too readily apparent. There was poor old Gymshoe Jim, clearly mentally unwell, stalking the streets and lanes at all hours, mind aswirl with who knew what. He was reported to the police and visited and questioned by Sergeant Sangster. Mad Tom was another, grilled until he had a fit and collapsed at their feet.

It was also around this time that another lurking evil voiced itself. A few of the more toxic of Minnie Page's enemies began to conjecture that Minnie Page might have engineered her disappearance to garner sympathy for her causes. They suggested her obsession for social reform had driven her to the extreme of concocting her own disappearance. Now she would miraculously reappear, they said, and her supposed assailant would never be found. It was all a fabrication. There were also murmurings it was a commercial ploy to feather her nest. Since she had disappeared, it had become even more desirable to own a Minnie Page painting. Her art now had the allure of a piteous end for its creator and there would be no more 'Minnie Pages'. Those who aired such comments, though, had to be sure of their audience for there was still much dread and concern abroad for Minnie Page and her family.

Tension was heightened when a young man was found dead near his father's house at Bottle Lake, to the east of Marshland, shot through the head. All indications, though, were of suicide. There was talk of thwarted romance but confusion too for the young man had been very popular. Another alarm was raised when the remains of a body were found on a farm at Styx, near Bottle Lake. Examination by a pathologist, though, revealed it to be months old. And as the search moved into a second week, a fire broke out at a house at Kaiapoi and burnt it to the ground before the brigade arrived. A sifting of the embers, to the great relief of the brigade and police, revealed no human remains.

TYRANNY OF THE RIGHTEOUS

As much as she twisted her wrists behind her, Minnie Page could not loosen her bonds. It had been easy to waylay her on her bicycle. That part of the park had been empty in the late afternoon, and the wad soaked with chloroform had worked a treat. It had been but a minute's work to place her in the trap and grab her bag that might have useful items. The chloroform he had obtained some weeks before by breaking into a cupboard at the hospital wher. he picked up chairs to be repaired.

She was tied securely to a chair in a shack by the ominously named River Styx, tucked out of sight amidst bush just north of Bottle Lake, seven miles north-east of Christchurch. The slight and sluggish River Styx emptied into the southern end of a lagoon which adjoined the mouth of the Waimakariri River. The main road was two miles to the west and a traveller there heading north would arrive within minutes at the bridge over the Waimakariri River. On the other side of the river was Kaiapoi. The shack with the corrugated rocf was invisible from the nearest track – the Lower Styx Road. It was also far out of hearing, being surrounded by trees and scrub with only wasteland between it and the road.

The ramshackle prison had been the perfect place for Adam Gibson to conceal Minnie Page. The spare, acidic-looking man from the meeting had planned the abduction for weeks and when he had seen her arrive at the hall on a bicycle (which was not surprising as she was well-known as a member of the cycling sisterhood}, he realised Providence was playing into his hands. The shack was already stocked with food and drink and rope. He had brought a chamber pot so she would not have to leave to relieve herself. The shack was a vestige of his childhood. He had come here with his late father Percy decades before to take advantage of the whitebait which ran then in the Styx River in late winter and spring. The shack had been sound in its basic structure when he had begun his preparations for the abduction of Minnie Page, but full of cobwebs and rodent droppings and its single window covered by vegetation. He had cleaned it up inside, leaving some of the vegetation obscuring the window so that even on the brightest day it was dim within. For Minnie Page, the grimy shack soured the whole world outside.

Gibson's obscure job as restorer of furniture for a second-hand emporium in the city had assisted him to remain undetected. While the other two raucous hecklers at the meeting had been quickly identified, Adam Gibson was known to few. During the day he worked alone in a room at the back of the emporium and at night, since his wife had left him the year before, he lived alone in a drab cottage on an acre of scrubby land at the north end of the city. The horse and trap were among his few possessions. A pity, he reflected, he could not have arranged leave from his job beforehand, but the great opportunity had to be taken. After abducting Minnie Page, he had driven her straight north through the thickening twilight and by the time he arrived at Marshland, it was pitch-dark. It must have been about then, he later realised, that her bag fell from the trap when she was coming out of the effect of the chloroform. She had kicked and lashed out and he had had to give her another dose just before they turned right on to Lower Styx Road. On arrival, he had bundled his comatose captive inside and secured her to a chair bolted to the floor. Then he had left the shack to remove the horse from its shafts and tether it in the bush where it could graze and drink from a rivulet.

She began to come out of the chloroform while he was tending to his horse. It was dark but vaguely, by the moonlight coming through the window, she became aware she was tied to a chair in a shack. She struggled against her bonds and cried out once, twice, three times. Only the sigh of the wind in the trees in reply. Then there was the heart-racing shock of the door crashing open and the shape of a man standing in the doorway. He stood there, still and silent, for what seemed forever. Then he stepped inside, lit a candle, and placed it on the room's small table. By the dim light, he was no more than an anonymous shape but she could dazedly take in more of her surrounds. A large and tatty mat covered most of the earthen floor and there was another chair besides the one she sat on, and a bunk with a pillow and blanket. On the opposite wall was a shelf upon which were three large tins. As she peered at these objects, her abductor stepped from the shadows with a strange mix of anger and triumph on his face. She recognised him instantly as the man from the meeting, cadaverous and intense, with scrutinous eyes. The attack in the park had been so sudden and unexpected, she hadn't seen the face of her assailant and neither had his face registered when she was coming out of the chloroform. Now, by the flickering light of the candle, she could see only too well her enraged heckler of the meeting towering above her, his eyes riveting her with hatred.

'Well now, Minnie Page. For the first time in your life, I expect, you will be taking direction from a man.' She writhed but could not loosen her bonds in the slightest. He looked with satisfaction at her helplessness.

'It's no use struggling. The bonds will only tighten.'

She sat frozen, unsure of the horrors to come. 'What do you want from me? This will only make things worse for yourself.'

'What do I want from you?' He let the question linger, enjoying her discomfort and dependence on him, and drew himself up, as tall as he could, like a figure of rectitude come to reprove and punish. 'I want my life to return to what it was. Before you and others of your evil sisterhood put notions into the heads of our wives. I want you to know the damage you have caused. I want you to feel the pain I have felt. I want you to recant your vile statements and tell your followers you were mistaken. How else would that happen except if I took you from your wicked collaborators? You must set aside your unwomanly pride and learn the humility of the righteous.'

She could see him becoming increasingly agitated as he talked, stepping this way and that, gesticulating, bending down occasionally to shout right in her face. And in this manner for one hour and then another it continued, Adam Gibson venting all his frustration and anger at her. Finally, he stopped and threw himself down on his back on the bunk. Minnie Page chose to hold her silence, not wanting to trigger another tirade. Soon he rose, prised a lid from one of the tins, and withdrew two cups, a container with water, and bread and cheese. As much as it made her guts squirm to eat and drink at his behest, she accepted she must comply to live. In this domain, Adam Gibson was King.

From that Saturday night, for day after day, he controlled when Minnie Page ate, when she listened and when she could doze. When she wished to relieve herself, she had to ask for her bonds to be removed so she could use the chamber pot. On these occasions he had enough decency to step from the shack. On return, he would secure her once again, take the chamber pot and empty it in the bush. Each time he left the shack, whether to replenish their water supply at the river, see to the horse, take his own relief, or do his ablutions, he would check her bonds before leaving. And each time he left, he took care to remain within the bush, out of sight of any prying eyes. The field beside the bush was desolate, scrubby, and stony, useful only when it rained and then only for the water fowl who foraged in its dips and hollows. It was a stunted, brooding place, apparently empty and there was no reason for anyone to come that way. Apart, that is, from Adam Gibson.

He wanted no interruptions to his programme of correction of Minnie Page. By day the shack was lit dimly by the few rays of sunshine which managed to penetrate the foliage and find the window. For Minnie Page, the physical hardships were bad enough but when she stirred from her fitful sleep each morning, the anticipation of the browbeating was worse. Time and again he would hammer home her mischief- making.

'You and your shrieking sisterhood caused my Dorothy to leave me. She was happily obedient until you came along filling her head with all your claptrap about the vote and the need for women to rise up and assert themselves. She hung on every word you uttered. Can you imagine for a second what that was like for me? To have her burst through the door after one of your meetings and toss your rubbish words at me as though they were gospel? Bad enough for me to listen to you myself, let alone have your words come to me through my wife.'

'I am not against marriage,' Minnie Page protested. 'Indeed, I am strongly for marriage, but a marriage of equals, where each respects the other and decisions are made jointly.'

'That is not marriage at all,' said Gibson. 'That is a ludicrous state bound to set husband against wife. Imagine the conflict if the wife did not vote as the husband directed. The home would be a pit of hell with argument from dawn to dusk. You must restore the man to his rightful position so he can guide, counsel, and protect his wife from the wickedness of the world.'

There was no reasoning with him or placating him, even when she spoke of her concerns for men as well as women. 'Many men work much too long a day,' she said. 'Many work 12 hours and go home to their wives and families exhausted. I know for a fact the attendants in the Sunnyside Asylum work on an average 13 hours a day.'

'Man is the breadwinner and will do what he must,' Gibson said. 'It is his privilege.'

There was one physical part of the ordeal nearly as bad as the mental. Whenever her hands were bound and he was shouting in her face, she was unable to take her handkerchief and wipe away his spittle. After the worst of his outbursts, there would be globules of saliva dripping from his pale moustache and globules running down her cheeks as well and soaking into her jacket. She could but grimace and try not to provoke him any more than she did by her very presence. Any attempted reasoning with him ended in a rant.

'You are going against the natural order of things. Name one authority which sanctions women to be at the helm. Name one respected body that has a woman chairman. The term speaks for itself – "chairman". There is no such term as "chairwoman". A woman, after all, is a creature of sensations and impulses. She is not a rational thinker. She needs the direction of man.'

And more, much more of the same until she could stand it no more and screamed for him to cut her bonds and set her free.

'Cut your bonds? Never!' he screamed back in her face. 'Cut your tongue from your head more likely.' Since then, she had realised any response only exacerbated his bitterness and she gave him nothing to fight against. Now, into the second week of her incarceration, in despair at the stark horror of her situation, she slumped exhausted in the chair with her head sunk most of the time on her chest, allowing his accusations to bounce off the walls of the shack unanswered.

As her exhaustion grew and her hope of release dissipated, Minnie Page became increasingly passive and silent. Adam Gibson saw that as the achievement of the first stage of her re-education. The time was approaching for the second part of his plan – a return to Christchurch to fetch his wife and bring her to meet her idol Minnie Page and appreciate the error of her ways. Not only could this be the resurrection of his marriage, but that of many others he knew as well.

When Dorothy Gibson saw the artist's sketch of the unknown heckler on a poster in the city, she felt her heart nearly bounce clean out of her body. That was her Adam, or rather, it had been, for the long years she now was grateful were behind her. His control had been even worse than that of her father. When she had married, she had foolishly imagined she was escaping the tyranny her poor spinster sisters had still to endure. Instead, she had left one form of bondage for one even worse. Adam Gibson had been a monster of control, deciding even how many pins, needles, and thread she could purchase. When she moved from his house to a boarding house in a far distant suburb, she took delight in leaving the curtains of her second-floor room pulled wide apart until it was dark as Adam Gibson had always insisted she close the curtains even before dusk. It had been a life of restrictions and confinement and since leaving him she had relished her freedom. It had been difficult making a living on her own but she was managing.

'Have you seen this man?' the police poster simply said, along with a plea to report any sighting. It had now been more than a week but tongues everywhere were still busy with the disappearance of Minnie Page. Most stories in the newspapers were one-day wonders, engrossing the populace one day and wrapping up their fish and chips the next. But Minnie Page was too famous to fade from the headlines. She aroused emotions that were too strong, one way or the other. And there was much sympathy as well for her son, a popular, well-regarded young man, and for her poor mother. The misery of both could be imagined. As soon as she sighted the poster, Dorothy Gibson hastened to the central police station and was ushered straight through to see detective Bernie Frost.

'I have only just seen your poster,' she told him.

'We have only just posted it,' he said. 'When nobody had identified the third heckler, despite all our inquiries, we had our police artist do us a sketch.'

'You have captured him exactly,' she said. 'There is no mistaking.' She looked again at the poster, confronting her now in Frost's office. It captured exactly the piercing eyes, the sallow face, the wispy moustache. He had nurtured his malice until his face pullulated with it. As she gazed, it was not, though, what she saw but words she remembered that made her cringe and be grateful she had exchanged life in his house for life in the small, stark room of the boarding house – the increasingly bitter and violent denunciations of women, especially of Minnie Page and of Dorothy herself.

'Where might he be found?' asked Frost.

Dorothy Gibson gave her husband's address and that of the second-hand furniture emporium that employed him and Frost sent squads to bring him in. He then summoned a shorthand typist and for the next hour she spoke of life with Adam Gibson, periodically interrupted by Frost requesting more detail. When reports came back that Gibson was not at his home ailing, as the furniture emporium's owner had assumed, and had been missing from his work for more than a week, he was confirmed as chief person of interest for the police.

'Did he have any family or friends to the north of the city?'

Dorothy Gibson wracked her brain. She could imagine the gravity of Minnie Page's situation. She had begun to think her husband was quite demented, even before she left him. She had seen the extent of his intolerance and his violent temper tantrums when crossed.

'He has no family at all in the city,' she said. 'They have all died. And no friend either that I know of. He kept to himself, and me.'

Once Dorothy Gibson had departed, Frost mounted a buggy and travelled to the furniture emporium to interview the manager and staff. Already word was spreading far and wide to find and bring in Adam Gibson. The interviews proved useless. Nobody could tell him anything. Gibson had worked in his own bubble, completely self-contained, exchanging no small talk with anyone. He would occasionally collect chairs in the city in need of repair and return them to their place of origin but would otherwise labour away incessantly in a corner of the emporium. He was a good worker and caused no problems.

Later that same day detective Frost told Toby and his nan of the breakthrough in the case. It was little relief for Toby as he had seen the hatred in Gibson for his mother up close. The ordeal continued as before with sleep broken and the daylight hours shot through with terrible imaginings that hurt him more than anything that might happen in the boxing ring.

◆ ◆ ◆

In the shack by the river, Adam Gibson was preparing to drive into Christchurch to fetch his wife. He had chloroform on hand if she did not respond to his reasoning. He had to return to town anyway as their food and other supplies were running low and Kaiapoi was too near to shop. He was confident Minnie Page would cause no problem in his absence as she was now yielding and compliant and gave little complaint. He had ensured she had eaten and drunk and relieved herself before his departure and that her bonds were secure. He took his empty provision tins to his trap and readied his horse which had fed well on oats that morning and drunk its fill of water. He had a last look at Minnie Page, slumped head down in her chair.

'I'll be back soon, with someone for you to talk to.'

She raised her head briefly at the closing of the door and then her head dropped back on her chest. She was trussed as tight as a chicken for the pot. There would be no breakout.

As he emerged from the patch of bush and crossed the scrubland back to the Lower Styx Road, the sun was up and shimmering over the way ahead. Adam Gibson was gratified his plan was working so well. He felt he was on the cusp of the resurrection of his life. Minnie Page had become pleasingly obedient and would now, he felt sure, counsel his wife on the error of her ways. Recalcitrant wives elsewhere would follow their lead and adopt the true path of duty and subservience. The family would be saved from conflict and separation. After more than a week of being cooped up in the shack with his prisoner, it was enormously refreshing to negotiate his way past a sagging, broken, barbed-wire fence and be out in the open. In the dusky blue of dawn, the air was coming fresh off the sea and the rising sun was over his shoulder chasing away the shadows and lightening his way. To the south he could see the trees of Bottle Lake. The horse itself appeared to be delighting in the journey, stepping out at a spanking pace.

They turned onto Lower Styx Road. As usual, there was no one in sight. They proceeded at a good, steady clip and were soon in Marshland, passing cottages and small holdings, every step bringing him closer to his wife and the reclaiming of his marriage.

But then, from his left, came something he could never have anticipated – the most terrible barking and a large dog rushing from a ramshackle property, growling and carrying on and worrying his horse. The horse whinnied in fear and swerved sharply away so that the trap was tossed completely onto its right wheel. Adam Gibson struggled to keep his footing and his grip. The horse was panicking, rearing and out of control, and the gig was lurching and leaping like a mad thing. Then with a terrible shout Gibson was gone, flung screaming straight out the front of the trap, high and far. For seconds he appeared to hang in space before crashing onto the gravel, his head landing with a ghastly crack and his body somersaulting once, twice, and then lying splayed. The horse bolted down the road with the trap fishtailing behind and was soon a speck in the distance. Opposite the dilapidated house, in the sudden silence and final swirls of dust, Adam Gibson lay crumpled and motionless. The dog had briefly raced after the bolting horse and now returned to sniff round the lifeless body.

The police manning the Marshland roadblock saw in the far distance the frightened horse racing towards them. They drew back in case it tried to jump their barrier and came down with the trap on top of them. But then it was as if the horse became aware there was no frenzied barking at its heels, no crazed animal dashing at it. There was only the quiet of the countryside and ahead, a great barrier impeding its progress. It slowed and then stopped altogether, tossing its head and breathing heavily, pawing the ground until it was sufficiently calm for a constable to bring it under control. Soon after, the body of Adam Gibson was found. Nearby were the three empty tins. Detective Bernie Frost was rapidly at the site. The scene was recorded and the body identified and removed to the mortuary at the hospital. Frost then ordered a blanket search of the land north, west, and east of the site for three miles. It would start within the hour and would take in all the country as far as the Waimakariri River to the north, the Groynes protecting Christchurch from the river's ravages to the west, and the ocean to the east. Every habitation in that area was to be searched and every stretch of bush, dune and beach combed. The finding of the tins, which had the lingering aroma of food, encouraged him to think the police might not be searching for a corpse. But being the good policeman he was, he had to consider another possibility – Gibson could have been on his way from concealing evidence.

AN UNEXPECTED DEVELOPMENT

For the rest of that day and the night, in her waking moments, Minnie Page listened for the sounds of his return – for the huffing of the horse, the opening of the door, and the barking of his voice from the doorway. By first light she needed to relieve herself and struggled with everything she had against her bonds, but she had to concede he was right – the more she fought, the tighter the rope became. By noon she had begun to wonder if this was how she would end her days – in bondage and alone. Only once in all her 38 years had she been so low – when she and her child had lost his father. The memory of that caused her to think yet again of Toby and her mother and the anguish they must be feeling. How she would feel in their position. Their faces floated before her, as if in a dream, giving her the strength and will to persist. By night her throat was parched and her knickerbockers were wet. She had never thought she would welcome his return but it seemed her only hope.

◆ ◆ ◆

Dorothy Gibson sighed long and deep on hearing of her husband's death. She felt no sense of loss. Rather, relief – never again could she be subject to his vile moods and bullying. That night her mind flicked back over their time together. At first it had been tolerable but then his craze for power over her had increased until she could barely do anything of her own accord. Her reflections, she realised, were part of her healing: she had to face what had happened, accept it, and move on. One thing, though, did nag at her, something she could not quite bring up from the past, something triggered by mention of Marshland and the Lower Styx Road, something relating to Minnie Page for the missing Minnie was always in her thoughts. What was it? And then it came to her in the night. Whitebait. Her late husband had spoken once, many years before, of fishing for whitebait with his father in the Styx River by a lagoon. She rose in the chilly darkness and hurried through the streets to the central police station. As she passed two drunks swaying and swearing, she took care to swing into the shadows. At the police station she introduced herself to the officer on duty and when she gave the name of detective Frost and said she knew where Minnie Page might be, there was a flurry of activity. Frost was there within 30 minutes and within the hour a search party with horses and lanterns was heading for the Styx River.

As the clatter of the horses rang through the silence of the night at Marshland, they passed the spot where Adam Gibson had lain the day before, skull split and body splayed. Detective Frost pondered on the damage and pain he saw each week in his work and how often it involved unbridled passion of one sort or another. Well, there was an opportunity now, perhaps, to put an end to the pain of Minnie Page and of the multitude who prayed for her. He urged his horse on a little faster.

Minnie Page heard the shout as the first faint sunlight penetrated the whare.

'Over here! A shack in the bush!'

Then, as if in a daze, there were relieved faces and then distressed faces, gasps of disgust and curses against her gaoler, a knife setting her free. A tent was raised and a nurse with the police party assisted her to change into fresh clothing and gave her drink and food. When she felt able, she was placed on a buggy with as much comfort as possible and taken to Christchurch Hospital for observation and recovery. Over the next few days, it was as if the city and nation had passed through a pestilence and emerged triumphant on the other side. Toby and his nan felt a great weight lifted and church attendance the following Sunday was greater than usual.

In the succeeding weeks, Toby and his nan saw a change in Minnie's demeanour. She was not as ready to bubble over into laughter and every so often there was a gravity which plunged them all into gloom. Minnie knew of the River Styx from her studies of art history as the river which divided the world of the living from the world of the dead, and she told her mother that in nightmares, she saw Adam Gibson as Charon the ferryman putting her in Hades. Henceforth, she was more selective where she went in the city. Hagley Park, once a place of joy for her, had become a place of dread, rancid with fearful memory. Then, for Toby, there was great sadness – Mr Goodwin died. It was not altogether unexpected; he was 68 and had been ailing of late. His death was devastating for Mrs Goodwin and her daughters, especially Priscilla who had seen him daily. There was huge change. A son-in-law, Robbie, able and personable, and his wife Jean, took over the property and Mrs Goodwin and Priscilla moved into their Christchurch town house. Toby remained on the estate but it was not the same. He had been almost a son to Goodwin and not a week had gone by without a summons from the house and the assignment of a special duty, whether to see to a favourite horse, talk to someone on Goodwin's behalf, travel with Goodwin and his wife and Priscilla to another grand house or tend to innumerable other things. Toby missed his jovial and affectionate presence more than he could have imagined.

With the terror she had been under since her abduction, It was a blessed release for Minnie Page to return to her painting. One week Toby got leave from the estate to travel with his mother and nan to Governors Bay where they rented a crib and pleased themselves how they spent each day. Walks along the beach and on the hills relaxed their bodies and cleared their minds. On the day before their return, Minnie dropped a bombshell on Toby.

'Mother and I are moving to Wellington.'

Her announcement took his breath away. He needed time to digest the news and its ramifications.

'As much as I love Christchurch, the city has too many bad memories for me now.' She paused and gazed across the sea at the horizon. 'It's not a sudden decision; I've been considering it for some time. As the seat of Parliament and such an economic hub, Wellington will provide me with many more commissions for portraits. Already there are two who have requested I paint them.'

Now that she had aired it, it seemed to him such an obvious move to make. He nodded, in acknowledgment of the sense of it.

'Besides, I can do greater good for the cause of women and families in the country's political centre.'

That, too, made sense. She was a mover and shaker and would be in her element in Wellington.

'Mother and I will purchase a small property in Oriental Bay and I will set up my studio there.'

He could see she had thought it all through and there would be no changing her. It was a plan based on both reason and emotion – he had seen the shudder when they had recently passed through Hagley Park.

'I'll miss you both dearly.'

As he looked at the two of them, the agonies of the past two weeks came back to make his heart race and his palms sweat. What must it be for his mother, to live again through the ordeal each time she cycled the streets of Christchurch? And he had heard Wellington was booming. With new settlers pouring into it from all over the world, it had even grandly dubbed itself 'The Empire City'. Yes, many of its politicians would doubtless be looking to immortalise themselves through a portrait by Minnie Page. Cynics had suspected subterfuge in her disappearance, and though that had not been so, they had been correct in predicting a boost for her paintings.

'Yes, I think you need to get away. A good decision.'

Minnie Page gazed with love on her forlorn son. She could see that Goodwin's death had hit him hard. Though she had done her best, she had been keenly aware all through his childhood that he needed a father. Once Toby had started working, Frank Wallis had been a godsend, and then Mr Goodwin had filled the role better than she could have dreamed. Toby looked at a loss.

'Why don't you come with us?'

The suggestion rocked Toby to the soles of his boots. He had never considered such a thing. Christchurch and Canterbury had always been his home. They were all he knew.

'Where would I find work?'

'A man with your talents with horses will always find work,' she assured him. He soon realised she had thought it all through not just for herself and her nan, but for him as well. 'I have been making inquiries and I know a place would take you on, I feel sure. The estate is in the Rangitikei and they are looking for an experienced and able groom. The estate owner is Mr Charles McAlistair. He has a large and well-appointed estate and races a fine team of horses based at the township of Bulls. It is in the district of Rangitikei, within a few hours' rail journey of Wellington.'

Toby puzzled at where he had heard that name 'Rangitikei' before. Yes, of course, the combined Hunt meeting at Goodwin's. Sir Robert Drake and his son Paul, visitors from the Rangitikei. And then the gift of the bottle of whisky at Riccarton Park. The memory of that set his lips in a hard line. The assault on him by the two hired toughs. They had had the advantages of surprise, size, numbers, and weapons but he had been fortunate they had been drunk and not versed in the art of the sweet science. Since that day he had never sighted the man whom he suspected of putting them up to it. It had been a strange thing indeed. A man dressed like a toff but acting like a common criminal. But Sir Robert and his son were fine people and the Rangitikei was said to be a prosperous part of the colony.

'You know me better than I know myself. I must admit I have been feeling restive.'

He was still happy enough at the Goodwins but the death of Mr Goodwin had changed everything. As for Josephine, they were still good friends. She was attractive and sweet and they were comfortable in each other's company but he knew it would never be more than friendship. And the thought of his mother and nan on the other side of the strait in Wellington was already painful. He liked the sound, too, of a fine estate in another part of the country and of working with racehorses. He still wanted to learn all he could of farming and this estate would doubtless have its own challenges and its own way of doing things. But to work more with racehorses was still his dream.

'Yes, I will apply.'

Minnie had all the details of application ready to hand. He obtained references from Mr Wallis and from the Goodwin family and posted it all away within days to the firm based at Marton which was handling the appointment on behalf of Mr McAlistair. There were then weeks of waiting which were very hard to take for by then his heart was set on the move and on the job. There was no mention in the application that he was the son of Minnie Page as neither mother nor son wanted prejudice against her to jeopardise his chance. Eventually, to the relief of Minnie, Nan, and Toby, he got word in January 1895 the job was his.

The Goodwin management said it would be sorry to lose him but wished him well. He made a point of visiting Mrs Goodwin and Priscilla in their townhouse to say goodbye. To their surprise, he enveloped each of them in turn in a great bear hug and kissed them on the cheek.

'Goodbye Toby. I will never forget you saved my life and Stanley never forgot that either.'

'He was a good man, Mrs Goodwin. I shall never forget him.'

'The best of luck to you. I have heard good things of Charles McAlistair.'

'Goodbye Toby,' said Priscilla. 'Take care of yourself.'

'You too Priscilla,' said Toby. He wanted to ask if she would accept the gentleman's proposal of marriage but sensed she was content to keep her independence and remain the family's beloved maiden aunt.

◆ ◆ ◆

It was with a rush of excitement that Minnie, her mother, and

Toby walked up the gangway of the SS *Penguin* at Lyttelton in a flaring sunset to travel to a new life. The vessel was of an older generation – launched in 1864 and with a single large funnel and a mast fore and aft – but its engine had since been replaced and soon, in darkness, they were churning down the harbour at a brisk 12 knots. As Toby stood in the chill on deck and gazed behind, the twinkling lights on the hillsides of Lyttelton gradually faded until the blackness was complete. Near the heads, far and faint to the right, there was the faint candlelight from a settler's homestead. A life there, thought Toby, would be so steady, regular, predictable, not like his own with so many unknowns ahead. As they entered the ocean, the vessel slowly dipped and rolled, reminding him their lives were in the hands of captain, crew, and Providence. He turned away and found the saloon where his mother and nan were comfortably settled with food and drink.

As he took supper with them, he looked around at his fellow passengers. Four well-dressed men were talking earnestly over drinks at a table, a curate and his wife and two children were playing cards, an elderly lady and a younger woman travelling with her had their noses in books and two men about his own age were smoking and chatting with beers in front of them. When two other men entered the saloon, Toby was all attention. One of them, a dapper-looking man of average size with a trim moustache, was Dick Mason of Riccarton whom he knew well. In his youth Mason had been a jockey but increased weight had taken him out of the saddle and now he was a celebrated trainer for the equally celebrated owner Mr G.G. Stead. He and Toby met with a handshake.

'Toby. What are you doing here?' He had with him a short lad of around 18 who Toby knew was a stable-hand. 'You know Jim Holloway.'

Toby shook hands with Jim as well and in no time, all three were talking horses. Mason heard with interest Toby's change of home and job. 'You should've come and seen me,' he said. 'I would've given you work.'

Mason thought highly of Charlie McAlistair and his team and hoped they wouldn't provide his four horses with too much competition at the Wellington Racing Club meeting they were bound for at the Hutt.

The voyage had settled into perpetual long dips and rolls and the Page family were mindful they should be restrained in their eating and drinking. A friendly steward, with a confidential manner about him, confronted the issue of mal de mer head on.

'I have heard the lot,' he said. 'Some old seamen used to swear by a tumbler of seawater. One of my passengers found it helpful to wear bright red spectacles and another, snow-boots. And one regular, piteously fearful, is always carried on full of drink and is woken at the end. There are some pass up on food altogether. But no need for that. You yourselves have dined very sensibly and the crackers will serve you well now the rest of the way.'

With the words of comfort ringing in their ears and hopefully passing the message on to their stomachs, the three of them rose and left for their cabins. Toby woke as usual around 3.30am, dressed quietly and closed the door on his cabin mates, young men sleeping soundly. He was sure he would never get used to the ship's pitch and roll. He tried not to fight it but move with it but the ship was lively that morning. Then he realised they were in Cook Strait itself. 'The windpipe of the Pacific,' someone had called it. Others had stronger names for it. He was happy to see Jim Holloway in the saloon. He had been up earlier tending to the horses. The two of them spent the last two hours of darkness discussing the prospects of the Mason horses and others that would be racing at the Hutt. Jim Holloway rated some of the Sir Robert Drake horses highly, as well as some of Charles McAlistair. Soon, the stewards were there with cups of tea and as the sun rose, the Page family sighted the lighthouse at Pencarrow and then the SS *Penguin* was entering Wellington Harbour, one of the great harbours of the world. The keen southerly wind whipped the smoke from the ship's funnel towards Eastbourne where it merged with the smoke rising from houses tucked into the bush. To port, cottages and the occasional more substantial building climbed all the way to the ridgeline. As the *Penguin* swung round Point Halswell heading for its berth in Port Nicholson hard by the city centre, the quarantine station of Somes Island lay far off to starboard while ahead were ships loading and unloading cargo, drays and other vehicles coming and going on the wharves, and, beyond, all the buildings and bustle of the Empire City.

 As Minnie Page eyed the pretty cottages of Oriental Bay where her heart was set on residing, she was keenly aware the passions in Wellington ran as hot as in the south. If anything, hotter, for this was where the elected with a political agenda gathered to vent their views. That morning, she would read in the newspaper that an old opponent, Henry Fish of Dunedin, still begrudged the vote for women and would overturn it if he could. She had to believe, though, there was not another so warped as Adam Gibson. She was sure, too, the constabulary would have its watchful eye on the extremists – the Empire City would want no kidnapping to sully its name. She had heard, too, that with people travelling from all quarters to the capital city, Wellington was a remarkably tolerant place, more than those where people stuck, along with all their prejudices. She could but trust that would be so. She determined, anyway, to forgo public speaking and to take a less prominent role in promoting the cause of women. For now, at least, she would sink from sight.

They breakfasted together in the city and then Toby saw his mother and nan to their temporary accommodation at the Britannia Hotel in Willis Street. The hotel promised 'a first-class table, every comfort and convenience, perfect sanitary arrangements and commodious sitting rooms replete with all the leading periodicals of the day', and Minnie and her mother vowed to make the most of it before finding a place of their own. After farewells with Toby, they watched him until he disappeared into Lambton Quay heading for the railway station, and then turned to each other and smiled. The move had been a great upheaval but there was the comfort all three of them were in the same island and in the southern part of it.

FLASHBACK

So slow was the train north for the first mile, Toby reckoned he could have kept up on foot. But it picked up considerably and township after township soon fell behind and he moved into a hinterland of plain and rolling hills, pasture and sheep and cattle, and much bush. Though the scenery was new to him and full of interest, the steady clickety clack of the train put him in a doze and it took the guard's stentorian shout, 'All passengers for Marton!' to stir him from his slumber. A moment later he found himself with his suitcase on the platform of the Marton Railway Station. Its most vehement supporter would have to concede the station was modest but it did afford a measure of protection from the rain drifting in from the north. Toby pulled his cap tighter and huddled into his jacket. As he looked down the platform, he realised the 'All passengers for Marton!' was himself. The guard blew his whistle, stepped back onto the train, and with a huff and a puff and much billowing of steam, it drew away. When the sounds faded altogether, the countryside was even more still and silent and Toby felt lonesome and a mite rattled. But moments later a buggy appeared with a cheerful lad at the reins. A cap was perched on his great mop of hair and he had a grin from ear to ear.

'You will be Toby then!' he called. 'Welcome to the Rangitikei.'

Jimmy Ford was a station hand of Charles McAlistair. He was a chummy sort and as they chatted, Toby began to feel at ease.

'There is the master, his wife, a son and two daughters, Clarissa and Sophie. The son, Harry, is a good lad but they keep a close eye on him as he's subject to fits.' He paused and looked reflective. 'Sophie is blind. The master and his wife have not, though, been brought low by it.'

Not brought low by it, Toby mused. Perhaps not on the surface but surely in their private moments they must reflect and grieve. That would be only human.

'Five permanent staff in the house,' said Jimmy Ford. 'Cook, parlour maid, kitchen maid, laundry maid and gardener. All live in and eat their meals together in the kitchen. They're a cheerful lot, all good sorts.'

'What about the stable?' asked Toby.

'They've got a few hopes there, I hear,' Jimmy Ford said. 'There were one or two slow as molasses. I know, because I did my money on them. But those are station hacks now and they have some good ones in. Norman Kelly's a good man and a good trainer and he'll tune them up, my word he will, don't you worry about that.'

As for the farm, Jimmy Ford said there were 48 staff but that could build to 100 at certain times of year. The estate was river flats, rolling hills and steep areas still in bush. There were some 40,000 sheep, mostly Lincolns and Romney Marsh, robust and good for both mutton and wool, and some 2,000 cattle. For the estate's own use there were dairy cows, pigs, hens, and a large vegetable garden. There was a large team of horses to pull the plough and carry and haul people and produce.

'Bert Sinclair is the station manager and reports direct to Mr McAlistair,' said Jimmy Ford. 'A tough man, but fair. He will rouse out the shirkers but give you credit when it's due. He's good with the swaggers and my word, we get a lot of swaggers through here. There are them who slack about and them who are tryers from first to last. "Shove along," Mr Sinclair will say to the first, and "Hang about a bit," he will say to the second. They all get a bed, a plate of stew and bread, and a cup of tea, for a night at least.'

Toby had always been intrigued by the swaggers at Mr Goodwin's estate. He had got to know many and had come to admire most of them. The loss of a job had often put a swag on their shoulder. He knew that these men (and they were nearly all men thank God; the life of a woman on the road he couldn't bear to think about) could be of great value at harvest and other busy times.

They sighted the McAlistairs' Glenview Station homestead some 90 minutes later. It was a grand, two-storeyed house set back from the road amidst gardens with many elm and other exotic trees. Toby considered its inhabitants, the master and mistress, Clarissa and the two damaged children. No doubt as groom, and general hand, he would meet them soon enough. They drove straight past to the station hands' quarters where he reported to Bert Sinclair and met with a frank, appraising look, and a handshake.

'Here's your man, Mr Sinclair,' said Jimmy Ford, removing

himself to tend to the horse.

'Thank you, Jimmy,' said Mr Sinclair.

Toby cast his own appraising look. Bert Sinclair was a tall, lean man with a clipped moustache. His grip was firm without being the oppressive clasp of someone trying to put him in his place. He was dressed not as one who might sit all day giving orders but as one who might mount a horse to see things for himself. He welcomed Toby to the estate on behalf of Mr McAlistair, confirmed for himself Toby's experience, outlined his duties, and showed him to his quarters in the bunkhouse. They then proceeded to the stables and the smithy where Toby met Frank Dunlop, the blacksmith he would at times be assisting, a short, thickset man exuding strength. Toby was then introduced to the horses that were not out working.

Over the next fortnight he was taken to all parts of the estate and learnt what was meant by the Downs and the Top Block, the Corner, and the Cliffside. He spent time, too, at the horse-training stable of Norman Kelly at Bulls, the private trainer who had the horses of Charles McAlistair and others as well. It was Kelly who introduced him to Mr McAlistair. They looked at each other for those two or three seconds that say so much. Toby saw a man in a soft felt hat with an open, friendly face, a neatly trimmed beard and a solid build. He could feel himself being weighed in the balance as he took the hand that was offered.

'Charlie McAlistair. Welcome to Glenview.' There was a slight smile and the look was intelligent and discerning. 'I hope you enjoy it here. We could use a man good with horses, as I've heard you are.'

Toby detected a faint Scottish burr. His mother had told him Mr McAlistair's family had emigrated from Scotland many years before. 'Thank you, sir. I will do my best.' Toby glanced down the line of loose boxes. 'You have some likely ones I hear.'

'Yes, they seem to be coming along nicely. The autumn meeting at Hutt Park should be interesting.'

While Mr McAlistair continued to talk with Norman Kelly, Toby turned back to his stable duties. He was pleased to have met the master and to have seen for himself he was not the cold and aloof sort. He was pleased, too, in subsequent weeks, that Bert Sinclair assigned him more to the stables than the farm, though he was all ears wherever they put him. All he did at first was work and sleep. But every day there was something to learn and at night he would take his pencil and record everything in his notebook. He discovered over the succeeding months he had a gift for teaching horsemanship. Some of the ability came from years of observation and experience with Frank Wallis and at the Goodwin estate, but he suspected that others he might have been born with. The station hands, other stable hands and even the jockeys appreciated his insights into the horses. Toby had the invaluable ability to see a horse's strengths and weaknesses and identify a minor problem before it became a major issue. Once, he stood in the middle of the track at Bulls, watched a horse gallop towards him, detected a fault in the action and had the shoeing altered to correct it.

The autumn meeting at Hutt Park was full of incidents from first to last. In the Railway Handicap, the McAlistair horse Sharp Promise was struck by the starting tape, reared up and lost lengths, but finished strongly for third. The stable's entry in the steeplechase finished second while others baulked at the fences and ran off, and in the open handicap, their horse ran fifth. Bobby Baxter, the stable jockey, told Kelly and Toby that a rival in the open handicap had tried to push his horse into the rail before the turn and Baxter had had to whip him off. Baxter could have been put over the rail or smashed his shin but Baxter, tall, thin, and wiry, had one priceless asset – once in the saddle, he stayed there. There was not as much rough riding now as in earlier times but there was still some and it could be deadly.

Toby relished his time with the McAlistair children. Clarissa, the eldest at 19, was already a talented horsewoman. Dainty and composed with her mass of dark hair usually in a long plait, she sat well on her horse and it was the more subtle things that Toby was able to teach her, such as how to pick up the stress messages a horse sent out and how to remove her own stress before she went to the horse.

'Think of your favourite place or your favourite song, and take a deep breath. Show the horse you are at peace. Have soft eyes and blink.'

With Harry, 16, Toby had to be vigilant to anticipate an epileptic seizure and ensure the boy was in a safe place. The first time there was a seizure, Toby was taken totally by surprise. Thankfully, Harry had been standing right by his side and when he lost consciousness and fell, it was only the few feet to the ground. Toby had watched aghast as his muscles went rigid, his breathing stopped, his skin went blue and all four limbs began to jerk. But, thank God, his breathing restarted. But then there was saliva foaming at his mouth. Toby's shout brought Mrs Elizabeth McAlistair rushing to the scene.

'Stand clear and don't touch him!' she said.

Mrs McAlistair was genteel in appearance and slight in build but had a large presence in the emergency. She cleared everything within five yards and then stood back, hands on hips, watching her son intently. In five minutes or so it was all over and Harry lay confused and sleepy before being helped back to his feet. He would have no memory of what had happened. The incident over, Elizabeth swept her cascading brunette hair back from her face and poured herself a brandy and ginger ale. She offered Toby one but he declined, reserving his drinking for after hours.

'If that ever happens when you're with him, just give him space and time,' she said.

Harry was on medication to help stay free of seizures. There was some opinion that bright lights or sharp sounds could trigger an attack. Toby tried to ensure there was nothing of that sort when Harry was with the horses. Harry of the tousled black hair and wide grin, never saw himself as handicapped and that might have been a hazard, but his parents were glad he was bold and fearless and prayed that in time, he would grow out of his affliction or that medical science would find a cure. He had his father's solid build and already, at 16, his father's gentlemanly manner.

Sophie, 14, was slim with fine features and blonde hair that normally tumbled to her shoulders like silk but today was in a messy ponytail. She had been blind from birth. Elizabeth had contracted rubella in the early stages of pregnancy and this had caused cataracts and blindness in the unborn baby.

Sophie needed an even closer eye on her than Harry for she had the same bold spirit as her siblings. She was devoted to her pony Maisie. Maisie – so placid you could crawl under her legs and tail and she would stand quiet as you liked. Sophie had discovered how Maisie liked to be touched and by guiding her hands, Toby was able to teach her yet more about Maisie. Sometimes they became so absorbed in the horse, Toby could even forget Sophie was blind. All trust and attention, she looked people full in the face when they spoke.

'See, she likes it when you hold your palm towards her forehead, nod downward, take a big breath and blow it out. See, she lowers her head just like you and blows out too.'

And Sophie would laugh as she and Maisie played copy-cat with each other.

Sophie had been blessed with a rare gift, as if in compensation – she had the most exquisite soprano singing voice Toby had ever heard. When she sang in the hall at Bulls, her heavenly notes transported the audience to another world. They would not let her leave, demanding yet another song. Some wondered afterwards if they had been hallucinating. Toby had felt as proud of her as if she had been his own daughter.

The children, in turn, were observant of Toby, and curious about his situation and his ambitions in life. He told them his father had been killed at riding and his mother and nan were in Wellington. He did not say she was the well-known Minnie Page as he had often found an extreme reaction for or against and would rather both he and she could live in peace, particularly after the kidnapping.

Clarissa made a frequent joke of his single status. 'Now Toby,' she would say, 'Aren't your mother and nan worried? Twenty-three and no wife on the horizon and no grand-children running around for them to fuss over. Do you need an introduction?' And she would name various lasses of the district who she was sure were looking for a husband. 'There's my friend Agnes for one. She is said to be very accommodating and would give you a ripping time but you would need great staying power to keep up with her'. And more of the same, which had Toby flummoxed and Harry and Sophie in stitches.

Mr and Mrs McAlistair could see how much enjoyment and value the children were receiving from Toby's tuition and he was allowed some time with them during the work day. But even on a Sunday, his day of rest, the children wanted to be with him, riding their horses.

As a capable horseman, Toby was invited to take part in the Rangitikei Hunt. So it was that one chilly winter's morning, he was hosted, along with Mr McAlistair, Clarissa and some 30 others, to breakfast at 'Closeburn' by Mr and Mrs Stewart and their three charming daughters. There were all sorts there, from the lithe equestrian in it for the ride to the gnarled veteran keen to show he still 'had it' and the fat dabbler in it for the company and for the nips of whisky before and after. One member was already having a sip at a whisky flask. He conceded, quite frankly, he needed it to face the fences. Others, perhaps to bolster courage, made extravagant claims for their horses.

'Jump?' Toby heard one exclaim. 'He can jump clean over a man's head!'

Another had great ambitions for success on the racecourse. 'I'll be thundering surprised if he's not lining up for the Great Northern this year.'

Clarissa had ridden with the Hunt since her days in pigtails and she kept Toby intrigued and amused with her observations. She drew his attention to two elderly men in sweeping moustaches, chatting animatedly in a corner.

'Those two fell out over something years ago,' she said. 'As the years rolled on, they couldn't remember what it was they fell out over but they were so bloody-minded they kept their absurd old sore festering. Then one day, passing in a lane, one nodded to the other and now the two old boys are bosom friends again.'

As Toby roamed around the green coats, red collars, and vests, he spotted Sir Robert Drake and his son Paul. They nodded in his direction. They remembered him from Canterbury and Paul Drake was also prominent in the Rangitikei Volunteer Militia, of which Toby himself was a member. Toby enjoyed the discipline of the drilling, the jumping of horses over fences and fallen trees, and the rifle-shooting competitions, and all the banter that went on around them. The members were nearly all hearty local lads, with a few older, ready to defend their country should any foreign power dare to invade. Then Toby caught his breath, stood stock still and stared. He felt lightheaded for a moment, as though his heart had stopped. There, beyond Sir Robert and Paul Drake, thick in conversation with three others, was the man who had stolen the bottle of whisky at Riccarton Park. Toby continued to stare. There was no mistaking it. It was no paranoic mistake. It was the young toff who had set the thugs on him. His companions were a large fellow with a walrus moustache, a man with mutton-chop whiskers with his hair swept to one side, and a dapper-looking fellow with a trimmed and waxed handlebar moustache. Toby moved to Clarissa's side and as unobtrusively as he could, drew her attention to the four of them and asked who they were.

'The walrus moustache belongs to Eddie Shaw,' she said. 'He farms near here and has interests in mining. Mr Mutton-Chop Whiskers is Henry Thompson. He parts his hair in that manner to cover a missing ear, shorn off by his horse's hoof when he fell at riding. The waxed moustache is Arthur Wilson, who has political ambitions. His father has a large estate and he himself has a property.'

Here she paused, and Toby detected a catch in her voice and a sincerity in her manner, with none of the flippancy of the earlier comments.

'The man holding forth at the moment, with the dark hair and blue eyes, is Simon Drake, second son of Sir Robert Drake.'

For a moment they both stared, each transfixed in their own way, before Clarissa moved away to speak to her father. Toby could understand Clarissa's obvious interest in Simon Drake – he was handsome and athletic with dazzlingly blue eyes.

Toby was shaken and confused. Surely the son of Sir Robert Drake would not steal his own father's bottle of whisky, gifted to Mr Goodwin, and then arrange for Toby to be thrashed for taking it back. The theft he was certain of – there was no mistaking the man and Toby had seen his action with his own eyes. The second was almost as certain for the ruffian had admitted to being paid for the deed and who else had the motive to pay? Then Simon Drake looked up, saw Toby and Toby knew for certain. Drake had looked at him at first with puzzlement and then his face had curdled and his body gone rigid. He said something and then all four were looking at him. Toby did not want to appear intimidated. While they gazed, he made a point of going to Mr McAlistair, now talking to Clarissa and Sir Robert and Paul Drake, to wish them all well for the Hunt. But Toby's ease had fled. He knew he had made an enemy and suspected the matter was not yet over.

Soon the riders were moving to their horses in a rollicking atmosphere under an iron-grey sky. Most of the horses were already warmed up, hacked there, towed behind the buggy, or even driven between the shafts, though some had been railed and then towed. One large man was mounting his horse from a gate. Charles McAlistair was well mounted on Buster, a flowing chestnut, and Clarissa on Molly, an excellent leaper. Toby had every confidence in his own Punch, a horse that looked sleepy until a Hunt began but then was all attention. Riders took their places behind the huntsman and his hounds, and the Master of the Hunt, Mr Dan Riddiford, a large, moustachioed man with a natural air of authority. The Rangitikei Hunt had a reputation for doing things by the book, typified by Mr Riddiford holding his whip erect, the tip resting on his shoulder, in the traditional pose for a Master. With discretion in mind, Toby stayed in the middle and to the side, well wide of Simon Drake and his companions. He could but hope that in time, Simon Drake would shelve his grudge against him, just as the two old boys had shelved their grudge.

In minutes there was too much happening for Toby to worry about Simon Drake. The hounds, tall, rangy, and fast, were onto a hare and the field was streaming after her. It was good, undulating hunting country, providing all manner of fences.

The music of the hounds rang clear over all the countryside, hastening the blood of horses and riders and warning the neighbours of an impending invasion. A few in buggies tried to follow progress from the road. The first two fences were straightforward post and rail, not too high. The third was gorse and higher and as Punch flew over, Toby saw how one horse had flopped into it and become entangled. No time to linger; there were horses pressing on both sides and behind. Its rider appeared to be unhurt. Onwards behind the tally-ho of the horn.

One elderly, red-faced, beaming gentleman said, as Toby went by, 'I do believe my bones are jumping out of my skin!'

Then a massive, boxthorn hedge was looming and even Punch was weighing up his chances. Some of the riders accepted it was too much and turned right for the easier option of a low gate. But up, up, up flew Punch and cleared the ditch on the other side as well. Toby patted it gratefully. To his rear, Simon Drake set his own horse at it and cleared it with a mighty leap. Two paddocks on, a high wire fence loomed. Many riders did not like wire, with the increased danger of the horse getting tangled, and would go sideways to avoid it. Drake rode hard to be ahead of Toby and as Toby readied Punch to take the jump at the wire, Drake cut him off and took the leap himself. Surprised and thrown suddenly off balance, Toby and Punch reeled sideways at speed. For a moment, Toby thought he must crash into the wire. He knew the wire could tear him to bits, shred the flesh off him, and Punch could break a leg and that would be the end of him. He resisted a fierce pull left that could take Punch off his legs and threw all his weight to the right. It took all his skill and nerve to stay astride and steady Punch. When the space had cleared, he swung back and around in a wide circle until he and Punch had calmed and their breath was normal. By then, the music of the hounds was faint and the field was a paddock away. He lined up the high wire fence once again and this time Punch flew it with ease. As Toby rode on, he tried to come to terms with what had happened. It had been more than accidental, dangerous riding by Simon Drake. It had been a deliberate attempt to maim or kill, just like the hiring of the two thugs to beat him up. He had to wonder at the depth of the man's bitterness.

Back at the house, he looked for Simon Drake to tell him what he thought. Son of Sir Robert Drake though he was, he had to be confronted. Toby knew that if he didn't speak up, Simon Drake would despise him as a lily-livered nobody. He tethered and tied Punch, and strode towards Drake who was standing with his friends, laughing. Drake's face slewed into a sneer as Toby approached.

'That was a low, vicious thing to do,' said Toby. 'My horse might have been killed.'

Drake looked astonished that someone would challenge him. A common fellow at that; a mere groom, Drake had heard.

'Bad as setting two men on another to maim him,' added Toby. That reference was a mystery to Eddie Shaw and Arthur Wilson but Henry Thompson knew what he meant.

Simon Drake's lip curled and his eyes narrowed. Toby saw his face flush and his body stiffen and Toby knew Drake wanted to hack him to pieces. But then Dan Riddiford, the Master, was suddenly there. Perhaps he had overheard the conversation or word had reached him from others of Simon Drake's selfish and dangerous riding. Whatever, he realised it was time to fulfil his duty as Master.

'Look here Drake,' he said, 'you should know by now the Hunt does not condone that sort of thing.' Mr Riddiford drew Simon Drake to one side to continue his reproof.

Toby turned his back on the others who were not laughing now. As he left to tend to Punch, he saw Sir Robert Drake glaring at the spectacle of the Master remonstrating with his son.

OF NATURE AND NURTURE

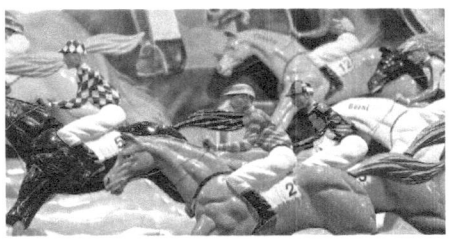

T oby used his holidays to visit his mother and nan in Wellington. With an early start, travelling by trap and train, he could be down there in a day. His heart always leapt when he arrived at the harbour and saw the sun sparkling off the water. Then it was a brief walk to Oriental Bay and into the arms of his mother and nan. Sometimes he still woke in the witching hours, distraught, and he doubted he would ever get over the anguish Adam Gibson had put them through. Minnie Page was as fervently devoted to her political and social causes as ever but she had never mounted the rostrum since that ill-fated time in Christchurch and her name was never these days emblazoned in headlines. Her influence was now behind the scenes. She was on first-name terms with leaders of the Liberal Party and other reformers and frequently brought issues to their attention. It was 1896 but still there were reports each week of horrific injuries in factories up and down the country and she pressed for improvement in conditions for all workers, male and female. Men in factories often worked unpaid overtime. In the city she saw women reduced to selling their bodies to any drunken slag. Some she helped to a better life. Above all, she pushed for greater opportunities and equality for girls and women – why should a male teacher receive £297 a year and a woman £129 for the same work?

Toby was pleased to see his mother as feisty and driven as ever. His nan, too, was revelling in life in Wellington and took secret pleasure in observing the affectations of the high and mighty who visited Minnie to have their portraits done. When she peeked through a door, she could see some of them primping themselves to look their best and others who posed like peacocks in mating season to achieve a noble presence. A part of her had to sympathise with them for she knew how difficult it can be to hold a natural smile without it turning into a death-like rictus. But it always staggered her, that however much they preened and presented their rosy side, her daughter captured their true selves in the angle of the chin, the look in the eye, the turn of the mouth. Their response at the final viewing was often a frozen gaze in silence, as they needed time to accept they were not Napoleon at Austerlitz nor Wellington at Waterloo, but themselves with all their blemishes and frailties. Any discomfort mostly dissipated when family, colleagues and friends heaped praise on the portrait and congratulated Minnie Page on capturing them so well.

In turn, Minnie and his nan were pleased to see Toby so content with his lot at the estate.

'What have you got brewing about a wife?' asked his nan. 'Have you got yourself a woman yet boy?' She had never been one to skirt around issues. After all, girls could marry at twelve and boys at fourteen and Toby was twenty-four. Many men his age had a brood of children by now. The question drew Minnie's attention as well.

Toby laughed and deflected the matter. 'You're as bad as Clarissa. Time enough for that later,' he said. 'I've got too much to do in the stables and on the farm for now.' Truth to tell, there was no one on the horizon but it was a situation he did want to remedy and he hoped to meet someone at a dance, fete, the football club, Hunt – anywhere.

Minnie and his nan then quizzed him at length about Mr McAlistair and his family. Toby's face lit up as the faces of the McAlistair family swam before him. His mother and nan were delighted to hear how much Toby liked them and how much life on the estate was agreeing with him, but they were dismayed to hear of Harry's fits and Sophie's blindness.

'It doesn't hold them back,' Toby assured them. 'We go on rides along the river and through bush trails and you would never know they have an issue.' He looked reflective. 'You know, I think it is those who would put limits on Harry and Sophie that have a problem. Perhaps dwelling on Harry and Sophie's challenges makes those people feel superior in themselves.'

'I think you're right boy,' said his nan. 'There are plenty of them that push others down to pull themselves up.'

Toby told them of Sophie's beautiful singing voice. Minnie nodded thoughtfully.

'Interesting,' she said. 'There are people I know who are always looking for brilliant new talent for the theatres and concert halls.'

Minnie was pleased that, although Toby did not yet have a family of his own, he had that family.

The days in Wellington flew by and then it was back to the Rangitikei and working from dawn to dusk with the horses or on the farm. Increasingly, Norman Kelly confided in Toby and even sought his opinion. They usually had a team of around 10. When Toby started, it had been a very mixed bag. Now, they were all either proven or promising horses.

'I've had to let some horses go,' said Kelly. 'You know how it is. They might look like world beaters but are not worth a pie. And then there are those that surprise you.' Toby had seen that himself down south. A horse that could not be mounted. He'd been told that if he tried, he'd be killed. A previous owner had beaten the horse. But Toby had taken his time and waited until it was ready. The horse had needed healing. It turned out to be sweet-tempered and in time Goodwin himself had ridden it to hounds and what a jumper it had been.

Toby nodded. 'I know what you mean.'

'Mr McAlistair has ambitions with them but it's more than the racing,' Kelly said. 'He loves the horses and will never ask for anything that will harm a horse or rider. Not like some of them.'

Kelly's face momentarily hardened. There had been the owner in earlier times who demanded his horse run despite its being lame, and the owner who had a heavy bet on another and wanted his own horse to be pulled out of the reckoning. Then there was the owner who insisted a meeting go ahead although anyone with a brain could see the ground was too slippery and dangerous.

Kelly's eye fell on a leggy bay gelding in the paddock. 'Talk about those that surprise you. Just look at Leap Year.' The horse was grotesque in its long, skinny legs and large head. 'It looks the queerest thing on four pins but can it jump! We have hopes for it at the Marton Spring Meeting at the Old York Farm.'

Toby was still coming to terms with the multitude of racecourses in the region. Rail was becoming more available to move the horses around but frequently horses were walked to the courses and every settlement with a scatter of houses and a pub seemed to have a racecourse.

Leap Year had been a fighter in his younger years and some of his riders had gone clean over his head. 'No good at all, especially with his queer-looking legs,' said the critics. But with firmness and easy, slow repetition, Kelly had gained his trust and Leap Year had learnt to channel that aggression. He was as ready as Kelly could get him for the Handicap Hurdle Race at the Marton Spring Meeting in November, 1896 but he had a weighty 13 stone to carry. Coming into the final bend, Leap Year had seen off 12 of his rivals and was second, three lengths behind the leader. One jump to go, a large brush fence imposing for a fresh horse let alone a tiring one. Clarissa admitted later she could scarcely look – with that weight on his back, this last fence could well find him out, no matter how big his heart. But it was the leader that faltered, slowed, half fell into it and barely scrambled over it. Leap Year took it at full gallop and with one mighty leap made up the three lengths and more and thrust on to the finish well clear as the

McAlistair family leapt in a joyous ring of arms on the lawn.

Norman Kelly and Toby sat one morning by the tack room and chatted about where the horses were at in their preparation, and their prospects. Most were well on and needed to be pitched at races. The two horsemen were joined briefly by Bobby Baxter. Baxter was lucky in that he lived with Kelly and his wife; some jockeys elsewhere were tossed a blanket and told to find somewhere in the stable. Baxter threw his pennyworth into their discussions.

'Mr McAlistair has his eye on the Rangitikei Cup in January for High Play,' said Kelly. 'The 1½ miles on his home course should suit him very well, especially if it's hard and fast.'

The others agreed. High Play, a four-year-old brown entire, was a long-striding horse that settled well yet had a good turn of speed at the business end of a race. He had already won six races and been placed several times and was the current stable star. The horses gazed over the doors of their loose boxes or munched contentedly at the fresh grass in the adjoining paddock as their futures were mulled over. Once Norman Kelly had all their thoughts and information together, it would all go to Charles McAlistair for he was the master and paid all the bills.

Toby looked forward to his Sundays with the children. Clarissa was often away with her parents visiting at a homestead, and sometimes Harry and Sophie went too. But otherwise, unless the weather was ghastly, the children would ride the river trails and wind through the bush with Toby, Sophie getting the feel of the land through sure-footed Maisie, and enjoying the wind in her hair and the sun in her face. Clarissa would lead if she were with them, otherwise Harry would choose their path. Sophie would follow and Toby would be 'tail-end Charlie' keeping an eye on them all. Harry was a naturalist and had the eyes of a hawk to go with it.

One fine day by the river he had a sharp intake of breath. 'Look at the paradise shelduck.'

Toby and Clarissa followed the direction of his arm and took in the life-and-death saga. The duck, in the distance, was giving a broken-wing display, intended to draw a predator – cat, rat, stoat or ferret probably – away from its chicks. Harry explained to Sophie what was happening.

'Oh no,' she said.

Toby felt a surge of exasperation at the human folly that had introduced the mustelids in the 1870s and 1880s to control the rabbits. The 'cure' had turned out worse than the 'disease'. Fortunately, on this occasion, the bravery and guile of the mother won the day. They watched, and Harry described for Sophie, how the duck drew the stoat well away and then flew back to her chicks.

Harry's observations brought the landscape alive for them all. On one ride, they took turns naming their favourite birds.

'The tui for me,' said Clarissa, 'with its cute little white tuft under the throat and its boldness and acrobatics. There is one other I do like more but I've seen it only once – the huia. You know, the beautiful feathers in Maori cloaks.'

'A good choice,' Toby said. He had never seen the rare huia

but he would never forget its song that he had been lucky once to hear. It had rung for hundreds of metres through the forest. Sadly, the huia seemed to be under great threat from introduced mammals.

'The welcome swallow,' said Harry. 'It's so eye-catching with its dash of red, and so gutsy – welcome swallows will mob a large predator bird threatening one of them.'

'The fantail for me,' said Sophie. 'How can you not love the fantail?' In her mind's eye she saw the little fantail or piwakawaka, so friendly, so busy. She had been deeply impressed when Harry said it would make up to four nests a year with some five chicks in each because of the toll taken by predators, and wasn't that a wonder in itself?

'Good choices,' said Toby. 'No doubt about that. But for me it's a toss-up between the bellbird or the kereru.'

The others understood his selection. The bellbird for its song and the kereru, or native pigeon, for its large size and striking colouring of white belly, dark-green and purple back and red bill and eyes.

At the annual district show day, Harry's observations brought everything alive for Sophie. Toby was mostly with the estate's horses that were involved in displays or competitions, but when he could, he went looking for Harry and Sophie. Clarissa was busy enough taking part in the jumping and mingling with her friends. To Toby's alarm, he saw Clarissa at one point with Simon Drake, sharing a joke, touching his arm. Toby had to admit that Drake was a dashing fellow and that he drew the eyes of the ladies, and not only those of the younger ones but those of some of the matrons as well. As he looked at the two of them chatting and laughing, he saw the whisky bottle, the two thugs coming at him and Drake cutting him off at the high-wire fence, and felt a stab of pain in his gut. He had heard stories, too, of the exploits of the self-named 'Hellfire Boys', Simon Drake and his toadies Eddie Shaw, Henry Thompson, and Arthur Wilson. As youths, they had degenerated into excess. They had discharged firearms in a bar and several staff were burnt but the four young 'bloods' had paid them off with hush money. Another time they had distributed cayenne pepper in a hall and many people had choked fit to die. Both times they were lucky not to be prosecuted. Family ties, it seems, had saved them. A frequent favourite trick, it was said, was to unhang the entrance gates of estates. Nothing could ever be proved – they were always long gone, believing themselves to be dashing jokesters. Toby was aware they were nothing more than a ratpack, more sneering and louche than lustrous.

'Toby, over here!' shouted Harry.

Harry and Sophie put a smile back on Toby's face, although it always worried him a little to see them on their own. There was such fun in the air – a band playing, children running, bells ringing and the music of the merry-go-round gaily ringing out. Balls were flying at a target to the cheers and hoots of the crowd, a man was dancing a jig and accompanying himself on a mouth organ, and a barrowman was shouting: 'Here we are, nice fresh bananas from the top of the tree where the monkeys can't get them!' Harry and Sophie were revelling in the noise, action, and excitement.

Toby could see Harry and Sophie were at a sideshow where contestants reached blindfolded into a large box and identified the objects within by touch. He was intrigued to see Sophie was wearing a blindfold. As Toby approached, Harry caught his eye and grinned and Toby knew what he meant – Sophie had the advantage of knowing no other state. A sign read 'Three goes and you're gone.' Three attempts to reach in and identify the heavily wrapped objects by touch. The sideshow attendant, a short, stout man in a hat, appeared to be in a strange mix of agitation and admiration.

'Oh my shakes young lady,' he said. 'I've never seen the like. Three goes and you've got three prizes, including my top prize.'

Sophie was laughing fit to bust. Her tactile expertise had found a rewarding outlet. There was no cheating about it – she was simply making use of a talent resulting from an infirmity. 'This is a great game Toby,' she said. 'We must play this at home.' Harry, with a mischievous grin, was holding her winnings: a cruet for use at the dining table, a moustache cup and a ladies' brush and comb. 'Here,' she said to Toby, 'the moustache cup is yours.'

'Home is where ye'll have to play it in future my lass,' said the man. 'Dang it, you would've done me in if you'd kept going.'

'Thank you, Sophie,' said Toby. 'A good win and a useful prize.'

As their group of three moved off, the sideshow attendant had to call out to retrieve the blindfold from Sophie as she had forgotten she was wearing it. He looked puzzled as they moved towards another sideshow where Sophie had as much chance as anyone – pushing down a lever with the arms to send a weight skywards to ring a bell. Charles and Elizabeth McAlistair had determined years ago that although she was blind, she did not have to be frail, and had set up a small exercise room where the children could lift and swing various weighty objects as well as swing themselves from a bar. At the sideshow there was a bell for ladies and a bell for men and with one mighty thrust, Sophie set the ladies' bell ringing loud and clear.

'Bravo!' shouted Toby while Harry clapped up a storm, not at all surprised she had won yet another prize. Sophie at just 16 had downed him more than once at wrestling when their parents were not around to see such tomboyish behaviour.

'What's next?' asked Sophie.

'Time for me to return to the horses,' said Toby.

'We'll come over soon and give you a hand,' said Harry, as he looked for the next attraction; Sophie just seemed to be warming up.

But Toby had not long departed when Harry suddenly screamed shrilly and crashed to the ground in an epileptic seizure. His frantic jerking of limbs shocked the by-standers and they could only stand and stare. The flashing lights or the noisy ringing of bells might have sparked it.

'Give him space!' shouted Sophie. 'If he vomits, turn him on his side. Otherwise let him be! Someone, please, tell me how he is. I am blind.'

A middle-aged woman, a nurse at the hospital on leave for the day, hurried to Sophie and clasped her elbow.

'It's all right my love. He'll be all right. I'll keep an eye on him.'

The distressing thrashing of limbs and heavy breathing was over in no more than three minutes but it seemed to Sophie to last for ever. The woman then helped Harry to his feet and Sophie embraced him in relief. He was confused and had no recollection of the seizure. With profuse thanks to the woman, Sophie asked for Toby to be summoned and Toby arranged transport for all three of them back to the house. He then returned to his duties at the show. It had been a sobering reminder of the children's vulnerability.

◆ ◆ ◆

As groom, Toby accompanied Mr McAlistair to the annual clashes for the Savile Cup – the Polo Championship of New Zealand, held over six days at various venues. Rangitikei was usually a leading contender and always beautifully mounted, thanks to Toby and others. Mr McAlistair took part himself. The cracks of the team were Dan Riddiford and Paul Drake who both made brilliant runs, electrifying the spectators. Nothing finicky about their games – bold as you like. Toby could see the palpable pride of Paul's father, who never missed a game and was prompt to congratulate afterwards.

Toby once saw Sir Robert rush on to the field after Rangitikei's last play against Auckland.

'Outstanding effort,' he said, grasping the hand of the captain. 'By Jove you chaps played well. A first-class performance. I've never seen such speed off the mark.'

Then Toby noticed it was not the hand of Rangitikei's Riddiford he was pumping, but that of the Auckland captain. What a gentleman Sir Robert was.

Toby was grateful Simon Drake did not usually attend. When he did attend, it was not to pay attention to the play but to gratify the well-bred women who flocked to the events. And he had no trouble finding them – he had but to rise and stride to a refreshment tent to have women swooning in his wake. More than once, again to his alarm, Toby saw Clarissa was among them. He wondered why, so often, it was the men with rogue in them who attracted so much attention from the women. Was it the appeal of risk and adventure – better a fling with an untamed man than a predictable life with a staid and stuffy one? Did he need a dash of roguery himself?

The district responded well when the Awahuri Racing Club held its first meeting in June, 1897. A settler between Feilding and Palmerston North had offered use of his paddock. Dawn greyness broke into blue and people came in droves, the bookies providing wonderful 'colour' and the track coming up trumps. A band of the oom-pah-pah variety struck up, quaint and amusing at first, but peculiarly irritating to most humans and possibly the horses too as the afternoon wore on. There was one lively, heated moment when an argument broke out amongst owners and stewards as to a horse's eligibility to start in a race for horses owned or trained within a three-mile limit. Was it as the crow flew or by road? Finally, it was agreed it was within a three-mile radius of the Awahuri Post Office. The McAlistair stable put on a good showing overall – Sharp Promise second in the Flying Stakes, another fourth and another well off the pace in a hurdle race, spooked by a wayward, riderless horse. The club was delighted with the close racing, the good turn-out and the profit, some of which went towards the local library.

There was one week in 1897 the district would never forget – the week of the flood. Toby was in it, literally up to his neck. An enormous amount of water filled the Rangitikei River until it spilled its banks. The river rose so fast the farmers scarcely had time to move their stock and thousands of cattle and sheep were swept to their death. Toby leapt on a horse and went to save stock where he could. He led tens of cattle to safety through storm detritus but further down the river another farmer was not so lucky. He was in the water with his legs up on his horse but the horse stumbled and he was thrown into the river and his body had not been found. When the river eventually subsided, the farmers could do nothing but bemoan their lost stock and crops and then shrug their shoulders, clear the carcasses and rubbish, claim what insurance they could, and begin to repair the roads, fences, and buildings. Mr McAlistair had been hit hard but others, he thought, had been hit harder and when a subscription list was opened in aid of sufferers, he gave generously.

Even a disaster can have a silver lining – the silt left on much of the river flats was of good quality and would increase the fertility. The farmers along the river set to with the optimism essential for those who work with nature. And so the Glenview Estate arrived at 1898 hoping for a better year.

EVIL ON THE LOOSE

T he first rays of the sun of 1898 cleared the mist over the Bulls racecourse and soon it was blue sky and the merest wisps of cloud. The people of the Rangitikei and even further afield began taking to their traps and buggies for a day at the races. Norman Kelly and Toby Page were well advanced in their preparations at the course before the first of the big crowd of 3000 arrived. They had entries in the sprint, the mile and the hurdles races and High Play in the Rangitikei Cup of 1½ miles, worth a bountiful 200 sovereigns to the winner. Bobby Baxter would ride all four. He had ensured he could make the light weight on one by sweating a couple of hours the day before in a manure pit. 'No need for that,' said Norman Kelly but Baxter was determined to succeed in his new calling and leave the days of milking cows and mustering sheep far behind. The manure pit wasn't much worse than the crude sweatboxes anyway.

The people came in their finery, the Marton Band impressed with their spirited renditions, and the refreshment tents spilled to overflowing throughout the day. As for the stable's racing, there was a rush along the fence for third, great jumping for second, and a dogged run for fourth. And then there was High Play. High Play trailed the leader coming into the straight and while others went for their whips, Bobby

Baxter continued to ride just hands and heels. While some at the rail screamed at him to use his whip, Baxter knew his horse well and High Play, to the joy of the McAlistair family, the stable and the screamers at the rail, drew majestically clear to win by two lengths. It had been a good day for Kelly and his team.

◆ ◆ ◆

The Glenview Estate had never looked so well as on the day of the Grand Social and Dance of March 1898. Guests emerged through the avenue of grey birches to see the fine homestead, freshly painted in fashionable light green, surrounded by splendid gardens full of colour. Exotic elms and oaks gave a stately presence at the sides while a remnant of native bush on the hillside formed a lush backdrop. When the fire brigade pulled up in front of the homestead in their dashing red uniforms with their bright red engine pulled by four horses, the vista became even more arresting. Smiles turned to frowns for those not in the know and they hastened to put their buggies well out of the way. But close attention would have revealed a delighted Superintendent Samuel Newbegin for there was a charity aspect to proceedings and his Rangitikei Volunteer Fire Brigade would be the beneficiary of the day's festivities. Soon, the Marton Band was on the lawn playing a sparkling rendition of *Verdi*, followed by a lively cornet solo.

As some 200 guests mingled, Clarissa and Harry joined the house staff in circulating with finger food and drinks, assisted by friends. As the band played on and the food and drink went in, inhibitions increasingly went out and the noise level went up until guests standing side by side had to lean closer. Charles and Elizabeth McAlistair ensured they greeted everyone in person. The fire brigade itself added to the occasion by demonstrating how quickly and efficiently they could dismount, unravel their hoses, and stand to. At the conclusion, Superintendent Newbegin smiled broadly and those who knew him well could see a burst of rhetoric coming on. Sure enough, he said his piece and stopped just as people were starting to get restless. A gymnasium group from Bulls then entertained with tumbling and club swinging. All the while, food flowed from the kitchen.

Toby helped where he could, assisting the newly arrived to tether their horses and tend to them, and pointing out where they might sit in more peace if they wished, or obtain a cup of tea, or comfort themselves. He had many friends amongst the guests from racing and polo and avoided the 'Hellfire Boys', Simon Drake, Eddie Shaw, Henry Thompson, and Arthur Wilson. Despite being well-known roisterers, they were all well-connected and all had means, and it would be a bold and perhaps foolhardy host who left them off a guest list. As the afternoon wore on, guests tended to form groups of family or close friends and Toby at one point found himself with racing friends but within earshot of Drake and his cohorts. Eddie Shaw, of mining interests, was holding forth.

'If the Chinks want to live here, let them sit a language test and let them pay an extra tax. Why should they be allowed to scavenge as they do and then take their earnings out of the country?'

Toby had heard Shaw was furious he had sold out too cheaply to six Chinese miners who had obtained some 200 ounces of gold when he had thought the area was worked out. Shaw should have been content enough with his earnings, Toby thought. He was known to drive his workers hard and pay them poorly in these hard times, despite making large profits from the asbestos quarries at Dusky Sound and elsewhere. Much of those profits was lost on slow horses.

'Quite right,' chipped in Arthur Wilson, with glacial hauteur, immaculate in his lounge suit, cravate and waxed moustache. He was a member of the Anti-Chinese League. 'If the influx of Chinese is not speedily arrested, they shall become as big a pest as the rabbits. If they ever form a union, look out!' Wilson was against most of the current movements: anti-teetotal, anti-small farms, anti the proposed old-age pension, anti the women's franchise and, lately, anti the Industrial Conciliation and Arbitration Act now before Parliament. His father owned a large estate and Wilson himself had speculated profitably in land and in businesses. 'Mark my words,' he continued, 'that Industrial and Conciliation Act will be used by the unions as a whip to beat us with.'

'There's no question. It's all stacked against the employer,' Shaw chipped in. 'What about this Workers' Compensation for Accidents Act. It will compel me to insure my mining workers against injury or death. No matter what stupidity on their part might put their lives in danger, I'm going to have to cough up for it.'

As the four of them supped on their beers or whiskies and Eddie Shaw and Arthur Wilson drew on their cigars and Simon Drake and Henry Thompson on their cigarettes, Toby cast his eye over the assembled throng and had to concede that most of them would agree with the views of the 'Hellfire Boys'. Except, that is, on the women's franchise and the place of women generally. He believed attitudes on that had changed considerably. As he looked around, he saw Elizabeth, Clarissa, Sophie, and scores more intelligent and capable women with minds of their own, but behind him came more snatches of the

Hellfire Boys' conversation.

'Getting beyond their natural sphere in life to be a wife and mother…Ridiculous to think women should hold authority over men…This Henry Fish speaks a lot of sense. Let women be educated, he says, not for its own sake but so they can more effectively do the work God has given to them exclusively.'

Toby heard Simon Drake describe what else women were good for and the others agreed amidst sycophantic guffaws. Toby was not a prig but there was something nauseous in the talk and manner of the Hellfire Boys and he moved well out of earshot. It was refreshing to find Harry and Sophie. Harry was never far from Sophie.

'I hear you will be entertaining us, Sophie.'

'I confess I am a little nervous,' she said, running a hand down her finely brushed blonde hair. She was gorgeous in a pink silk blouse with black sleeves and a black velvet skirt reaching to her ankles.

'I am sure you will be a sensation,' said Toby. 'I remember how everyone loved your singing at the hall in Bulls. For myself, I can never hear enough of you.'

Harry was already smiling and full of pride at the thought of everyone there gazing on Sophie, enchanted by her singing. His 'handicapped' sister with the remarkable talent.

'Dinner is in one hour at the woolshed and then there is the concert followed by dancing,' Harry reminded them. 'Let me know if you want anything from the house Sophie.'

'My music,' she said. 'Could you fetch that for me soon please Harry. I've left it on my dressing table. Margaret will need that.'

Margaret was Miss Margaret Fairbairn, 22, dark-haired and vivacious, a teacher of pianoforte and dance. She had been home-schooled by her mother, a well-read settler from Scotland, and already had her music qualifications from England. She had been a dancer herself, of the highland fling and the hornpipe, of jigs and reels and free expression. Though a pianist and dancer, she was not unacquainted with the broom and dustpan. Toby had met her parents, hard-working small farmers, and knew it was a household not afraid of work. As the eldest child, Margaret would have done her share of household chores, besides helping with the younger children. She was an encouraging but demanding teacher and her school in Marton had as many pupils as she could cope with.

As they spoke, who should approach but ebullient Miss Margaret herself, checking on her star performer and dispelling some of her own nervous energy. Toby felt drawn to her and suspected it was reciprocated, but he was also aware he had a crippling shyness regarding Miss Margaret. He wondered, at just twenty-six years of age, if perhaps he had already spent too long on his own and was becoming too used to his own company. But, deep down, he sensed the main reason for his hesitance regarding Miss Margaret was the attraction he felt for her. Greetings exchanged, they moved into the house to see Mr and Mrs McAlistair and ready themselves for the rest of the evening. Soon, guests were strolling the short distance to the woolshed which was shining like a beacon in the encroaching darkness. Just beyond were the stables, the station hands' quarters, and the swaggers' bunkhouse. Mr McAlistair had ensured the station hands had eaten especially well that night, to share the festive spirit.

The guests entered the woolshed through a single door and wisely, Toby had been placed just inside to encourage people to keep moving and not stand and stare and jam the doorway. The interior was spectacular, imaginatively decorated with palms and other greenery and drapery of bright crimson. Overhead were baskets of clematis, lycopodium and bracken, and signal lamps shed a warm glow. Large supper tables soon beckoned seductively. No sooner were the guests seated than the processions of food began until the tables were groaning with platters of roast beef, mutton, veal, pork, bacon, sausages, tongue and game bird, fillets of haddock and other fish, bowls of roast potatoes and parsnips, carrots, and greens, with the cutlery declaring dessert was to follow. For such a rural gathering, the lingering whiff of sheep enhanced the ambience. There was such a hubbub that it seemed to Toby everybody was talking and nobody was listening. Then, with the sharp and imperious ting of spoon on tin plate, the hubbub died away and Mr McAlistair rose and welcomed all to supper. With grace said, an observer might have thought the throng had been shipwrecked and starving, instead of plied with food all afternoon. Faces turned ravenously to the feast before them. With the beer, spirits and wine flowing freely, the woolshed rang with good will and merriment.

An hour or so later, as the guests burped and sighed in content and the empty platters and bowls were on their way back to the house, Mr McAlistair proposed a toast to all who had contributed to the day's activities and Mr Newbegin thanked the gathering for its generosity. 'We're never quick enough but we do our best,' he said. Sir Robert Drake thanked the hosts on everyone's behalf and then the Master of Ceremonies, Maurice Bee, announced the concert and Miss Margaret Fairbairn took her place at the piano. Mr Thomas Sebastian mounted a small dais at the front of the woolshed and lustily sang *My Pretty Jane* with much extravagant gesture, Mr Trevor Hatton provided a lively sailor's hornpipe and Mr Percy Burnett a resounding clog dance. Mr James O'Connor's *Love Serenade* showed his wells of emotion ran deep. Miss Berenice Ineson lightened the mood with her reading, *The Tipperary Policeman and his sweetheart Biddy*, and Miss Fenella Fraser charmed with her ditty *Come the Day*. It was then the turn of Sophie McAlistair. Harry took her hand and led her to the dais, warning her of the step up.

Sophie's first note of *Robin Adair* hushed the hum of conversation. Margaret Fairbairn provided all the accompaniment she needed. Sophie's voice rang as clear and pure as that of the first bird of a dawn chorus. Her simple songs stirred nostalgia and put a reflective, faraway expression on many faces. She followed with *Cradle Song* by Johannes Brahms and then Donizetti's *I Was Dreaming* and Schubert's *Ave Maria*. The tinge of sadness in her voice touched souls and when she finished, there was a contemplative silence. Then people were on their feet applauding, time and again. Congratulations were showered on Sophie and Margaret Fairbairn, Mr and Mrs McAlistair and even Clarissa and Harry.

'My dear girl,' Lady Pamela Drake said to her, 'you'll be charging £100 a concert soon.'

'Utterly charming,' said Sir Robert. 'Never heard better.'

As the McAlistair family fielded praise, Sophie thanked Margaret Fairbairn and chatted with the other performers seated up front. No jealousy there – Sophie's special talent was so evident.

Time now for dancing. Willing hands stacked the tables at the back of the hall and placed chairs and even some couches at the sides for those who wished to sit and talk and sip tea or something stronger. Margaret Fairbairn was joined by other musicians and soon the springiness of the woolshed floor was making some dancers look better than they were.

With her time in the public eye finished, Sophie craved the company of Maisie. It was often Maisie she sought after something especially emotional. As much as she loved the dance music, her performances did leave her somewhat spent. She had been preparing for the night's concert for weeks and now that it was over, the adrenaline was draining out of her. She slipped unseen past the people dancing and the knots of people talking, out the door and into the darkness. She could find her way as easily by night as by day around the homestead and the nearby farm buildings. The stable was the easiest building of all to find as she was guided as much by the pungent earthy smell she loved, as by the familiarity of it all. The sounds of revelry from the woolshed drifted to her through the still, night air. The door squeaked open and she made her way along the stalls to Maisie. It was as if Maisie knew she would be coming for she was waiting to be petted and caressed. Sophie began stroking the way Maisie liked, softly downwards around her eyes.

But Sophie's departure from the woolshed had not gone unnoticed. Simon Drake and the other 'Hellfire Boys' had been lolling by a rail in the darkness, watching as some of the guests left early. Some guests had a long way to go and others were more into eating and drinking than dancing. The four of them were sipping from their whisky flasks and smoking.

'Now then,' said Simon Drake. 'Here's a bit of a lark. I've never had a blind one. She's probably never had it before. I'd be doing her a favour.' The magnitude of his suggestion dismayed the other three. In the 'dives' with the sawdust and spittoons on the floor, or even in the drawing rooms with the fine furnishings and lace, they might have been up for such a proposal. But at the house of their host and with his daughter, blind at that! It left their moustaches twitching fiercely and their minds racing.

There had been no pranks from the Hellfire Boys today. The presence of so many of the worthies of the district had had a subduing effect on them. They were also having to accept they were now in their mid and late 20s, 'boys' no longer, and the pranks did not have quite the satisfaction of before. Other factors also muted their spirits. Shaw's gambling had put him in financial strife and creditors could soon be lining up; he needed to keep on good terms. And Wilson, who had political ambitions, knew people would not vote for a clown. Thompson had an issue with neighbours about the smell from his soap factory.

'Let it go,' said Eddie Shaw. He was as foolhardy as any of them and not many weeks before had stripped naked in a bar, astonishing the young and disgusting the old. But Simon Drake was making him uneasy.

Arthur Wilson, bully that he was, believed woman was born to serve man, but something had strangely moved him in the girl's singing and he too urged caution. 'Give it a miss old boy. You'll get better elsewhere.'

'Better to visit Poxy Lily's,' advised Henry Thompson. 'She'll be open for business now.' He also was disturbed by Drake's words. His father was a lay preacher and chairman of the Rangitikei Charitable Aid Board and the son had sat through enough church services to have some awareness of sin.

Invariably before, they had followed where Simon Drake had led. He had taken them on more capers throughout the district and beyond than they could remember. Capers satisfyingly filled with women, for there were always women on the fringe not required by him but available for the rest of them. But tonight, even they could see with crystal clarity, despite the alcohol muddling their brains, that Simon Drake was going too far.

Too late. Already he was gone from them, a dimly visible shape at the stable door.

ATTACKS IN
THE NIGHT

'Who's there?'

Sophie, for the first time ever in the stable, felt a stab of fear. The squeak of the door told her someone had entered and the silence that followed said danger. She withdrew her hand from Maisie. Maisie gave a strong, blowing-out breath, rolled her eyes, and pawed the ground. Sophie could hear footsteps approach, and heavy breathing. For her, the stable was black day or night; the newcomer would have the dim light of the stable lamp.

'Who is it? Stop! You're frightening me!'

Hands grabbed at Sophie, throwing her to the ground and tearing at her clothing. As she screamed and went down in a heap, her attacker pawing at her, Maisie went berserk and the other horses whinnied and stamped. As Sophie writhed in pain and shock, the hands were ripping at her in a silent frenzy, trying to remove her underclothing. The attacker was panting and gasping and his breath was hot on her throat.

This was not the love-making of her dreams. The crash onto the floor had knocked the wind out of her and at first made her helpless. But then the alcoholic stink in her face and her rage at the barbarous assault, put such a fury in her that she began to fight back. She found one of the grasping hands and grabbed the thumb, pulling it back as hard as she could. She heard a groan of pain but still no words. That was when she realised the attacker was known to her. She also sensed he was surprised at her strength and resistance, and she struggled yet harder. She started to scream but a hand slammed over her mouth, stifling her.

Outside, Thompson, Shaw and Wilson had heard the commotion of the horses and were already at the stable door. They burst in to see their worst fears realised – Simon Drake grappling with Sophie on the floor. They rushed forward, pulled him off and dragged him cursing to the door, while Sophie, overcome with the ferocity of it all and the sudden removal of her assailant, lay sobbing and distraught.

As the 'Hellfire Boys' plunged back into the darkness, heading towards their buggies, Toby Page responded to the noise of the horses. He had heard them whinnying and thumping when outside farewelling guests. He walked briskly through the dark the 70 yards or so, his thoughts racing. Was it fire? An animal on the loose? What? When he opened the stable door, he stood for a few moments, looking and listening. The horses were still restless. Then, in the dim light, he saw a bundle on the floor by Maisie's stall and heard a sobbing. As he stepped towards it, puzzled and concerned, he recognised Sophie's dress. So distracted was he by the sight of it, and so distraught, he was oblivious to the attack coming at him from behind. The piteous sight of Sophie was the last thing he saw for the vicious blow on his head left him sprawled unconscious on the stable floor.

Simon Drake looked with satisfaction at the result of his blow. He had wanted to do that ever since the 'uppity nobody' had removed the bottle of whisky. His crowding of Page at the high wire fence at the Hunt had been abortive but he had laid him out now well and truly. Damn, bloody, interfering upstart. Page had somehow inveigled himself into the lives of the McAlistair family but flat on the stable floor, bloody and bruised and in a state of darkness, was where he deserved to be for his interfering. Drake paused to look ruefully at the dishevelled bundle that was Sophie, before a hand clamped on his shoulder and led him away. It was Thompson who had rushed back first on realising Drake had returned to the stable. He had been just in time to see Drake smash Page to the ground with a crowbar that was to hand.

'Damn it all Simon,' Shaw said when they were outside. 'You've gone too far this time. You've got to keep that bloody thing inside your trousers. What a bloody pickle is this.'

'You worry too much Eddie. They all of them want it.' While the bashing of Page had been something to savour, Drake was mightily frustrated over the other matter and had an aching thumb to boot.

But moments later, by the time they met up again with Wilson and Thompson at the hitching rail, Eddie Shaw realised Drake's assault on Toby Page, though mad-headed, presented an opportunity.

'It was Page who attacked the girl,' Shaw said slyly. 'We were outside having a smoke, we heard the horses carrying on and we went to the stable to investigate, as good citizens would.' He looked around the others, now gazing back at him in admiration. 'It's our word against anyone's else's.'

'He's often with the McAlistair children,' said Thompson. 'At the polo, fetes and elsewhere. Would people believe it?'

'All the more reason,' said Wilson. 'Harbouring his secret desires. Waiting his chance. A nobody like him, at the family's beck and call. When he saw the girl go into the stable, it was his chance to have it off with her and when she resisted, he attacked her. And that's the end of it.'

Shaw turned to Drake. 'You were at the back of us, right? Henry went into the stable first, followed by me, Arthur and then you. We saw the girl on the floor and a man near her and Henry grabbed the crowbar and struck him down. It turned out to be Toby Page.' He noticed Drake massaging his thumb and wincing. 'For God's sake tidy yourself up Simon and brush yourself down. And leave your bloody thumb alone.'

From the urgency of the others' demeanour, Simon Drake began to get a glimmering of the gravity of the situation. He rubbed the stray bits of straw off his jacket and trousers and straightened his clothing. Unusually, he had no smart quip to make.

'Now then, come on,' said Shaw. 'We must be quick and get our story in first. Henry and Arthur, you go back to the stable and mount guard over Page.'

Drake hurried after Shaw to the woolshed. Shaw burst through the door shouting for attention and with Drake crashing in behind him, he had it within moments. In the sudden silence, his words were shattering. 'Sophie McAlistair has been attacked in the stable! Henry and Arthur are mounting guard over her assailant.'

Mr and Mrs McAlistair and Harry rushed for the door. Some guests had been standing closer and raced ahead of them and others followed until everyone except the infirm had poured out of the woolshed. Some were audibly praying for Sophie while others were cursing her attacker.

When the first of the shocked guests burst into the stable, Toby Page was still prone on the floor, but beginning to stir. In an instant, men were surrounding him and a boot crashed into the small of his back, holding him down. Women rushed to Sophie, kneeling by her side, some talking to her, all agitated.

All Toby saw through glazed eyes as he swam in and out of consciousness was not a face, not a helping hand, but shoes. Vaguely, he remembered a bundle whimpering on the floor by Maisie's stall. He put a hand on the ache at the back of his head and looked in confusion as it came away covered in blood. Then he was being roughly hauled to his feet, amidst incredulous cries of recognition.

'Toby Page!'

'What's Toby doing here?'

'Where's the attacker?'

'Page was the attacker!' This from Henry Thompson, who then regurgitated the story concocted minutes before by Eddie Shaw – how they had burst in and seen, by the dim lamp of the stable, a man standing by the girl, and how Thompson had struck him down with a crowbar.

'Who would have thought,' said Eddie Shaw, pressing through the crowd now jamming the stable.

'But how many times that's the case,' said Arthur Wilson, on his heels. He drew a hand down each side of his moustache. 'It's the one in plain sight, waiting for the opportunity.'

Curses were heaped on Toby Page who was still groggy, still unable to comprehend the situation, and able to stand only because of the hands holding him upright in restraint. He did remember that Sophie had been in trouble and he was deeply anxious for her. She was now out of sight behind a wall of attendants. Some of the guests, his closest friends, refused to believe he was the assailant and scoured the stable for someone else. But there was no one hiding in the shadows.

Mr and Mrs McAlistair, Clarissa and Harry had rushed to Sophie's side, barely glancing at the man prone on the floor. When assured she had suffered no permanent physical harm, and was on her feet and in their arms, they turned to the monster who had attacked her. Toby was now coming to his senses and beginning to struggle against those who were pinioning his arms to his side.

'Toby!... Never,' said Elizabeth McAlistair.

Charles McAlistair and Harry were too dumbfounded for words. Toby had been a confidant of Charles on polo excursions and a trusted companion of the children. They looked at him in confusion, faces blank, waiting for his denial. All the while, the Hellfire Boys were pouring their poison into the surrounding ears, and some of the ears were only too ready to accept it. As Toby gazed at the parents and Clarissa, Harry and then Sophie, his memory began to clear, despite his pounding headache.

'Sophie, what happened?' he asked.

Sophie looked blankly in Toby's direction. She had no idea who had attacked her and was still partly concussed from the crash onto the floor and traumatised by the assault. She nodded her head slowly back and forth sideways as she was assisted by her parents past him and out the stable door.

'See that, he's trying to weasel out of it but she'll have none of it,' Shaw said.

By the time the two policemen arrived later that night to haul Toby Page away, Shaw, Thompson, and Wilson had spilled out their false statement so often, the 'Hellfire Boys' had almost come to believe it themselves. Simon Drake did his only wise thing of the evening in staying back and staying mostly silent.

'Terrible business,' he said, to anyone who inquired. 'Page is a blackguard, make no mistake.'

The McAlistairs were pale and unsteady, shattered. Their beloved daughter Sophie had been viciously assaulted, perhaps even violated, and the chief suspect was a trusted employee and a confidant of their children. The guests were also in turmoil. Their evening had been brought to a shocking, juddering stop. As they drove away, some were in stunned silence, trying to digest what had happened, while others endlessly gabbled.

'Fancy. Such a horrid thing. And to such a lovely girl.... Can you believe it?... And Toby Page, so close to the family...Heaven help us that such things can happen... That poor family. What they must feel...Beastly business...Wicked thing...Lucky Shaw and the others happened upon it... Guttersnipe...Bloody good whipping with hard labour if you ask me.'

Margaret Fairbairn was utterly crushed. The lovely girl she had spent countless hours supporting and nurturing, accompanying that glorious, God-given voice, foully attacked. And the man Margaret had begun to feel drawn to, accused of the heinous act. The truth of the attack was before her very eyes. As to the truth of the accusation against Toby Page, she was bewildered and shaken. The evidence seemed incontrovertible, but it was so unlike the Toby Page she knew.

Later that evening, Sophie McAlistair was examined by a doctor and sedated. Meanwhile, Toby Page was on his way to the Wanganui Gaol and the 'Hellfire Boys' were consolidating their story before their appearance in court. Clearly it was indecent assault, said the doctor, but felonious assault, not rape. A great mercy for the girl and the family. For Toby Page, the charge might as well have been murder as felonious assault, for he was sunk in the gloom of the innocent condemned by all. As for the 'Hellfire Boys', they were almost disbelieving of the fortuitous turn of events. They were the saviours of the day; disaster turned to triumph. Simon Drake woke the next day with a headache from the drink and a tender thumb, but with deep content that Page was in custody and shortly to be condemned in court, and that he would have a part in it.

The next day Sophie tearfully recalled the events to her mother: leaving the woolshed to visit Maisie, entering the stable, being tossed to the ground, and then somebody tearing at her clothes and striking her. All soundless, until the gasp when she grabbed the attacker's thumb. And then feet hurrying away. As Sophie shuddered and sobbed at the recall, her mother comforted her. She and Charles had been so proud of Sophie at the concert, overcome, yet again, that they had a child with the voice of an angel. And then the horror of the barbarous attack on her in what should have been the sanctuary of home. In a cruel twist of fate, it had been Sophie's love of Maisie that had taken her from the protective ring of the family. Elizabeth flayed herself with guilt as she hugged Sophie. Why hadn't they kept watch over Sophie? And then there was that other torment – had there been a devil in their midst and they hadn't seen it?

It was as if Sophie read her mind. 'It would not have been Toby,' she said. 'Toby would not have attacked me.'

Elizabeth McAlistair could not bring herself to say his name. At first, she had thought the same as Sophie but as she and

Charles mulled it over through the night, she was plagued by doubt and by morning had come to the painful conclusion it could well have been Toby.

'Toby could not have done it,' Sophie repeated to her in the morning. 'It wasn't Toby...I don't know who it was, except it was someone who knew me for he took care not to speak.' She broke into fresh sobbing and for minutes they just held each other. When Charles, Clarissa and Harry entered the room, it was a group of five that hugged and comforted one another. Harry broke the silence.

'They're holding Toby in the Wanganui gaol.'

Elizabeth and Charles now felt a physical jolt at mention of the name.

'It would not have been Toby,' said Harry. 'I know he could not have done that. Not Toby.'

'Me too.' Sophie recalled the stink of whisky in her face, the hands grabbing at her. Then, she had a thought. 'Toby drinks more beer than whisky.'

'But he was the one that Henry Thompson and the others came upon. He was the only one there,' Clarissa said. She was confused and didn't know what to think. She had been horrified by the attack and shocked that Toby Page was chief suspect. It was totally not the Toby she knew. She was gratified, though, that Simon Drake had been one of those who had come to the aid of her sister and prevented further abuse. Even as she held her sister, she saw Drake's remarkable blue eyes.

'Whatever, I know it could never have been Toby,' said Harry.

And in such manner the McAlistair family struggled through the day, torn by love, pity, hate and confusion, until exhaustion gave them rest.

The attack was the talk of the district. There were some, like Sophie and Harry, who could not believe the Toby Page they knew could have attacked Sophie McAlistair. But others saw hidden depths of depravity, perhaps aware of what they themselves might sink to when deep in their cups and driven by lust.

'How well do you really know someone?' was said over the farm gate.

'I did wonder he was so often with those children when he should have been out and about with a woman,' said another.

'I always found him a nice young fellow,' said a third. 'He does have many friends amongst the women.' He might have added his daughter Freda was keen on Toby Page and he himself would be very pleased with the match.

But the police had few doubts. There was only one suspect and they were buoyed by the testimony of Shaw, Drake, Thompson, and Wilson and saw no need to call any other witnesses apart from Sophie McAlistair herself and the doctor. Since the incident, the 'Hellfire Boys' had become figures of substance in the community. The public were deeply appreciative of their timely arrival on the scene and gratified they would be witnesses for the prosecution. Their days of levity and mischief were forgotten. They were fine young men who had rescued the beloved Sophie McAlistair.

But Mr Douglas Percival, 52, barrister for Toby Page, an avuncular-looking man with a white moustache, was not convinced by the 'Hellfire Boys'. He sensed something murky there. He had seen enough of life to be little surprised by people. He had once been on the receiving end of one of their pranks, racked by a cough after the distribution of cayenne pepper in a hall, and he recalled their suspicious, sudden disappearance beforehand. Now, he heard them singing from the same songbook but he would not have been surprised to hear one of them had made up the words and the others had parroted. There was something else – he knew Toby Page from horse racing and polo and he was not one of those ready to jump on the bandwagon of hatred and revenge. He began to make his own inquiries at the McAlistair estate.

A STARTLING DISCLOSURE

Minnie Page was horrified to read in the Evening Post newspaper of the assault on Sophie McAlistair by an unnamed assailant. Soon after, she was shocked to her roots to receive a letter from Toby telling her of his arrest for it. Then his name was in the newspaper charged with the assault. As yet, the newspaper had not linked his name to hers. That would not take long, she knew. The notoriety of that did not concern her. She knew in her soul he was innocent and she was already on her way to Marton. Alighting from the train, she hired a cab to take her to the McAlistair estate. Her conversation with the cab driver was brief, especially after the driver said, 'Terrible business up there the other night. Miss Sophie attacked and one of the house hands arrested.' Minnie's heart was breaking and her mind was in turmoil. She had given no notice of her visit. Fortunately, Charles McAlistair was at home – he felt his place at this time was with his family. When the housemaid took her directly to him, she saw a puzzled stare and then a jolt of recognition and the semblance of a smile.

In the last two days, Charles McAlistair felt he had aged 10 years. And now there was the unexpected visit of one he had not seen for 23 years, except for a photograph once in the newspaper regarding the notorious kidnapping. He requested cups of tea and refreshments and withdrew with her into the drawing room, while Elizabeth wondered why the famous suffragist and painter Minnie Page had come to visit and why she was ensconced with her husband. The two of them were barely seated when Charles received yet another shock.

'I shall come straight to the point,' Minnie said. 'I am here because of the dreadful attack on your daughter and the charge against Toby Page, your groom. Toby is my son. And your son.'

Charles reeled back at the words, his hazel eyes wide open and rivetted on her. With his first sighting of Minnie Page at the door, the years had rolled back to this same house in 1872 when he had befriended a small, vivacious housemaid. He was 17 and she 16 and one night, irresistibly attracted to each other, they had transgressed the barriers of class and position and made passionate love. It was the first time for both. Some weeks later, Minnie was gone from the house, vanished. Charles had loved her dearly and been deeply upset, but what could he do? Their social positions were too disparate. They could never marry. He was told she had taken a position elsewhere. Now, he recalled something his father had once said: 'In the McAlistair family, it takes but a rattle of the bedroom door handle for there to be a child.'

They sat in silence. Time had also retreated for Minnie Page. She remembered a caress with Charlie observed by his mother, the first tell-tale bump and then morning sickness. A McAlistair uncle had become involved, money had changed hands, and Minnie and her widowed mother had moved to Christchurch. There, Toby had been born, taking Minnie's surname. Within a few years, she was commonly thought of as Mrs Page, widow of a man killed in an accident involving a horse.

Finally, he managed to speak, faintly. 'Toby is your son.'

'Our son.' It was a lot for him to take in and she gave him more time. 'I want nothing from you,' she said.

He waved away any suggestion that was what he was thinking. He was still coming to terms with it. There was a lot to think about. When Toby called him 'sir' and 'Mr McAlistair', he was addressing his father. When Toby had been with the children, he had been with his half-sisters and half-brother. In assaulting Sophie – if he had assaulted Sophie – he had assaulted his half-sister. It was monstrous.

Minnie continued. 'I am here because of the charge against Toby. He would never have assaulted your daughter. I know my son. He can be hot-tempered and physical, but only when there is cause. He would never, ever, attack a woman.'

Charles looked intently into Minnie's eyes. He could see the concern and pain. 'How has it come to this?'

They both knew there were boundaries not to be crossed but that raw emotions could tear codes of behaviour asunder and a quirk of fate could make a nonsense of the best-laid plans.

'You would have heard, I suppose, of my ordeal in Christchurch.' He nodded. 'Afterwards, I needed to leave the city.'

At this point the door of the drawing room opened and Mary the parlourmaid appeared with tea and sandwiches. Charles thanked her and she withdrew.

Minnie picked up her explanation. 'Toby had been much shaken by my abduction and was ready for a change. His first employer, Mr Frank Wallis, a livery stable owner, had been like a father to Toby. Toby still wanted to work with horses but also wanted to learn about farming. He then took a position with Mr Stanley Goodwin.' Charles McAlistair nodded in recognition. 'Toby looked to Mr Goodwin, too, as a father. Soon after my discovery and release, Mr Goodwin died. I felt, with all the upheavals, that Toby should know his real father.' She paused to wipe away a tear. 'I encouraged him to apply for the position here. If I did wrong, I am sorry.'

Charles McAlistair turned to pour the tea as his mind spun. His life had been turned upside down twice in a week. Father to another son, father to the man being held in gaol prior to being put on trial for felonious assault on his own half-sister. Bad enough for Sophie to be assaulted and bad enough that it be by a trusted estate employee. How much worse that it be by a brother! And what of Elizabeth? She knew nothing of his being the father of Toby. He couldn't think straight with everything going through his head.

'Toby is innocent. I am sure of it,' said Minnie Page. 'Somebody, or more than one, is putting their own evil twist on it.'

Charles knew through his business dealings and his horse racing how jaundiced people could be and how manipulative for their own ends. There were those who would stoop to anything. Treacherous devils. As he sipped the tea and sat in thought, he remembered his first disbelief on seeing Toby was the accused. And the disbelief of Elizabeth and others of his family as well. Father of Toby, he reflected. He recalled what a good companion Toby had been to him, and how good he had been with the children. He had been already like a member of the family, bonded to them all.

'There is much to consider,' he said. 'I need time.'

As they left the drawing room, Elizabeth McAlistair urged Minnie to stay for lunch. Elizabeth was a great admirer of Minnie's social agitations and had been mortified by her abduction. She was intensely curious about the reason for the visit and put out 'feelers' but both Charles and Minnie answered briefly and vaguely. Minnie departed soon after and as the taxicab disappeared down the driveway, Charles took Elizabeth aside and told her that Minnie Page was the mother of Toby Page. He did not, though, add that he was the father of Toby Page.

◆ ◆ ◆

A brief trial in the Lower Court established there was a case to be answered and Toby Page would now be tried in the Higher Court before a jury.

Harold Graves, prosecutor, was a spare man with an ascetic, deeply lined face and the intensity of the soapbox evangelist he occasionally was. 'Repent ye ways ye sinners,' was his mantra. He met with Douglas Percival beforehand and fixed him with a cold, cod-like eye. 'For the sake of God, get him to plead guilty man. It would be a mercy to spare the poor girl the ordeal of the trial.'

'How can he plead guilty when he is innocent?' said Percival.

There was no more to be said and Graves departed for a meeting with his witnesses Drake, Thompson, Shaw, and Wilson. Rumours had reached him of shenanigans in the past, but they were well-bred young fellows and Graves was confident the weight of their testimony would be overwhelming. Page had strayed from the true path, thought Graves, and succumbed to his baser instincts. There were some who should be whipped and gelded.

Later that day, Toby Page had a visitor. He and his mother embraced for so long she worried she would be told her time was up, and she broke free. It was not so many years before that she had been the prisoner and he had been the one outside in confusion and anguish. All the way from Wellington she had wondered if now was the time to tell Toby of his parentage, but since she had spoken to Charles McAlistair her mind had cleared. Charles McAlistair had had to know it was his son accused of the heinous attack on Sophie, and now Toby had to know Charles McAlistair was his father.

'We were both so young,' she said. 'I was a housemaid and he the son of the master. We were in love but could never have married. When his mother saw us embrace, I was obliged to go, and when it was apparent I was pregnant, the family assisted in my leaving.'

Toby's mind was whirling. Always it had been his mother, his nan and him alone in the world and now he had a father, step-mother, brother, and sisters he loved as well. But if anything, it made his present situation even harder – accused of betraying his own family by felonious assault on his sister.

'You suggested I come to Glenview,' he reminded his mother.

'I thought you deserved to know your father. I didn't tell you earlier because you were too young to understand. As you grew, I realised I could not be both mother and father to you. I saw you drawn to men you admired like Mr Wallis and others at the stable and livery and at the boxing gymnasium. And just like your father, you were drawn to the horses. When Mr Goodwin died, and I was moving north myself, I thought it was time for you to know your father.'

She could see his mind was churning with so much to take in and hugged him once again. He was so stunned at her words he did not at first respond, but then he hugged her close.

'I'm pleased you did what you did,' he said. 'I love my family.'

Minnie told Toby to keep the knowledge of his father to himself. 'For Charlie's honour,' she said. 'He will tell his family when the time is right. Elizabeth and the children do not know.' Minnie sobbed as they embraced, both with the relief of her disclosure and the knowledge of the charge against Toby, and Toby himself shed tears. The father he had thought long dead was alive and a man Toby greatly admired. So often he had thought of his father and wondered what sort of man he really was. Now he knew, but to his anguish he was reminded, as the guard banged on the cell door, that his father must believe Toby had assaulted his beloved daughter.

◆ ◆ ◆

The Judge, Mr T. M. Robertson, proceeded two days later with the hearing of the case in the Wanganui Court House. The building was of ample size to easily accommodate the usual cases of theft, drunkenness, or affrays, but such was the interest in this case, some were left standing in small groups on the footpath. Places had been reserved for Mr and Mrs McAlistair, Clarissa, and Harry to attend, and a place also for Minnie Page, when it became known she was the mother of the accused. The four key witnesses for the prosecution took up half a row themselves. They were in their Sunday best, thriving in the occasion and eagerly awaiting their time in the spotlight. Simon Drake's eyes glinted in satisfaction at the sight of Toby Page in the dock. He had had the pleasure of punishing Page in the stable and now the court was doing it for him again. The arrival of the McAlistair family had silenced the crowd while the arrival of Minnie Page had started tongues wagging again. What? Mother of the accused? Those with an ounce of pity could only imagine what a cold tremor ran through Minnie Page as she took her place.

Harold Graves began his case before the jury of 12 men with suitable gravitas. First, he established the crime had been committed, calling for the doctor who gave his opinion it had been a felonious assault. The silence was then absolute as a clerk of the court led Sophie McAlistair to the stand. Haltingly, in a quiet but clear voice, looking in the direction of Graves, she gave her testimony. It was stark and factual, but the terror and shock of the attack was readily apparent. She finished with the description of the attacker violently pawing her one second and then gone the next.

'There was a curse, footsteps fading and then just the noise of the horses, frightened.'

Graves let her final words hang on the air, piteously, before he sat down. As Douglas Percival rose to cross-examine, he saw two of the jury in tears and another on the verge.

'Miss McAlistair, it was a dastardly attack on you and my deepest sympathy. I am intent on getting to the bottom of this.' The suggestion it could be anyone other than the accused appeared to take most in the courtroom aback, as frowns and furrowed brows appeared. 'Miss McAlistair, do you know the accused, Toby Page?'

Sophie was pale, but her voice was steady. 'Yes, he is a groom on our estate and frequently takes us out on the horses.'

'During this wicked attack, was there anything to suggest the accused, Toby Page, was your assailant?'

'Your Worship, objection.' Mr Graves had shot to his feet. 'How could the poor girl know? She is blind and was knocked half-senseless and is probably still in shock.'

'Miss McAlistair still has her hearing and other senses,' said Mr Robertson. 'We must give her the opportunity to answer the question. Objection overruled.'

'No, there was nothing to suggest Toby Page was my assailant,' she said, to a murmur in the courtroom. She could be seen fighting back her own tears. She swallowed and spoke again, loud and clear. 'I know Mr Page very well and I am sure he did not attack me.'

The smirks of the four 'witnesses' vanished, replaced by frowns.

Mr Percival continued. 'Miss McAlistair, to elaborate on that. Was there any reason to indicate Mr Page did **not** attack you?'

Mr Graves began to rise but the judge gestured for him to sit back down.

'There is,' she said, steadying herself with a hand on the front of the witness stand. 'Mr Page, so long as I have known him, is a drinker of beer, not of whisky. The man who attacked me had a breath heavy with whisky.'

There was a buzz of comments in the courtroom. The 'Hellfire Boys' looked at one another mightily discomposed and Simon Drake swore violently. His Worship had to call for order and issue a warning.

Mr Percival continued. 'Miss McAlistair, in your testimony, you described how you fought back, grasping the thumb of your attacker and drawing a groan from him.'

She nodded. 'Yes, that is so.'

Mr Percival, turned to the jury. 'And yet, when I had a doctor examine Mr Page, he found no indication whatsoever of a strained thumb.' He handed the doctor's signed declaration to the clerk of the court. 'Thank you, Miss McAlistair.'

The moment she stepped out of the witness box, Mr Graves was on his feet. 'How desperate is the defence that they trumpet the thumb of a blacksmith not appearing strained! The man works constantly with his hands, hands which he turned to atrocious intent on the night in question. Gentlemen of the jury, I have no doubt the attack of Mr Page on Miss McAlistair stopped short only because of the timely intervention of my next witnesses.'

The thumb reference merely irked Graves but the whisky reference troubled him. The girl had told him at interview she did not recognise her attacker and had downright refuted his suggestion it was Page. Her murmurings at the time of whisky breath he had discounted as trivial and of no account. Now damn Percival had got hold of it and it had come back to bite him. The prurient element of the case made Mr Graves very ill at ease and the sooner the thing was settled and the odious fellow put away, the better. He thanked heaven he had heavyweight witnesses in waiting.

AND NOTHING
BUT THE TRUTH

Mr Graves called Toby Page. Toby had winced at the harrowing testimony of Sophie McAlistair but been deeply relieved she had spoken up for him. He knew very well though, that the district had been simmering with hatred since that night, intent on vengeance for the attack on the beloved Sophie, and that it was his name that had been widely cursed. He could see the loathing in the eyes of many of those before him but could only look on in impotence, feeling helpless against the machinations and lies of the Hellfire Boys.

'Mr Page, you have pleaded not guilty to the charge of felonious assault on Miss McAlistair and yet you were found at the very scene of the crime, and not only by one person, but by four, immediately after the offence had been committed. Indeed, while your victim was still on the ground, distraught from the assault. No other person was seen in the building, or leaving the building.'

Mr Graves put it to Toby Page that he had inveigled himself into the confidence of the McAlistair family until he could take advantage of Sophie McAlistair's trust. That he had been able to close on her in the stable without suspicion and take her by surprise. That he had subsequently been thwarted by the unexpectedly strong resistance of the victim and prevented from fleeing by the timely arrival of Messrs Thompson, Shaw, Wilson, and Drake.

Toby writhed at each accusation. At the height of Mr Graves's invective, he glanced at the McAlistair family, saw the confusion and hurt, and never looked that way again. He saw the anguish of his mother and knew she would be burning to get to the truth of it and clear him. At each vile allegation, there was glee and gratification on the faces of the 'Hellfire Boys'. Basking in their role as deliverers of the girl from evil, they were again unconsciously putting on airs, Eddie Shaw running a hand down each side of his walrus moustache, Henry Thompson pulling his shoulders back, Arthur Wilson adopting a frosty hauteur and Simon Drake smiling, trying to catch the eye of a pretty lady in the gallery.

When Mr Graves had finished vivisecting Toby Page to his satisfaction, he nodded to his key witnesses who returned the acknowledgement.

Mr Percival now rose. 'Mr Page, please tell the court what circumstances took you to the stable that night and what happened there.'

Difficult though it was, Toby Page felt relief that at last he could tell the district his story. He recounted hearing the horses, crossing to the stable to investigate, seeing a woman lying on the floor, realising it was Miss Sophie, and then being struck down from behind and recovering consciousness to find himself accused of a heinous crime. The courtroom was transfixed. Many there knew him personally and had been astounded at the charge. But then again, he had been found at the scene and there was no other suspect.

It was time for Mr Graves to call in the heavy brigade. Henry Thompson took the stand. Thompson was determined to make the most of the occasion. His business interests in the rabbit-tinning factory and the soap works had never presented the opportunity to address such a throng. And it was a rare occasion for Thompson to have the supportive eye of the community upon him, in particular the supportive eye of his father Alfred, chairman of the Rangitikei Charitable Aid Board. In ringing basso profundo, he vowed to tell the truth and nothing but the truth so help him God, and eagerly awaited his counsel's lead.

'Mr Thompson, can you tell the court what took you to the stable on the night in question and what you saw on entering.'

Thompson paused, aware that in that moment of time, his words had never, ever, been so anticipated. 'Myself and the gentlemen with me heard the horses in the stable making a racket. "Look here," we said, "we must look into that." ' He looked around the courtroom and then focused on the jury. 'I was first through the door. By the light of the stable lamp, I saw a figure standing by a woman lying on the floor. She was moaning something awful and had clearly been savaged by the man.' The courtroom hung on his words, in appalled silence. 'I grabbed the nearest weapon, a crowbar, and struck the villain on the head with it. It turned out to be Toby Page. Fortunately, the blow knocked him cold and he could not make a run for it.'

'Objection, Your Honour,' said Mr Percival. 'Speculation on the part of the witness. There is no proof Mr Page would have made a run for it.'

'Sustained,' said Mr Robertson. 'Please confine your comments to the facts, Mr Thompson.'

Thompson finished his account, embellishing it as much he could, and looked disappointed when Mr Graves had finished with him.

It was now the turn of Mr Percival to cross-examine. 'Were you aware Miss Sophie McAlistair had entered the stable before you investigated the noise of the horses?'

Thompson looked momentarily nonplussed as the 'Hellfire Boys' had focused in their pre-trial discussions on the events in the stable after Drake had struck down Toby Page, and Sophie McAlistair's arrival at the stable had scarcely been touched upon. He looked at his three co-witnesses. Shaw was nodding his head and mouthing something. Thompson picked up the nod as affirmation.

'Yes, we saw her leave the woolshed and go in the direction of the stable.'

'You appear uncertain,' said Mr Percival.

'Not at all,' said Thompson, recovering his composure. 'The noise of the horses alarmed us and we were concerned for Miss Sophie. She is handicapped with her blindness after all.'

'Mr Thompson,' asked Mr Percival, 'where were you when you saw Miss Sophie McAlistair leave the woolshed?'

'Standing outside with these gentlemen here.'

'By gentlemen I take it you are referring to Messrs Drake, Shaw and Wilson.'

'Yes of course.'

'What were the four of you doing standing outside when everyone else was in the woolshed or preparing to leave?'

'We were having a chat and a smoke.'

'Nothing else, Mr Thompson?'

Thompson reflected, momentarily puzzled. 'And having a drink of course.'

'What were you drinking?'

'Whisky, from our flasks, like everyone.'

'Not everyone, Mr Thompson. Miss McAlistair has stated Mr Page does not drink whisky.'

'Well, plenty do,' said Thompson, in remonstrance.

Eddie Shaw, Arthur Wilson, and Simon Drake then testified in turn, corroborating the story of Henry Thompson. Mr Percival let them tell their story without interruption, until it sounded repetitious, like the concoction of co-conspirators that it was.

Mr Percival called two further witnesses. His time at the estate interviewing staff had not been wasted. Matthew Mataira, 32, was the youngest son of a large family on the East Coast. Hard-working, amiable and of sober habits, 'Matt' Mataira would have been described by many of the Europeans on the estates, as a 'good' Maori.

'Mr Mataira, please tell the court what you saw on the night in question.'

Mataira took in the courtroom. The prosecutor Mr Graves was looking at him warily and the 'Hellfire Boys' with mingled contempt and curiosity.

'I was having a smoke with Calamity Rush by our quarters when I heard the horses playing up. I looked across to the stable and saw Toby Page going in the door to sort it out. Just after him, there was another went in. And then, shortly after that, a group of them, shadows in the night. Three or four maybe. In the darkness, I couldn't be sure.'

'You did not see Miss McAlistair enter the stable, or anyone else before Toby Page?'

'No sir. It was the noise of the horses that drew my attention. I looked that way when the horses played up.'

'How could you be sure it was Toby Page?'

'I know Toby Page very well. I see him most days. Even in the dim light of the stable lamp when he opened the door, I could tell by the shape and movement it was Toby Page. The others, I couldn't say.'

'You say another went in just after Mr Page. Thirty seconds? One minute? Two minutes?'

Mataira scrunched up his face and thought back. 'No more than 30 seconds.'

'Thirty seconds at most,' said Mr Percival. 'Thirty seconds for Toby Page to go to the far stall, toss Miss McAlistair to the ground, grapple with her, rise and be standing half-way back across the stable when struck unconscious by Mr Thompson. I think not.'

Simon Drake's knuckles were white and a nerve twitched on his cheek. Eddie Shaw fidgeted and Thompson and Wilson looked on in dismay. Their story had not entirely collapsed but it was now shot through with doubt. They looked at Percival and Mataira with loathing.

Mr Graves, rising to cross-examine, fixed the witness with a disbelieving eye. 'Mr Mataira, would you claim Mr Page as a friend?'

'Yes. Toby Page is a good fellow. Friendly to us all. Not stuck up.'

'A friend you would keep from gaol if you could?'

'I am just saying what I saw.'

'What you saw in the darkness.'

'In the moonlight and the light from the stable lamp. There was enough light for me to see the opening of the stable door and people entering.'

'It could have been two minutes, three minutes. You had no watch.'

'It was 30 seconds at most.'

Mr Graves turned to the jury. 'So, what do we have here? Mr Mataira, an itinerant, half-caste station hand, gazing in the darkness from one building to another, with no watch, favours a friend with his estimate of time. His testimony, gentlemen, is of no value whatsoever.'

Mr Percival then called William James O'Sullivan, aka Calamity Rush, to the stand. The swagger showed to best advantage in the dim light of dawn or dusk as his life had been onerous and he was not one to dandify his appearance. The bright lights of the court room showed every bump and disfigurement. But he was not there for his appearance. Most crucially, he corroborated the testimony of Matthew Mataira.

Mr Graves rose eagerly to cross-examine. He had heard the ripple of surprise that a swagger should give evidence and intended to pin him to the wall like a rare and particularly unpleasant specimen of moth. 'Mr O'Sullivan, would you kindly explain to the court your calling in life and why you are known as Calamity.'

'Sir, I am a swagger. I travel from estate to estate and get work where I can. Calamity, because I have seen many men brought low by life and assist them where I can. Rush, sir, because I am never in one.'

Mr Graves, like everyone else in the courtroom, was unaware that William James O'Sullivan had been classically educated at Trinity College in Dublin but was blessed or cursed with the unquenchable spirit of the rover. A life on the road was more to his taste than a life within the cloisters of a university.

'How well do you know the accused, Mr Page?'

'Well enough to see him entering the stable by the light of God and man sir.'

'A man you scarcely know because you are a shiftless shirker,' Mr Graves spluttered, 'and yet you have the effrontery to appear in this courtroom and swear to his sighting.'

'Sir, I could have picked you out, had you been the one.'

'With the eyes of an owl no doubt,' said Mr Graves, voice dripping with sarcasm.

'No, by the peculiar bent of you sir, as you thrust your head at me now.'

Graves drew himself up amidst general sniggering, pointed an angry finger at Calamity Rush and exclaimed to the court, 'At the end of my finger is a vagabond and an ass!'

'Which end would that be sir?' asked Calamity. There was a burst of laughter from the court.

Mr Percival, in his summing up, drew the attention of the jury to the outstanding character references of the accused, and to the several anomalies in the prosecution's case. He had built a compelling case of doubt. Mr Graves, acutely aware his 'watertight' case now leaked like a colander, spoke more shrilly than he would have wished, while the mouths of his four key witnesses were set in grim, straight lines.

The Judge, in his summing up, said that in a case of this sort, the court had to be particularly careful regarding the judgment.

More often than one might imagine, the life of the individual rests in the hands of others, with the decision riding on information true or false, attitude impartial or biased, reasoning objective or self-serving, disposition assertive or subservient. When the jury retired and the court was adjourned, Toby Page could but pray the twelve men would sift the truth from the orchestrated outpouring of lies. His life was in the balance.

Many were surprised at how quickly they returned.

'Not guilty!' declared the foreman.

'Mr Page, you are free to go,' said the Judge.

Toby, more relieved than elated, and too wrung out to rejoice ebulliently in the verdict, thanked Mr Percival and shook his hand. The first in his arms was his mother, followed by Sophie, Harry, and Clarissa. Mr and Mrs McAlistair congratulated him, their strain plain to see. Mr McAlistair, looking benumbed, shook his hand and told him to take leave and spend time with his mother. Norman Kelly and other well-wishers shook Toby's hand while those who had trumpeted his guilt scurried off. The 'Hellfire Boys' slunk away dismayed.

Shaw turned to Drake before leaving. 'Your prick will get us all into trouble one of these days.'

Drake smirked. 'You come with me by choice, old man. You've had plenty, thanks to me.'

'Not like that I haven't,' said Shaw and he turned his back on him.

FOR QUEEN AND COUNTRY

T oby Page took the instruction of his father and spent a week with his mother and nan in Wellington. The three of them revisited the circumstances of Toby's birth and as the days passed, Toby began to adjust to a fresh view of the world and his place in it. The discovery of a living father, as well as a brother and sisters, was an immense circumstance to come to terms with. As his mother, his nan and he strolled by the harbour and had tea in Willis Street and Lambton Quay, his mind constantly drifted back to the estate and the faces of his other family. Minnie Page occasionally saw a pang of sadness and pain in her son and recognised it as the same sadness and pain she had felt after her release from the shack at the Styx River. To be imprisoned, through no fault, and, even worse in Toby's case, to have the hatred of the community heaped upon you, was an abhorrence almost too ghastly to bear and it would take time to soften the memory.

Toby, indeed, was in turmoil. To see Sophie whimpering on the floor, dress dishevelled, had been heartrending. And then to find himself on the stable floor and be hauled to his feet and accused of attacking her had been beyond his worst imaginings. He had always protected Sophie as though he were her brother, which, to his amazement, he now knew he was. His mother's revelations had forced him to look anew at both her and his nan. He had never been one to pass high moral judgment on others for so-called 'loose behaviour'. He readily accepted he was by strict definition a 'bastard' but his mother and father had loved each other and only the social structures of the time had prevented marriage. As the week passed, he continually re-evaluated the situation. One evening, in the Trocadero restaurant, he looked at his mother over their oyster supper and saw the 16-year-old girl discovering she was pregnant and being terrified her child might be taken and given to strangers. And looking at his nan, he saw the mother discovering her daughter had transgressed and realising there would be consequences, some beyond their control. Each time he re-assessed, he realised there was no one to blame. It was life in all its infinite variety. There are crossroads when a choice, even on a whim, can change a life profoundly. Of one thing he would be forever grateful – there was much love in both his families. He hoped that one day, eventually, the families could come together as one.

There was, too, the ongoing enmity of Simon Drake to be considered. The depth of bitterness in the man appeared fathomless and occasionally the thought of it preyed on Toby. He raised the matter with his mother and nan.

'It started with a bottle of whisky at Riccarton,' he said, recounting what had happened, including the attack on him.

His mother and nan looked at each other aghast.

'I don't know Simon Drake,' said Minnie. 'I've met Sir Robert, his wife Lady Pamela and their son Paul. 'It was at a function at the Club Hotel. They were all very charming. The father and son were like two peas in a pod. Gentlemen both.'

'It seems that you stumbled into more than you knew, boy,' said Nan. 'What you did was right. You recovered what Sir Robert intended for Mr Goodwin. But you took something Simon Drake saw as his due. He must be choked with bitterness. A grudge against father, brother, or both.' Nan's eyes were hard and her face grim as if remembering incidents from the past. 'Jealousy can be a terrible thing. You be careful of him boy. There are some will nurture their spite and never let it end.'

After the week in Wellington, Toby returned to Glenview and resumed his duties as groom. But as warmly as he was welcomed back, things were not the same. Each time he entered the stable, he saw Sophie huddled in misery, sobbing. He saw the fingers pointed as he was led away under arrest and he saw lingering doubt on people's faces in the present. For the case remained open – the attacker had never been found. Even when he was out on the far reaches of the property, where the foothills vanished into a hazy range, accusing faces swam before him. The McAlistair family themselves could not have been more open-hearted and generous. Toby knew they all accepted his innocence and that they would always now be his family, along with his nan and mother. Yet Toby felt with all his being, that he must put time and distance between himself and Glenview. It was as if he had to take himself away and put himself together again. Too much had happened, both outside himself and within himself, to simply carry on as before.

He discovered a vacancy of stable-hand on the estate of Mr Richard Howard at Heretaunga, just north of Wellington, swiftly applied and was appointed. He was still a member of the volunteer militia and when he transferred from Rangitikei to Wellington, he instantly had rugged companions, full of friendly banter and pranks. He visited his mother and nan when he could and he wrote every few weeks to his family at Glenview, addressing each letter to a different one of them each time. They fell upon his letters and passed them round. A few months later, in October 1899, the talk amongst the militia was all about a war in South Africa and a declaration by the Premier, Sir Richard John Seddon, that a New Zealand Contingent would be sent to support Britain and its Empire. Toby knew immediately he needed to be in the Contingent.

Things then happened so quickly he could scarcely believe it. The Premier, it seems, wanted to make a statement of loyalty as well as, perhaps, deter the enemy from fighting. Just days after the declaration, Toby Page was one of 204 men ticked off as they boarded the SS *Waiwera* in Wellington's Port Nicholson, bound for Africa, half a world away. A tumultuous crowd on the wharves had heard Premier Seddon declare that the First Contingent of New Zealanders would be fighting for 'one flag, one Queen, one tongue, and for one country – Britain.' Toby understood there were English settlers in South Africa at odds with Dutchmen, called Boers. The Boers had established their own republics of the Orange Free State and the Transvaal and had now given the British an ultimatum to withdraw their troops from the Transvaal. The ultimatum had expired and the Boer Republic was now at war with the British territories of Cape Colony and Natal. The Contingent's horses were already on board. Toby had every confidence in his Trojan, a big, strong horse surprisingly agile on his feet.

At dusk the ship departed, to the waving of handkerchiefs, umbrellas, canes, hats and ribbons and wave after wave of wild cheers from people cramming the wharves and the escorting vessels. It was soon apparent one essential man was missing. As the *Waiwera* hove to in the harbour opposite Worser Bay, a small ship came alongside and a man was hoisted on board by means of a rope. Yes, a vital man – the baker. And then the *Waiwera* pushed out into Cook Strait and was on its own.

'Quite a lark, eh,' said a short, stocky man leaning on the rail beside Toby. Lonnie Sparks, at only five foot five inches, was barely tall enough to meet the required height for recruits but he was a proven performer under pressure, a well-known footballer in the half-back position. Toby had played some football himself and was sure the game was good preparation for what they were going to. He had heard a bystander remark at one rugby game, 'They might as well take a ball in one hand and a gun in the other.'

'Talk about extremes,' said Toby. 'A banquet, bands, Lord Ranfurly, Premier Seddon, other fish-heads and half the country to see us off and now just the empty sea and a seagull or two.'

Lonnie chuckled. 'We can't get there fast enough for King Dick. Shoulder to shoulder with the Mother Country defending the English there.'

Toby nodded. Some had suggested in newspapers and on the street that the war was trumped up in the interests of mining millionaires, for there was gold and diamonds in the Transvaal, but there was such a zest for war in the air, those cynics had to mind their tongues.

'Our country needs to pull its weight,' he said. 'We can't expect to have the protection of Britain without doing our bit to help.'

'I don't think all the boys here share your noble sentiments,' said Sparks. 'I know of at least one who goes by another name in the city. He's running away from a wife, the police, or a creditor.'

'Yes, I expect there'll be all sorts, including some who just want the adventure of it all,' said Toby.

Gazing into the rough weather and the tossing waves, Toby had to concede he was both running away and seeking adventure. Running away from false and gruesome accusations. And as well, he had to concede, perhaps running away from commitment to someone else besides his mother and nan. As the ship rocked through Cook Strait carrying the nation's hopes for glory, the troops soon had to turn away and tend to their horses and get some tucker into themselves as well before addresses by Major Robin, the overall commander, and Captain Davies, the commander of the North Island Company. As the ship pushed on through the strait and then out into the Tasman Sea and New Zealand slid away in its wake, so too did the traumas of Glenview estate and Toby's thoughts raced ahead to those fabled continents, Australia and Africa.

The crossing of the Tasman was rough but finally the wind dropped, the seas calmed and there was fine weather to Albany at the bottom of West Australia. Coaled up, the *Waiwera* pounded across the vastness of the Indian Ocean to Port Elizabeth in South Africa and then, on 23 November, their destination, Cape Town.

As Toby led Trojan on to the wharf to join the others of the 1st New Zealand Mounted Rifles and took in the bustle of men and horses around him. his eyes were drawn inexorably to the massive bulwark of rock overlooking the city. Table Mountain hinted at the huge hinterland teeming with exotic animals, where some had carved out a life on the land for themselves and others had come to dig out the mineral riches. The Contingent had but a few days to exercise the horses and ready themselves for combat before moving north by train to join General French, commander of the Cavalry Division. The Boers had advanced down the railway and occupied Arundel.

The journey on the train seemed to go on for ever.

'I don't like what all this travel is doing to our horses, Lonnie. It's bad enough on ourselves.' Toby looked with concern at Trojan, listless and off his fodder after nearly four weeks at sea and hours of trundling north on the train.

'Not good,' agreed Lonnie Sparks. 'My Paddy's the same. They've got rust in the works with all the standing around.'

'And now they've got no time to acclimatise,' said Toby. 'They're going to be badly knocked up if we push them hard. We'll lose a lot of them.' He caressed Trojan around the eyes. 'Don't worry old fella,' said Toby, 'We'll get you through it. This war should not last long.'

But Toby was wrong. Perhaps he was influenced by the jingoism at departure or had overestimated the might of Britain and its empire or underestimated the skill, courage and resolve of a people fighting for their freedom and equipped with the latest weaponry from Germany. Over the next three years there would be 10 New Zealand Contingents and of the thousands of horses that came with them, just one would return home.

The Contingent's first action was at Jasfontein farm. The troops were roused at 2.45am and in eight minutes were dressed, saddled, equipped, and mounted, each with 150 rounds of ammunition. They were not cavalrymen, fighting on horseback, but mounted riflemen, dismounting to fight while one in every five held the horses. Two miles short of the farm, the Royal Artillery poured shells into the area and then the troopers charged in. Suddenly, 300 Boers appeared in dominant firing positions and the artillery had to be called back to drive them off. There were close calls: Trooper Tubman with a bullet through his overcoat and wallet, Trooper Maunder with his water bottle pierced, Trooper Casey with a bullet hole through his rifle and, grievously, farrier/trooper George Bradford dead, dying of wounds in Boer hands. Toby Page, for the first time in his life, realised he had to seriously consider the prospect of death. Somehow, it sharpened his appreciation of life. He pondered his far-distant family and realised how much he missed them.

Death stared them in the face again at Slingersfontein farm from 9 January, 1900. Toby Page and Lonnie Sparks were part of a half-company of the New Zealand Mounted Rifles hotly engaged in an attack by the Boers on an advanced British position. A company of the East Yorkshire Regiment, along with the New Zealanders, held a high, steep hill. On 15 January the Boers poured in heavy and continuous fire from long range and, at the same time, advanced on the eastern side of the hill where there was cover. But then this attack was seen to be a ruse – the Boers were launching their main attack up the steep western slope, creeping up behind rocks as cover. When they knew they had been seen, they increased their fire. The British commander fell, badly wounded, and the sergeant major was killed. The Boers rushed on and the British force was in danger of being swept off the hill, with heavy casualties.

'Come on you men!' shouted Captain Madocks of the Royal Artillery, commander of the New Zealand half-company, gesturing to Page, Sparks, and a few others. He led them to the western side where more British troops had fallen and rallied the remainder there. 'Fix bayonets!' he shouted.

There was the rattle of steel and then Madocks was charging. Fuelled by the frantic nature of it all and by surging adrenalin, Page, Sparks and some 20 others were on his heels. The leading Boers were shocked by the wall of steel suddenly coming at them and turned and ran. Others sprang up from the ground and joined them. Madocks shot dead the top-hatted Boer leader in a point-blank rifle duel and the British forces poured fire onto the retreating backs. The Boer force pulled back with many wounded and 29 Boers lay dead. The initiative of Madocks had turned the battle and he was promoted to major. There was also much pride for the New Zealanders when General French named the battle scene 'New Zealand Hill'. But, when the tumult was over, there was a grim aftermath – the New Zealanders had to bury two of their own, Sergeant Samuel Gourley and Private John Connell.

Major Robin said at the funeral, 'Lads, our comrades there have done more for their country than we have; they have died for it and we still live.'

By now the British forces in South Africa had been reinforced and the commander-in-chief, Lord Roberts, decided the time had come to relieve Kimberley to the north-west and to advance from there on Bloemfontein, the capital of the Orange Free State. French's mounted troops, including the New Zealand Contingent, advanced rapidly towards Kimberley in early February. They outflanked the besieging Boer force and entered the town on the 15th. There had been little fighting but the march had taken a terrible toll on both men and horses. The distances had been vast, the grassland and scrub boundless, the hills and the hidden little kloofs treacherous. When on trek, the men slept in the open in numbing cold and the occasional stunning display of stars wheeling overhead made Toby yearn even more for those he loved back home – his mum and nan, his family at Glenview, and Margaret Fairbairn. For most of the journey they were in alternate storms of dust and rain and on half-rations of mainly hard army biscuits. They were ragged, dirty, and lousy.

'It's what I feared Lonnie,' said Toby, looking askance at his beloved Trojan, once strong and stalwart, now all sinew and weariness. 'At this rate he won't last much longer.' The final stages of their route had been marked by discarded equipment and dead horses.

'My Paddy too,' said Lonnie, looking close to tears. 'The poor old thing got shot in the rump but he's carried me 50 miles since then. All our horses need rest and building up.'

For many of the remaining horses it was too late. They sickened and died and the New Zealand troops had to use the remounts provided by the British, which were generally inferior. They preferred the captured Boer horses or other locally bred horses. Toby did his best to push the painful things to the back of his mind and dwell on the good and generous. Such as the trooper who had used his tongue to draw a tiny piece of steel from the eye of a man.

The Second New Zealand Contingent sailed into Cape Town on 25 February and the Third disembarked at East London a month later. On 17 May British forces lifted the siege of

Mafeking and back in New Zealand celebrations began. The whole of Wairoa was reported to be 'jubilating' with bells ringing, gongs beating, flags flying and rifle volleys firing while at Dunedin night was immediately turned into day with merrymaking. Feilding was calm with people expected to enthuse the following day.

The Second and Third New Zealand Contingents now joined the First Contingent at Kroonstad on the railway line between Bloemfontein and Johannesburg and all three were organised into one regiment under Major Robin. Toby and Lonnie took part in the advance towards Johannesburg. Near the city, at the end of May, in an intense skirmish, they captured more than 50 Boers, a gun and supply wagons. Johannesburg fell to the British forces on 31 May and five days later, 50 kilometres to the north, Roberts took Pretoria, capital of the Transvaal.

The Boers, though, still had Toby's respect as a force to be reckoned with. They used guerrilla tactics, striking out of nowhere and vanishing back into the veldt. A Boer leader, de Wet, was especially active in the Orange Free State. The New Zealanders themselves had a great reputation as horsemen and scouts and Toby Page, Lonnie Sparks and other New Zealanders were among a detachment of mounted infantry sent south in operations against de Wet. At the end of July, they had the satisfaction of seeing 4,000 Boer surrender, but de Wet and his own commando evaded the net.

'It's like trying to put your finger on a piece of quicksilver,' said Toby Page.

By this time, he was riding a captured Boer horse. Trojan had died back in camp, the hard campaigning too much even for his mighty heart and will. For Toby, it had been like the death of a bosom companion. Lonnie Sparks, too was riding a locally bred horse, captured on a Boer farm. His Paddy had broken down and been shot in mercy. Illness and battle casualties had reduced the strength of the three New Zealand Contingents to only about 300 men. The force was further reduced when some departed for well-paid jobs with the South African police, military, railways, or post and telegraph service.

'No show of me staying here. I've been here long enough,' said Lonnie Sparks. 'It's back to the Wairarapa for me when this lot's finished.'

'Yeah, back home for me too. I miss my family too much,' Toby said. And as he spoke, he saw in his mind's eye Minnie, his nan and the McAlistairs. And then, lingeringly, Margaret Fairbairn. But would she still be available on his return? A lovely and capable young woman like that would surely be spoken for before too long. The thought threw him into a sombre mood. That night he wrote two heartfelt letters – one to his mother and one to Margaret – and immediately felt better for it. It would be many weeks though before he could hope for a reply.

In August, the Contingent was involved in the relief of Rustenburg. In September, 75 New Zealanders led by Colonel Robin, as he was now, were part of a remarkable cross-country march through mountainous country the Boers had deemed impassable. All went well until they approached the target of Barberton. Then, on the flank of the advance, Lonnie Sparks rode directly into a Boer outpost. In the shocking sudden crackle of the firestorm, he took a bullet in the body and two in the legs and his horse collapsed dead under him from bullets in the head. Toby, close behind, was struck in the thigh but stayed astride. By great good fortune both did not die there for the air was full of Boer lead. Lonnie scrambled to the nearest clump of rocks and brush while Toby Page slid off his mount and rushed it to the refuge of the rocks.

'Sooner we're out of here the better mate,' said Toby.

He wasn't especially worried about his own wound but he could see Lonnie was in trouble. Toby crawled to his side, dragged him back to his horse and hoisted him across the saddle, expecting to be hit any time. But his mates were pouring in so much fire, the Boers could not get a clean shot. As Toby led them away, running beside the horse, he could hear bullets whistle by and others bury themselves with a vicious whir-r-r-p in the ground behind. But the fusillade from his fellow troopers kept most Boer heads well down and to Toby's surprise and relief, the bullet with his name on it never came.

'Thanks mate,' Lonnie Sparks said much later, recuperating in the hospital.

The soldiers were a laconic lot, not given to effusive statements, but their few words could say a lot. At 26, Lonnie Sparks already looked up to Toby at 28 as an older brother. It was not just because he was the younger – there was a rare maturity about Toby Page. It was as though he had faced whatever life could throw at him and emerged wiser and without bitterness. He was not to know there was more ahead that would test him to the limit.

MAN DOWN

For his action in rescuing Lonnie Sparks, Toby Page was mentioned in dispatches. Some thought a yet higher award was merited but Toby was just grateful to get the two of them back alive. The British took the township of Barberton, a prize capture for it was full of Boer rolling stock and stores, and it became the base of most of the New Zealanders for the next month. For the first time since they had landed in South Africa, the troops could take blessed rest. The leisure even extended to cricket matches against other units.

The First Contingent was originally to return to New Zealand as a body, but so great was the toll on the men that some were permitted to return at once. Toby Page now yearned for home and family. His year of physical and mental hardship on the veldt, with the hovering presence of death, had helped bury old demons. To his relief, his mention in dispatches put him on the ship – the authorities reasoned that a war hero back in New Zealand would be a useful tool for recruitment. Lonnie Sparks qualified for return through his serious wounds. On 23 October, with an officer and 40 other men, they left for home. After days more of veldt and weeks of sea, they arrived back in Wellington on 25 January 1901. There was little of the jingoism of the departure. Indeed, there was mourning as

Queen Victoria had died just three days before. Most people had known no other monarch. Her son Edward had once said, 'Most people pray to the Eternal Father but I am the only one afflicted with an Eternal Mother.' He would now succeed her as Edward VII and it was 'God save the King!' From Wellington, Lonnie Sparks, now with a permanent slight limp, headed back to his father's farm.

Toby and Minnie Page locked in each other's arms on the wharf. She broke the embrace to speak. 'Mum died while you were away.'

He clasped her again. His loving nan had always been there for him. Before he had left for Africa, he had noticed her skin had become papery and she was often weary.

'I sent word but it will be somewhere out on the ocean.'

Arm in arm, mostly silent but deeply relieved to have each other, they walked around the wharves to Oriental Bay. Over the next week, talk about people and events spilled out of Toby. Scarcely anything of the fighting but much about the living conditions, the leaders he looked up to and the good mates he had made, especially Lonnie Sparks. Minnie knew of him as a prominent footballer. Every so often their thoughts would turn to Nan and each week they visited her grave in Karori.

'She was hugely proud of you,' said Minnie as they gazed one day on the gravestone, high above the city.

'And of you,' Toby said. 'And she got so much fun from her peeks at the worthies sitting for you.' They chuckled as they recollected Nan's miming of the worthies' affectations.

Back home, Toby broached a subject that had worried him in Africa. It was something scarcely talked about there.

'The British have started putting Boer families in camps,' Toby said. 'It's a rum thing. Mostly women and children jammed up in shocking bad conditions. Blazing hot during the day with damn blowflies everywhere, and freezing at night. It sticks in my craw. The officers say the families are providing the Boers with food and shelter but it should be a fight between the men, not the women and children.'

'Nothing in the newspapers of that,' Minnie Page said. 'I will mention it to my political friends.'

Toby felt better for airing the issue. The friends Minnie spoke of were men of influence who would bring the matter into public light.

It was Minnie Page who, casually as you like, brought up the subject of Margaret Fairbairn, asking if Toby had been in touch.

'I wrote to her from Africa,' he said, 'and got one reply. She was busy at her teaching and delighted with Sophie's progress.'

The mention of Sophie made them both reflective for a moment.

'Don't leave it too long before visiting Margaret. I'm sure she would be pleased to see you.'

Toby nodded. He certainly did intend to see her. She was

increasingly on his thoughts. Now, he was looking to return to Glenview and his family there and Margaret would be close by in Marton. There was one obligation first – to attend a ceremony in the capital to receive from Governor Ranfurly a citation for his mention in dispatches. Such a spontaneous action, he thought, over in a flash, and such a fuss being made of it. Lonnie would have done the same for him, he was sure. As he walked back through the streets of Wellington afterwards in his civilian clothes, he passed a line of boisterous young men at a recruitment post. At a stroke he was back in Africa, with the veldt stretching to the horizon, dust on his lips and the horse labouring beneath him. It had not been all bad – there had been good mates and camaraderie.

'Good luck boys,' he said.

'You should join us mate,' one of them called.

They waved hands in good will at his disappearing back. Their lives would soon be changed for ever and so – though he didn't know it – would his.

Toby contacted Mr McAlistair and checked there was a position for him back at Glenview. To his relief there was. He then visited Mr Howard at Heretaunga, passed on his respects and resigned from that position. He was grateful for his time there and Mr Howard understood his wish to return to his family.

Glenview was just as Toby remembered it but he was immediately aware people were looking at him differently. Before the trial, many had looked at him with dread and after, with relief, but still with some discomfort from the cloud which had hung over him. Now a year had passed and he was returning as a war hero. Clarissa, Harry, and Sophie raced into his arms and then probed him for details of his life in South Africa, especially of the fighting and the action which won him his citation. Toby gave them enough to satisfy their craving for vicarious excitement, omitting the ghastliness. There was a hug too with Elizabeth. She and Charles had read of the death of his nan and commiserated. Toby was acutely aware of the change in his relationship with Charles – the friendly look with playful, crinkled eyes was as warm as ever but more contemplative and lingering, and the grasp of the hand was firmer and longer.

'Well done,' said Charles. 'We are proud of you.'

'We have followed it all in our atlas,' Elizabeth said. 'Your great voyage and treks. It has been like a geography lesson for us all.'

'Best of all, your voyage home,' said Sophie. 'Every day Harry gave us an update to the chorus of, "See the Conquering Hero Comes".'

'Good on you,' said Harry. 'We're so proud.'

Toby saw with relief that Sophie appeared to have put the molestation behind her. She was as vivacious and at ease as he remembered from before. As the days turned into weeks and he fell back into the rhythm of life on the estate and in the stable at Bulls, it seemed as though that dreadful disruption in all their lives was a thing of the past. At the first opportunity he visited Margaret Fairbairn at Marton and his shyness fell away at first sight. It seemed the year apart had lowered inhibitions and brought them closer. They embraced, though a little awkwardly, talked non-stop over cups of tea and her home-made biscuits, and toured her garden. So far as he could tell, there was no other suitor, but he realised he could not be sure. He did not yet feel quite ready to ask for her hand – the married couple's quarters at Glenview were not a patch on her cottage and he could not expect her to exchange one for the other. No, the time was not yet right but he knew there was danger in delaying too long. He was aware that many a loving heart had been left to wither in silence.

As before, on Sundays, if the weather was not too rough, Toby often rode with Clarissa, Harry, and Sophie on the river trails. Now, he was riding not with the children of the station owner, but with brother and sisters. He knew something they did not but he did not consider it his place to tell them. His father knew and he had clearly not said anything so Toby kept the knowledge to himself, tucked up warm inside him.

Harry, for a time, turned their treks into ventures across enemy territory.

'Up ahead on the left in the kopje,' he whispered. 'A Boer advance party preparing an ambush.' Instead, a hawk, roused by their party from its kill of rabbit, flapped suddenly skywards from a patch of grass. Again, 'There, in the shadow of that rock, a movement, major.' A hare leapt out and, in a few giant strides, vanished into scrub. And, looking down the valley, 'Colonel, where shall we position our snipers?' And the laughter of them all chirrupted across the valley.

Toby was surprised to receive an invitation to lunch from Sir Robert Drake and Lady Pamela. Sir Robert was hosting the Duke and Duchess of Cornwall who were visiting New Zealand in June 1901 following the opening of the Commonwealth Parliament in Australia. They were also taking the opportunity to thank New Zealand for its support in the South African war. Before the war ended in 1902, 71 New Zealanders were to be killed in action or die of wounds and another 159 die in accidents or from disease. Toby realised he would be on show as a local military hero. Fernbrook, Sir Robert Drake's estate, had never looked better. The gravel was meticulously combed and the lawns were smoothly ironed. Sir Robert and Lady Pamela were graciousness itself and Paul Drake, Toby's commander in the Rangitikei militia, shook hands warmly. At one point, though, he noticed Simon Drake eyeing him venomously with a curled lip, and a shadow fell on the afternoon.

'Here is our hero from Africa,' said Sir Robert, introducing Toby to Prince George Frederick Ernest Albert, Duke of Cornwall and York, and the Duchess Mary. Toby had read that the duke was not at all loud and flamboyant like his father, Edward VII, more content to collect stamps than to carouse. Even so, he was taken aback by the contrast between the slightly built man of average height, with a neatly trimmed moustache and beard, and what he represented. The social divisions of Home were weakening in the colony where 'Jack' vied to be as good as his master, but as he shook hands with the Duke, Toby was acute aware that one day this man would be King of Great Britain and Ireland and its vast Empire which Toby had fought for in Africa.

'Well done,' said the Duke. 'Marvellous. We are very grateful.' His attractive, dark-haired wife, the Duchess, murmured her appreciation as well. Toby's rehabilitation in the public eye could not have been more complete.

As Toby mingled with other guests, he came eventually within earshot of Simon Drake.

'Spray the things round like confetti,' Drake was saying. 'So many awards and mentions in dispatches that every Tom, Dick and Harry is getting one.' Toby could see Drake glancing his way to ensure his barb was striking home. Toby shrugged and turned back to his conversation with friends from racing and the Hunt. He would not allow Simon Drake's toxic tongue to spoil his day. He would have lots to regale his mother with on his next visit to Wellington. How she would have loved a commission to paint the Duke and Duchess. How his nan would have loved to hear of any quirks and foibles. He felt a pang of loss but then recalled her joy of life.

As the months rolled round, Clarissa was increasingly absent from the Sunday treks. Now 24, she was more often socialising with the sons and daughters of the district's estates. Toby occasionally saw her on the fringes of the polo crowd and amidst racegoers on the lawn. She had blossomed into an effervescent, dainty beauty, allowing her riotous black hair to fall to her shoulders and charming all with her free and easy manner. Sophie and Harry, too, and Elizabeth appeared to have put that horror of the past behind them and were relaxed and untroubled. But for Charles, the shocks of recent times had been more difficult to handle. The attack on Sophie and the arrest of Toby had pained him more than he had shown. And then the revelation Toby was his son had piled emotion on emotion. He had thanked God that Sophie had not been violated and then that Toby had been exonerated and then yet again at Toby's safe return from Africa. But at times he found himself more easily distracted than before, and more anxious.

Toby felt compelled to mention it to Elizabeth.

'I am only too aware Toby. Events have taken a great toll on him. But don't blame yourself for any of it. It was all far beyond our control. He is delighted to have you as one of the family.'

In truth, Charles needed the help of a doctor of disorders of the mind to come to terms with the trauma of the attack on Sophie and move on. But in 1901, people did not do that, certainly not hardy sons of the soil, and he continued to carry the trauma deep within. It came to a head one Wednesday afternoon in spring. The meeting of the Rangitikei Hunt, hosted by Mr and Mrs Lochie Irving, was on easy, rolling hill country near Hunterville with a great variety of fence – hawthorn, gorse, post and rail, stone wall, sapling, light gate, and, one special challenge for the most bold and fearless, a barberry hedge with a post-and-rail in it, a wire on the top and a ditch beyond. That would add some ginger to proceedings and test the 'sand' in the riders.

The day dawned with drizzle from dark, lumpish clouds but then a wind came up, clearing the sky, and the sun blazed forth, chasing away the gloom. With such ideal hunting country and now a day of blue sky to rejoice in, there was the best turnout of the season. Charles, Clarissa, and Toby were all riding and Elizabeth, Harry and Sophie had come along to follow the action from a buggy on the road as best they could. As the riders mounted and took position behind the huntsman and the Master, Elizabeth was interested to see Simon Drake engaging Clarissa in close conversation. She was not surprised they were showing interest in each other – her daughter was a beauty with an engaging personality and Simon Drake, well, she could see how the women looked at those eyes of sapphire-blue, the tossing black hair, the lithe body and dazzling smile. Her younger self, she was sure, would have been equally drawn. She was reminded of a comment of Lady Pamela she had once overheard: 'His good looks will be the downfall of him and, unfortunately, others.'

Harry, too, had noticed the close conversation. 'Clarissa seems more interested in a Drake than a hare today.'

'Tell me about it Harry,' Sophie said, intensely interested in the flirtations of her sister. It was usually Clarissa who kept Sophie up-to-date with the district's liaisons, both official and unofficial, though sometimes the favour was reciprocated as Sophie's hearing was incredibly acute.

'Simon Drake is paying great attention to Clarissa and Clarissa to him.'

Sophie certainly was interested in this tittle tattle. Simon Drake had never turned his charms on her but she had heard much talk of his affairs. She would question Clarissa later – there were sure to be some laughs in it.

And then the Hunt was on the move. It had barely started before a rabbit was sighted and speedily demolished by the pack. Away the pack went again and this time at a terrific pace. A huge hare was bounding away on the far side of the paddock. The first fence loomed, a post and rail, and the field flowed over it, except for one gentleman who lurched sideways, lost his reins, and came out of it with his arms around his horse's neck. The blood of hounds, horses and riders was now well up and raging and there was a depth and richness to the hounds' music. Charles could feel his Buster quivering with excitement and then rising at a fence hard beside two others. They hung suspended for a moment as though one, before thudding to earth and splitting free. The hare had run straight at a cracking pace but now she turned up a slope towards the cover of bracken. The deep-throated hounds were in ecstasy, surging after her in a body but the hare was gaining ground up the slope. Charles looked at the best hunting country he had ever seen – gently rolling green fields intersected with fences and dotted with elm and oak trees, pine, poplar, and gum, with a stream running through the middle of it. A distant mist was turning the far hills to lilac. The thought may have crossed his mind – would there be a better way to go than on his favourite horse in this superb countryside with his family close by? But the horse beneath him had no wish for the adventure to end. The spunky chestnut jumped for the joy of it and careered up the slope after the hounds towards the bracken. Alas for the hare, there was no refuge there, for the hounds had shot straight in and driven her out. Now she was flying straight for the barberry hedge flanking the paddock beyond. Charles turned his attention to Buster as the field swung left towards a stiff gorse hedge.

'What a mighty run!' shouted someone to his left.

'The best yet!' shouted another.

'Just listen to those hounds!' said a third.

In their buggy on the road to the left, Elizabeth and Harry marvelled at the spectacle. So fine, with the charging hounds, the stream of horses and the smart green coats of the riders. Sophie was just as involved as Elizabeth and Harry, through the music of the hounds, the thud of the hooves, the faint shouts of riders and the running commentary Harry provided.

'The hare's still half a paddock to the good. Mr Riddiford's at the barberry hedge with the wire. He's over. There's others back a paddock. Dad's cleared the gorse hedge and Clarissa too and they're running on. Oh hell, half a mo! Horse running loose and lady rider down, back at the gorse hedge. Lady getting up. Dad's now with a pack of others half-way to the big barberry hedge. About 10 of them. The riderless horse has joined them. Buster's getting set to jump.'

Charles lined Buster up at the barberry hedge with the post-and-rail and wire and the ditch beyond. There was a light gate as an alternative but that would mean taking a deviation. Buster gathered himself and began to launch at the barberry hedge like the fine steeplechaser he had been in his prime. Was it age that found Buster out at last? Did his hind feet slip on mushy ground? Was it the riderless horse pressing in from the left? Was it the hard-mouthed, green horse on the right? Were there just too many going for the same stretch of fence and rail? Or was it distraction and hesitance running down the reins from the rider? Whatever the cause, whether one or several, Buster slewed sideways, a hoof hit the wire and he crashed into the ditch in a fearsome great flurry of legs. Charles was tossed clean over his head, flew forever, and crashed to the ground beyond where he lay in a heap, deathly still.

'Oh my God!' said Harry. 'Dad's down.'

Elizabeth felt her heart had stopped. And then it was thumping so hard she might have fainted.

'Is he up?' Sophie asked.

Harry was willing his father to move, to spring up like that other time he had fallen. Every rider knew they did this sport at their own risk. There was scarcely one who hadn't fallen at some time and sprained an ankle or broken a bone or two. They were a rugged lot. Once, after Clarissa fell, she jammed her handkerchief over the cut on her head and then jammed her hat over the handkerchief and carried on. And Harry remembered the story of the surgeon horseman who had dislocated his arm. The surgeon had instructed another man to hold the arm just so; the arm clicked and went back into position and the surgeon hunted on for another hour and a half.

But Charles continued to lie unmoving. While most of the other horses flowed onwards, Buster stayed back with his master.

'What's happening?' asked Sophie. She and her father had felt the other's hurt and pain intensely since that night at the stable and had hugged even more since.

'Not up yet,' said Harry. He leapt out of the buggy and raced across the paddock to his father. Elizabeth quickly tethered their horse to a fence and she and Sophie followed. Sir Robert Drake was there already, with Clarissa and Toby.

Sir Robert rose as Elizabeth approached. 'He's breathing,' he said. 'But he's in a parlous state.'

They looked down at Charles. He was on his side, still unconscious, with his coat and pants torn and his boots soiled. The force of the collision had broken Buster's girth and torn off the saddle.

'Can we use your buggy to get him back to the homestead?' Sir Robert asked Elizabeth. 'I'll take him on to the hospital.'

Charles was conveyed as carefully as possible, Elizabeth by his side, while another buggy was sent for Harry and Sophie. Soon all four were in the spacious carriage of Sir Robert bound for the hospital. A cursory examination indicated damage to shoulder and rib, but most worrying was the head injury. Charles did not regain consciousness for nearly two hours.

The hare, after providing the Hunt with a long, fast, and glorious run of more than five miles, got clean away. Most riders would have agreed with that ending.

CHORUS OF MOURNING

The journey to Palmerston North Hospital was torturous for Charles and distressing for Sir Robert, Elizabeth, and the Sir Robert's long-time employee Dick Roake, gardener/chauffeur. Charles kept drifting in and out of consciousness, with occasional convulsions and vomiting, prompting fears in Elizabeth of permanent brain damage. She stayed in a nearby guest house overnight. The next day, Clarissa, Harry, and Sophie joined her at the hospital. They had boosted their spirits on their bleak journey to Palmerston North by being as positive as possible. Even Clarissa's description of the incident emphasised the normality of the Hunt.

'He was just ahead of me, travelling well. Buster was full of himself, clearing the fences with ease. He did get a bit squeezed up at the barberry hedge, with that horse running loose and a big field, but nothing too out of the ordinary. Then, for whatever reason, Buster faltered and went into the fence.' She didn't add what she and Harry would never forget – their father hurtling through the air and smashing into the ground beyond the ditch.

'Dad's fallen before and bounced back quickly,' said Sophie. 'And I've heard Palmerston North Hospital has two excellent doctors and a good team of nurses.'

'And mum's been with him throughout, making sure he gets everything he needs,' Harry said.

'We'll get him back to his old self,' Clarissa said. 'Norman Kelly wants me to pass on his best wishes and he's given me a rundown on the horses' preparations and which races he thinks they should be placed in. That'll get dad's attention.'

There were, though, long silences between their exchanges. At the hospital, embraces with Elizabeth soon turned to earnest conversation.

'The doctor has told me it will take time,' she said. 'He does remember something of the Hunt but nothing of the journey to Palmerston North. His confusion has been a concern for them. His brain has taken a battering but mercifully, there is no fracture of the skull.'

They exchanged grateful looks for that. The hard hat had clearly helped.

'He will rest here four more days for observation and then it will be for us to help him recover at home.'

The looks they exchanged spoke of their determination to get husband and father back to the capable, responsive person he had been.

There was another visitor to his bedside. Toby had told his mother of the accident and the news had chilled her heart. Her visit had been no comfort. The sight of him so pale, bravely smiling but with signs of bewilderment, shook her more than she said. She stayed only briefly, wanting Charles and the family to know of her love and support but not wishing to intrude. It was their husband and father to be brought back to life. In recent days, Minnie had thought it was time Elizabeth and her children knew that Charles was Toby's father and the children's half-brother and had thought to raise the subject with Charles. But no chance of that now. She would have to wait until he recovered.

When Charles returned to Glenview, he was to all appearances the master once again, well turned out and with gentlemanly presence, but those close to him knew differently. Elizabeth saw he struggled to do the estate accounts and would forget he had meetings. There was the terrible time she had found him standing in the doorway bemused, tears running down his face, knowing there was something important he had meant to do but with no idea what it was. The children did their best to clear his confusions, jumping in with prompts when he struggled to recall and coaxing him with recollections from the past. But his frequent befuddlements left them shaken and anxious. Toby felt he had found his father and then lost part of him. Charles was simply going through the motions. Norman Kelly could see the difference in a flash. Charles had always been at one with the horses; now, he strained to even remember the names of some of them. A mordant air lay over the house.

Elizabeth consulted with the family doctor, Timothy Armitage, 55, bespectacled and portly, a much- revered figure in the community, on call virtually any time of night or day. Once he had even swum a flooded river and another time tramped for hours through country more suited to birds and goats.

'We can medicate to lessen the agitations from damage to the brain but sometimes, alas, there is little we can do to heal the underlying damage. You can but ensure he has rest and is not subject to undue pressure. Time can be the great healer.'

The words were little comfort for Charles appeared to be getting no better. The estate, also, had the immediate problem of lack of governance. Things were in a state of limbo. There were scores of staff and a multitude of tasks to manage. Elizabeth took more of the responsibilities on herself but finally one day had a full and frank discussion with Charles. He was at first reluctant to put any more on her but when she produced the calendar of meetings for the next month and then the pile of letters and accounts requiring action, his head slumped. When he looked up, she saw eyes full of despair.

'Why don't we use Bert Sinclair and Monty more, until you're well,' she said. Bert Sinclair, station manager, was highly competent and Monty Powell, their accountant based in Marton, was a family friend as well as a trusted business confidant. He had always been a good back-up and she was sure he would much rather step in now than face trouble later.

Charles nodded in resignation. He had never been one of those gentlemen estate owners operating at a distance. The satisfaction had been in hands-on, close to staff, supervising and encouraging in person. To have a muddled mind was hugely frustrating. Recently he had shaken the hand of Norman Kelly, gone to address him and the name had escaped him. When once he could have given the breeding of his horses for generations past, now, when he watched them at work, they could have been the animals of a stranger. Several times Norman Kelly had seen him standing at the track, alone, looking totally befuddled. Kelly had mentioned his concerns to Elizabeth and she had instructed him to put his observations about the horses and his plans for them on paper for Charles to consider at his leisure. The stable could not be allowed to moulder through inaction.

Elizabeth was aware, too, that the future of the estate itself must be secured. It had been in the McAlistair family for three generations. The property even had its own small cemetery, fenced and trim, with McAlistairs in two small rows with space for more. Thomas Kirkpatrick McAlistair had emigrated to New Zealand from the family farm in Argyllshire in 1852 and been much taken by the river flats and rolling hills of the property he named Glenview. When he died in his bed, to the lamentations of the entire region, his son Craig succeeded to the property. Craig McAlistair served the public in many capacities as well, further enhancing the family name, and ensured his son Charles had the best of educations. He had attended Wanganui Collegiate School which had flourished since it was established as the Native Industrial School in 1854, and he had befriended the sons of many leading men of the colony. Craig McAlistair, tragically, died before his time at age 52 when a cutting was being put through the property and a spark from a lighted fuse fired 90 pounds of blasting powder unexpectedly. Charles had succeeded him aged only 32. Now Charles, at age 46, could feel the McAlistair grasp on Glenview slipping away. He tried secluding himself in his library, with the ledgers of the estate before him along with the seasonal and yearly plans, but his head would swirl with a host of confusing images and he would leave in distress with barely a page turned. The dismay on the faces of his family pained him more than he could say and there were times he muttered an apology and hurried away before further humiliation.

Plunged into depression, Charles turned to alcohol for comfort. He had never been more than an occasional social drinker but now, to the family's despair, he began taking to the liquor cabinet mid-morning and there was nothing prissy about the glasses he poured. When Bert Sinclair and Monty Powell arrived in the early afternoon one day to go over the estate's business with him, his breath was heavy with alcohol and he was slurring his words and drifting into sleep. The session ended shortly after it began when Charles violently vomited. Later, Elizabeth remonstrated with him.

'Charlie, the doctors say you mustn't drink, that it will react badly with the medications you are taking.'

Charles was hollow-eyed and pale as a drained sky. 'My love, the medications do nothing for me. When I wake in the morning, my head is as damn crocked as the day before. People and places float in and out, past and present all jumbled up, and I can't get a grip on any of it. I can see what I am doing to all of you but, I'm sorry, I can't sort myself out. The drink helps me forget. It's a comfort.'

Sophie was hovering nearby. His words broke her heart and she approached and held him tight. Clarissa, Harry, and Elizabeth joined the embrace.

Timothy Armitage visited. 'Charles, the alcohol is poisoning you. If you persist, there will be more vomiting and seizures. You must give nature and the medications a chance to help heal you.' He ordered the liquor cabinet to be locked and spoke intensely to Elizabeth on departure.

'The poor fellow is not at all himself. A head injury can be a cursed thing. I'm sorry Mrs McAlistair, but there is nothing more at this stage we can do.' He looked in pity at the distraught wife wringing her hands. He was devoted to his calling but a visit such as this was excruciating. 'Except the one thing we must do – keep him away from alcohol.'

Besides conveying their love, and praying for him at church on Sunday, the children now had another way to help their father. It became, though, a macabre game of hide and seek as Charles continued to crave the solace of alcohol and they continued to try to block his access to it. But one way or another, he obtained his whisky, brandy, gin or other spirit and Clarissa and Harry found empty or partially empty bottles all over the estate, usually after observing their father leaving the site.

One mid-morning Toby came across Charles in a dressing gown, slumped on a chair in the stable by Buster's stall, a glass of gin in his hand and his favourite dog Holly, a golden retriever, at his feet. He looked at Toby sadly. They sat in silence for a minute.

'How can I help?' Toby had so much respect and love for the man his father had been, to see him in this woeful state was heart-rending.

Charles's face was drawn and sunken. 'Just be here my boy.'

Weeks passed. There was no improvement in Charles and his furtive drinking continued. The mood in the house was sombre and disquieting. There were times of desperation when Elizabeth would have welcomed any healer, however outrageous, who claimed he could lay his hands on Charles and heal him. She looked with interest at the pamphlet of an American lady practitioner of faith healing who claimed her thoughts could travel through space from one side of the earth to the other, if need be, to cure disease or disorder. It was as well that Arthur Worthington, the faith healer who had propounded his own religion from his Temple of Truth in Christchurch, had fled two years before for Australia. Elizabeth and Clarissa increasingly took on Charles's duties. Monty Powell was now visiting weekly and order was being restored at the estate. Toby, without making a conscious effort to do so, found himself more and more involved with Norman Kelly in the decision-making at the racing stable. Charles McAlistair, the owner and the payer of bills, sunk in his cups, surveying the detritus of his life, was now scarcely involved at all.

On the rare occasions when Charles appeared to have no access to alcohol, Elizabeth would take heart that his mind and body would be recuperating from the dreadful buffeting they had taken. But there were more days when Charles, with the connivance of an estate worker who cared more for the health of his pocket than the health of his master, would procure a bottle without the knowledge of Elizabeth and the children. One such day matters came to a head. Elizabeth had been meeting with Monty Powell to go over the estate's accounts. When they emerged from the dining room, they saw Charles in the kitchen, drunk and babbling to himself, barely able to stand. It was too much, even for Elizabeth's steely resolve, and she broke down for the first time in the sight of others, her body wracked by huge sobs. Monty Powell did what a friend would do – put a consoling arm around her shoulders. Then Charles turned, saw Elizabeth being comforted and took his first decisive action since the accident. He went to the study, got the key to the gun cabinet, selected a hand gun, went through a side door to the wash house, and shot himself dead.

Elizabeth and Monty Powell heard the gunshot as she was seeing him out of the house. They raced in the direction of the shot. Bert Sinclair was first on the scene, Elizabeth and Monty second. Elizabeth's worst fears were realised. Her beloved Charles lay sprawled with his head a pulpy mess of blood and brains. As she collapsed on the ground distraught, Bert Sinclair ordered the gristly scene sealed off and went inside to summon the police and the doctor.

When Dr Armitage arrived, he confirmed death had been instantaneous and dispensed medication to the family and some of the estate workers for shock. The doctor was barely holding back tears himself.

'I can only say, my dear, Charles was a fine man and I will miss him more than I can say.'

Elizabeth now went beyond sorrow to profound despair. Charles and she had adored each other. Henceforth she would forever torture herself with the thought that Charles had seen the arm of another around her shoulders, although it was totally innocent, only the kind action of a friend. That night, the plaintive howling of the golden retriever Holly rang through the house and stable and deep into the Glenview estate. Other dogs took it up and turned it into a chorus of mourning.

There was once a time in the old countries when those who had killed themselves were buried ignominiously on the high-road with a stake thrust through their body, and without Christian rites. As if the misery that had driven them to the act had not been punishment enough in life. It was a degree of mercy that Charles McAlistair was remembered for the fine man he had been. Hundreds came to his sad farewell as the whole district mourned, and the Christian rites were delivered. Sir Robert Drake delivered a eulogy. The McAlistair family clung to one another and Minnie Page and Toby clasped each other tight. Margaret Fairbairn stood by the family, with them in spirit. In that whole gathering, only Minnie and Toby were aware that Charles McAlistair was Toby's father and both knew this was no time to reveal the truth of the paternity. As the crowd dissolved after the ceremony, they joined Elizabeth, Clarissa, Harry, and Sophie.

'We will carry on with the estate,' Elizabeth said. 'Charles arranged some years ago to bequeath everything to me in the event of his death.'

Toby was relieved to hear that. When there was no male in the immediate family, many wills bequeathed everything to a male relative, sometimes to an uncle or even a cousin. There was of course Harry but when the will had been drawn up, Harry had been a small boy with a severe disability. In leaving the estate to Elizabeth, Charles had been ahead of his time in his thinking. It was evident, too, that Elizabeth had emerged from her despair and was looking to the future.

'Clarissa will assist me,' said Elizabeth, 'along with Monty Powell and Bert Sinclair. And Norman Kelly will run the racing stable, with the assistance of Toby.'

Charles need not have feared the Glenview estate would slip from the grasp of his family.

WEDDING OF
THE YEAR

Elizabeth had to concede that the drive which had sustained her in the months leading up to Charles's death, had been in the vain hope he would recover and take the reins once more. Now, as the reality of his death sank in, and with her will sapped, she decided to retain ownership of the estate but appoint Bert Sinclair manager and move permanently to The Elms, their town house in Tinakori Road, Wellington. Clarissa, Harry, and Sophie would remain at the estate. Norman Kelly would continue to run the racing stable, assisted by Toby Page.

Six months later the world turned on its head when the district's wedding of the year was announced – Simon Drake and Clarissa McAlistair. Elizabeth had grave misgivings from Clarissa's first intimations of something more than friendship. She discussed it with Clarissa until there was nothing more to say and she feared their communication would break down altogether. She could see that with the death of her father, Clarissa was emotionally vulnerable and easy prey. Sophie, too, was fearful as she had heard much of Simon Drake's wayward ways. Harry put his trust in Clarissa's judgment. She had always encouraged him to try new ventures despite his seizures and now he would support her in her decision. There had been talk of Harry and Sophie staying at Glenview with Clarissa and Simon after the marriage, and Simon said that was quite acceptable to him. But Sophie insisted on moving to The Elms with her mother and Harry would go with her. Elizabeth made it clear that she would retain ownership of the estate and that Bert Sinclair would continue to manage it, in consultation with Clarissa and Simon.

Lady Pamela Drake sighed with relief as she and Sir Robert prepared to travel to St Stephen's Church at Marton on the morning of the marriage.

'Thank the Lord Simon is getting married and to lovely Clarissa.'

'It should be the making of him,' Sir Robert said. 'It's time he had the responsibility of a wife and family and duties. He's been too thick with that lot he knocks around with.'

Lady Pamela nodded in agreement. 'I must admit it's a huge relief to me.' She did not like Simon's companions and she had long been discomforted by his romantic dalliances. She even suspected an affair with one of her married friends.

They were also pleased the Drakes were connecting with another fine estate. Estate succession could be such a difficult business, particularly with more than one son and the wish to keep the estate as intact as possible. Paul Drake was heir apparent of Sir Robert and Pamela's Fernbrook, and the other boys Simon and Ralph had to find their own way. There were of course the four girls to marry off as best they could to the town or rural aristocracy. The McAlistairs were a fine family and

Charles's accident at the Hunt had been wretched bad luck. But now something good was taking place and the district could move on. Glenview was a magnificent property and Simon had fine prospects.

With Paul well settled and Simon at 30 now marrying well, Sir Robert was struck by another thought.

'My dear, we need to talk about Ralph.'

Ralph, seven years younger than Simon, presented them with a quite different challenge. It was a battle waged not before the eyes of the world but within themselves for Ralph was involved in a crime not to be named among Christians. At boarding school, he had discovered he was sexually attracted to males and at 16, had fallen hopelessly in love with another boy of his year. For self-protection, it was a clandestine affair and perhaps the more passionate for that. This was no passing phase. Lady Pamela and Ralph's sisters had suspected it long before Sir Robert commented on Ralph's distinctive voice and walk. His sisters adored bubbly and sensitive Ralph but they and his mother feared for him deeply as the Liberal Government in 1893 – though so reformist in several ways – had passed legislation making any sexual activity between men unlawful with penalty of imprisonment as well as the possibility of flogging, whipping or hard labour.

'Let's marry him off quick smart,' said Sir Robert, straightening his collar in front of a mirror. 'There must be a pretty filly in these parts that will bring out the stallion in him.'

Lady Pamela doubted that. They loved all their children and they had worried about all of them at different times, especially with childhood diseases so prevalent, but she worried most of all about Ralph. His path would be arduous and full of danger.

◆ ◆ ◆

On the morning of the wedding, Clarissa was warned that Simon had run into a door in the dark and sustained a black eye. But when she walked up the aisle of exquisite St Stephen's Church on the arm of Harry and turned to look up at Simon, she was taken aback by the extent of the injury. The entire area of his left eye was black with bruising. She squeezed his arm in sympathy and murmured, 'Bad luck, my love.' He grimaced back at her, recalling the giant fist of the outraged husband coming his way during the last bachelor 'bash' of the 'Hellfire Boys'. His huge purple bruise was a great embarrassment to him, and painful as well, but so many had been invited, including the elite of the district and far beyond, there was no postponing the day. When he rose to deliver his speech at the reception, he felt every eye was on the bruise and certainly some guests did scrunch their faces and recoil at the sight of it. But then he saw Sir Robert, Lady Pamela, Paul, and Paul's wife Dorothy looking at him and began to relish his moment in the spotlight. Not only was he coming out from under the shadow of Paul and greatly enhancing his position in life, he had a beautiful, vivacious bride. There would be the bonus, too, of no interfering father-in-law looking over his shoulder.

At the reception, Simon Drake was eventually able to extricate himself from guests offering congratulations and talk properly with Eddie Shaw, Arthur Wilson, and Henry Thompson.

'Come over when I return from Rotorua and we can talk about the mining venture and the racing stable,' he said.

Shaw's eyes lit up. He was already making much money from his own mining interests but his life style was extravagant and he could never have enough. Mention of the racing stable was also compelling – Shaw, as a heavy gambler, liked nothing better than inside information. He could empathise with Simon Drake on his black eye. He had his own tender spot. That morning, still groggy from the night before, he had stumbled on entering his library and thudded against a bookshelf, dislodging a heavy volume which struck him on the back of the head. It had had a greater impact than any book. But now, at mention of the mining venture, he was all attention.

'I can get my people to assess prospects for you,' he said. 'From what I have seen myself of Glenview, I believe there might very well be asbestos in the upper regions and who knows, even platinum.'

'Let me know if you need additional capital,' Arthur Wilson said. He had speculated profitably both in land and mining. His sights were particularly set on the seventeen percent of New Zealand land still owned by Maori, much of it undeveloped, and he was pushing for a more straightforward way to get access to it. But now, Simon Drake's venture might put land and mining into his lap close to home.

'Likewise,' said Henry Thompson. With his money coming from unfashionable tallow and rabbits, land and mining would be welcome.

Toby was appalled at the marriage. He, too, had seen the mutual attraction of Clarissa and Simon long before and though some of it no doubt on Simon's part was physical, he was certain the allure of the McAlistair estate and the horses was the main part of it. He was also appalled at the prospect of Drake being the master of the house and of having to live under his aegis, even in part. As guests mingled afterwards, he raised the future of the racing stable with Elizabeth.

She looked contemplative. 'Nothing has been said. I have no idea what his hopes are Toby. We shall have to wait and see.'

Already, Toby was considering his options.

On return from their honeymoon in the hot lakes district, Simon Drake moved into the McAlistair homestead and that same evening he hosted Eddie Shaw, Henry Thompson, and Arthur Wilson to dinner. Toby could hear their revelry from his quarters at the estate. As he heard cheer after cheer, he could imagine the toasts to their unsavoury leader. A miasmic sense of evil and intimidation seemed to swirl from the house and envelop the whole of Glenview.

Within the week, Drake was in Wellington with a proposal for Elizabeth. It was phrased more as a statement than a proposal. 'I will purchase the racing stable from you and run it as a business quite separate from the estate.'

Elizabeth had suspected there might be something of the sort. She knew of his fervent interest in horse racing. The stable had always been the passion of Charles, not of her, though she had always taken more than a passing interest. And, despite the occasional thrilling win, the stable had made only a modest profit. He gave her a price. It was certainly a handsome sum and would provide a useful investment for the family.

'Let me consider it,' she said. 'I must discuss it with Clarissa.' Elizabeth saw the stab of annoyance on his face that Elizabeth should want to discuss it with his wife.

He had no wish to linger and chat with his in-laws and they, in turn, were not sorry to see him turn and go. He had never been especially friendly with them, except Clarissa. He was also a reminder of the horror in the stable. With Toby exonerated, some despicable other must still be running loose and that continued to trouble many.

The next day Clarissa entrained to Wellington. There was a joyful reunion with mother, Harry and Sophie and much talk about the wonders of the Rotorua thermal region. Then, at Clarissa's urging, Elizabeth withdrew with her into the drawing room and Elizabeth at once saw a dramatic change in Clarissa's manner.

'Mother, you must agree to the sale,' she said, eyes pleading. 'It means more to him than I would ever have thought. He talks about nothing else.' She wrinkled her face in dismay. 'There is another thing. He has a dreadful hatred of Toby. And I'm pleased you weren't there to hear the comments of Simon, Eddie Shaw, Henry Thompson and Arthur Wilson about Minnie Page.' She shook her head in disgust. 'I am also worried about Simon's plans for the estate. Eddie Shaw is keen to prospect on the property for minerals and Henry Thompson and Arthur Wilson are speaking of the four of them forming a business consortium if anything is found.'

Elizabeth quaked at the thought. Glenview had been developed by generations of McAlistairs into prime agricultural land. The only areas not productive with crops or stock were the steeper hills which had been left in native bush to protect against erosion. She shuddered to think what Charlie would have thought of the pasture or bush being gouged for minerals. The very idea of Simon Drake chewing over the future of Glenview with his drinking companions hugely rankled. Drake had no sooner got into Clarissa's bed than he was looking to take over both the racing stable and the estate.

'The racing stable is one thing,' she said, 'the estate quite another. He will not get his hands on that. I will call a meeting to make it perfectly clear where responsibilities lie. Bert is the manager, reporting to me and Monty. The role of Simon is to assist the estate to run smoothly. His suggestions are more than welcome but he must be told he has no authority whatsoever to implement them of his own accord. Certainly not to invite prospectors onto the estate.'

Elizabeth pondered the information about Simon Drake's ambitions for Glenview. It gave further reason for selling the racing stables to him – his zeal over the stable might absorb his energies and take his attention off the estate.

'I will not be bullied into a sale of the racing stables,' Elizabeth said. 'I will sell only if it is in the family's best interests. Anyway, I can't give him an answer immediately. I must discuss it with Monty.' She studied the anxious and crestfallen face before her. She had never seen such dismay and lack of confidence in her daughter. 'You must remember, Clarissa, you are the mistress of the estate and are not to be coerced into running around at his beck and call.' Elizabeth would never have thought her spirited Clarissa would need her spine stiffened. Clarissa had always been the strongest of them all. Whenever a decision had had to be made about putting down a household horse or dog, Clarissa had cried but had given her assent when appropriate and made the arrangements. Moments later, to Elizabeth's relief, she saw her daughter pull a face and shrug in acceptance that she would not be returning with news of the sale. But Elizabeth did not want the matter dragging on. 'You can tell him I will give him an answer by the end of the month.'

Over lunch the family talked about the momentous change of Elizabeth, Harry and Sophie living permanently in Wellington. There had been the huge advantage for Sophie of greater access to her singing teacher, Madame Probert, as well as more liaison with other musicians and more concerts in which to perform.

'It can be a bit draughty in the capital,' said Harry, 'but there's no denying there are opportunities.' With his buoyant personality, Harry could have picked up many jobs in sales, with a liberal expense allowance to boot, but he dearly wished to pursue his interest in the natural world and was seeking advice from scientists in the city.

Later that week, after a meeting with Monty Powell and due diligence, Elizabeth decided it was in the family's best interests to sell the racing stable. The sale would in no way affect the estate which would continue to be owned by Elizabeth and managed by Bert Sinclair in discussion with Clarissa and Simon. Once the decision was made, Elizabeth and Clarissa went to the racing stable and told Norman Kelly and Toby personally. Drake had said nothing about who would be training his horses but both men determined it would not be them. They had heard and seen too much of Drake. They would serve out the month of their notice.

No sooner had Simon Drake signed the documents of sale than he was driving his trap to the stables at Bulls. Norman Kelly was grooming a horse and Toby was putting feed in a manger when they heard the rattle of the hooves on the paving stones. Norman Kelly took two steps towards Drake while Toby stayed where he was and looked on.

'I presume you've heard the news.'

Kelly nodded.

'Vernon McCardle will be taking over,' said Drake.

Toby and Norman Kelly exchanged a look. They were not surprised. McCardle was a knowledgeable and skilled trainer in his 30s but he was not beyond stooping to low practice and would be pliable in the hands of Drake. There had been talk around the stables of concoctions he had fed to horses. The other trainers knew, as well, that McCardle frequently ran horses that were far from ready, using the racing purely for training purposes while the punters' money went down the drain. McCardle and Simon Drake would be well suited to each other.

'You've got two weeks,' Drake said.

'Mrs McAlistair has told us one month,' said Kelly. 'We are being paid for that time.'

'We'll see about that,' said Drake. 'Vernon McCardle will be here in two weeks. Have your gear out by then.'

And just as abruptly and coldly, two weeks later, Norman Kelly and Toby Page were seen off the premises. After years of dedicated service to Charles McAlistair and his horses, they were out on their own. It did not take Kelly long to find another training position – he was popular amongst the owners and was snapped up by a Wellington beer baron. As for Toby Page, he had plans of his own.

A LIFE ON THE LAND

T oby moved that night into the hotel at Bulls. The fare
was good and the bed comfortable. He was sad to leave
the McAlistair family, Glenview, and the racing stable,
but relieved to be away from Simon Drake. As he lay in bed
with the hum of talk and occasional shouts drifting up to his
room from the bar, he mulled over his future. Matters had
come to a head quicker than he had expected but there had
been an idea brewing even as he had gazed on the Indian Ocean
when returning to New Zealand from Africa.

'A farm of my own,' he had said to Lonnie Sparks.

'Me too,' said Lonnie. 'I won't get my dad's one. 'There's two
ahead of me. But I reckon he'll help me into a small one of my
own. Nothing flash.'

'That's what I'm looking at,' said Toby. 'But not yet. When the
time's right.'

Now, lying in his bedroom that was too tiny to swing a possum
in, he decided the time **was** right. A place of his own that he
could put his heart and soul into and then ask for Margaret
Fairbairn's hand in marriage. It had worried him tremendously

that on his last visit to her at Marton, a local school teacher had come by when he was there and Toby suspected he was vying for her hand. Time now to get started and put a stake in the land. Frank Wallis had encouraged him to save. 'There's too many finish up with nothing,' Wallis had said and Toby himself had seen money going through men's hands like water. He had been saving money regularly for years. His food and keep had cost him nothing at both the Goodwins and the McAlistairs and neither during the South African War, though there had been no money from that. As closing time was called below and the last footfalls faded into the night, Toby turned out the light and lay thinking in the darkness.

'Time to visit Lonnie,' he said to himself.

Lonnie Sparks was repairing a fence when he got word he was wanted at the homestead. After huge grins and a hearty handshake, Toby broached the matter directly.

'What do you say about going shares in a farm?'

They repaired inside to talk about it over a cup of tea and a scone. Properly drawn up business contract, said Toby. Put the same amount in, work it together, expand as they were able and eventually split it in two or one buy the other out. He had lit a fire in Lonnie. By lunchtime the family started arriving from their tasks all over the property. Lonnie's large family were thrilled to meet Toby Page they had heard so much about. Toby Page who had fought beside their Lonnie in Africa. Toby

Page who had saved their Lonnie's life. After lunch, Lonnie drew his father aside and put the proposal to him. Noel Sparks was an astute businessman. Astute with people as well as figures on a balance sheet. Before buying the Wairarapa farm, he had worked for a bank as a rural adviser and he had always said he could tell within 10 minutes if people were good for a loan. He had no qualms about lending to his son but he was concerned about the dual ownership. He had seen other such ventures break up in acrimony.

'I can understand why you want to team up,' he said to Toby. 'Double the money should give you a property with decent potential. But the legal agreement must clearly delineate each party's commitments. Will you still want to be farming together in five years' time? In 10 years? I have my doubts. You must declare in writing from the start how your assets will be split at the end of the partnership.'

They discussed possible locations. Many of the large estates were being broken up and the government was also purchasing undeveloped, Maori-owned land for settlement. Both Toby and Lonnie were keen to remain in the lower North Island where they were close to family and familiar with the land use. Toby already had his eye on a largely undeveloped block in the upper Rangitikei district, near Manui, some 40 miles north of Hunterville. He ran it past Noel Sparks.

'Much of it's still in bush. It's rolling country with a good area of flat land each side of a stream that joins the Rangitikei River. Those flats are swampy but that's kept the price down and put it within reach. I believe we can drain the swamp and turn it into good agricultural land.'

This business venture was hazardous but Lonnie and Toby had

the bond of facing death together and depending on each other for their lives. Noel Sparks agreed to look at the property with them. It took three days and much journeying on horseback through mud and slush to get there. At the end of it, on a high vantage point, they looked over some 2,500 acres of bush, scrub, bracken, swamp, and rough grass.

'It'll be hard yakker boys but it's a good one,' declared Noel Sparks. 'There shouldn't be much of a problem with flooding and there's no sign of slips. You'll have to keep some of the land in bush though.'

'Bloody great,' said Lonnie. 'Can't wait to rip into it.'

'First thing will be to knock up some sort of shelter,' said Toby. 'Make it more liveable as we go on. You at one end, me at the other, away from your snoring.'

'That's enough of that,' protested Lonnie. 'No one's ever said I snore.'

'That's because no woman's wanted to sleep with you,' said Toby. 'There was one night on the veldt I thought a train was coming through, with all your huffing and puffing.'

With the banter flying, they proceeded to Mangaweka where they put in a tender for the property. When that, to their joy, was successful they drew up the legal document detailing their commitments. By now they had a name for the property which paid homage to the highest and lowest points of it – Ridgeburn. Returning two weeks later, they cleared a site suitable for a temporary homestead, erected a slab whare with a totara bark roof, and cut a bridle track to it. Driven by their dream, with success depending solely on themselves, they took to the work with gusto. Each night they were whacked but could look back with satisfaction on how much they had achieved. They lived austerely, sustained mainly by mutton, milk, and vegetables and by the satisfaction of shaping their own destiny. While they were draining the swampy land by the stream, men with saws arrived to start cutting the valuable timber out of the bush. Proceeds from the sale of this were ploughed back into the farm. Thousands of fence posts were cut from the smaller puriri trees and buried in deep pits. Toby made sure he marked the location of the pits as accurately as he could for retrieval later. Some stands of large trees close to the site of the future homestead were left so the timber could be used for the homestead and farm buildings. Everything else up to 2½ feet in diameter was felled. Progress came at a fearful cost: a man broke a limb jacking logs, another was concussed by a falling branch and many had broken and poisoned hands and feet. Months later, in January 1904, after the debris from the bush-felling was dry and the wind was right, the burn began. For weeks the sky was filled with smoke, ash fell thickly for miles around, and the sun was a blood-red ball.

While the property flamed and smouldered, men with pitsaws cut lengths of timber from the preserved stands of trees and other men brought in roofing iron and windows on pack horses. On a natural plateau overlooking the stream, Toby and Lonnie, under the direction of a builder-friend, erected a permanent home and metalled the access road to it. No longer would horses be belly-deep in mud. Amongst the first guests were Lonnie's family and that night the house rang with merriment. They laughed at the unusual design of a bedroom at each end but Toby and Lonnie pointed out that there was plenty of room for bedrooms to be located at the rear in the future, when one of the existing bedrooms could become a lounge.

'Or a nursery,' said one of Lonnie's sisters to more laughter.

With the fine house now available, Toby and Lonnie, with the urging of Mrs Sparks, advertised for a live-in housekeeper. Though they were both whip-cord hard, they had to acknowledge they were not eating properly. A widow, Mrs Crichton, was the successful applicant and proved to be warm-hearted and capable. Toby and Lonnie purchased an Angell washing machine for her.

'The time I've spent washing!' she said. 'If I'd had one of these earlier, it would have added 10 years to my life.'

A fenced-off garden and an orchard was planted out and a fowl house with two dozen hens was erected.

Since Toby had moved to Ridgeburn, many letters had gone back and forth with both his mother and Margaret. His letters to his mother were signed with 'love' and his letters to Margaret with 'kindest regards'. Margaret was increasingly in his thoughts but in the restraint of the times, he didn't feel it proper yet to tell her he loved her in a letter. He delivered and picked up at the Post Office attached to the store at Mangaweka. In 1890 there had been only standing bush there but by 1893 there was a smithy, a store, and a boarding house, though service at the boarding house was basic – the menu stated: 'Boarders will find dessert in the garden.' By 1901, with farms being established and the railway pushing ever northwards, there was a main street filled with businesses. In mid-1904, when Minnie Page first visited, she stood in wonder at the bustle around her.

'My goodness,' she said, 'who would ever have thought? Here was I thinking you were living in the wilderness and there is a hairdresser and tobacconist, a watchmaker and jeweller, and a draper and a tailor, besides the butcher, bootmaker, and the rest.'

Toby chuckled. 'You don't know the half of it. There is also a school, a newspaper, a Chess and Draughts Club and a Literary and Debating Society. First stop is the millinery shop where the owner's putting on an afternoon tea to encourage ladies to buy her hats.'

Afterwards, with a new hat gifted by Toby – an extraordinary creation in crimson with many bows and feathers that were not entirely to Minnie's taste – she climbed aboard his trap and, with a shake of the reins, his reliable Susie clip-clopped out of Mangaweka. One hour 30 minutes later, she delivered them to the homestead where Mrs Crichton had a Devonshire tea waiting. The housekeeper was garrulous by nature and had looked forward immensely to chatting with the famous Minnie Page. As the talk went this way and that, on everything under the sun, Minnie marvelled at what a wonderful subject Mrs Crichton would be for a portrait. Her face spoke volumes: the skin was weather-beaten, the creases plunged deep, and the smile ran from ear to ear. A life of toil, and much humour, was there for all to see. Minnie tucked the thought away for another day when she would bring her palette, brushes and paints and transfer that delightful, infinitely wrinkled face, to canvas.

When Lonnie Sparks arrived, he and Toby took Minnie for a tour of Ridgeburn close to the homestead. Each side of the rustling stream, on the flats, she saw rich fertile soil begging for grass. The drains had worked a treat. But for the rest of it, she looked on utter devastation. The hills and flats were heaped with ash and debris and here and there blackened skeletons of trees stood like sentinels. Toby saw the look on her face.

'Don't worry. You will be amazed how fast nature comes back. With a little help.'

That look on her face convinced him that he should wait a few weeks before inviting Margaret Fairbairn. That night Minnie and Toby discussed his other family, the McAlistairs.

'Harry and Sophie are fine and Harry's been free of seizures,' she said. 'He's studying zoology at Victoria University and loving it. Sophie is rapidly making a name for herself as a singer. I frequently see her name in the newspaper. She recently performed in the Wanganui Opera House.' Minnie's face then crinkled in displeasure. 'I am, though, worried about Elizabeth and Clarissa.'

Toby's latent fears about them came flooding in.

'Simon Drake,' said Minnie. 'Elizabeth tells me he is riding roughshod over Clarissa and angling to have a bigger and bigger part in the running of the estate. And he appears to be a brute of a man.'

Toby winced at what Clarissa had got herself into. If Minnie knew more about his treatment of her, she did not elaborate.

'Clarissa says his friends have made Glenview a second home

and the liquor cabinet needs replenishing every week. She has remonstrated with him but it only makes things worse. Elizabeth's only comfort is that the estate has not been passed to the eldest daughter and her husband on their marriage. She remains the owner.'

They sat in silence, pondering the situation.

'I'm visiting them soon at the townhouse,' Toby said. 'Perhaps I can meet there with Clarissa, too.' He missed them all hugely, especially at night when the body was resting and the mind could roam.

'And I will keep in touch regularly with Elizabeth,' said Minnie. 'I may be able to help her talk through the issues.' She paused, her brow creased. 'Toby, there is another thing.'

He braced, wondering what other plague had struck them.

'It's Margaret. Elizabeth tells me she has a serious suitor. A buyer of sheep and wool who lives in the locality. You know how fast word travels in the country. He is said to be visiting her regularly. If you want her, you have to act fast son.' Minnie could see from the look on his face that the news had struck home.

Toby had already arranged to see Margaret on his pending visit to Wellington. His heart sunk as he began to wonder if she would tell him of her engagement to the sheep and wool buyer. He wrote to her that night and posted the letter the next day. Never had he poured out his heart in such a manner. It was by any measure a proposal of marriage. But had he left it too late? He had a sleepless night and there was no blaming the faint sounds of Lonnie's snoring at the other end of the house.

Margaret, alone in her house at Marton, was in a quandary. Month after month she had waited for Toby while he was in Africa, forever fearful of a black-edged letter in the post. Then, on return, he had promptly vanished into the back-blocks of Rangitikei, absorbed in a joint farming venture. Really, how interested in her was he? Was her future elsewhere? She craved a happy marriage and family but was she waiting in vain? Toby had always been attentive and a gentleman, speaking and writing politely, but there had been nothing heartfelt. Was his passion directed elsewhere, or was he simply one of those hamstrung emotionally, unable to express what was inside? Would that reticence condemn them both to a solitary life? She recalled her shock at looking at a friend's family tree and seeing so many single people, alone through a dearth of men after the world wars, the custom of a daughter looking after her parents, the call of the church, social awkwardness, and whatever other cause. She was now 26, and already, she suspected, a confirmed spinster in many people's eyes. It was not as if some men were not interested. There was the school teacher, Stephen Bannister, for one...

Toby still had one vital duty to carry out before leaving for the capital. Once the heat had gone from the ashes, Toby and Lonnie, along with hired help, put a bag of seed on either side of their horses by their knees, and eight of them formed a slowly moving row, flicking handfuls of grass seed as they went. Pack trains of horses laden with extra grass and turnip seed followed. When the sowing was finished, it was time to wait for nature to do its part and time for Toby to take the train to the capital.

After embraces with Harry and Sophie at the Wellington Railway Station, Toby stood back and looked at the transformation in them. It had been two years. Harry, at 25, was a smartly dressed university man with a trim moustache while Sophie, 23, had matured into an elegant woman, fashionably dressed in a long, flowing skirt, jacket, and hat. They in turn gazed on a man leaner than they had known, with face hard as leather and brown as a nut.

'Tell me what you've been doing,' he said as they hired a horse cab to take them to The Elms.

'It will take the rest of the day and half the night,' Harry warned.

'That's all right. I've got the rest of the week in Wellington.' He smiled to himself – he would not only be staying with his mother and catching up with her, but catching up as well with Margaret Fairbairn who would be in Wellington supporting one of her most gifted pianoforte players at a concert. After his heartfelt letter, he was on tenterhooks about their reunion.

At The Elms, there were smiles, hugs and kisses with Elizabeth and Clarissa but later, when talk switched to Glenview, grim faces.

'I had no idea of the extent of his feasting and drinking,' Clarissa said. 'Eddie Shaw, Henry Thompson, and Arthur Wilson are practically living in our pocket. But when **my** friends visit, he's very cold to them. Two of them he's forbidden me to invite again. And he's awful to the staff. I overheard Mary say in the kitchen, 'Put on as many grand airs as he likes, he'll never be a gentleman.'

'Is there nothing good about him?' Toby asked.

Clarissa paused, and gave a grudging, coy smile. 'He's good in bed, when he's sober.' She saw their discomfort and moved on. 'He's good to his friends. Too good. I believe he's lent Eddie Shaw some money. From what I gather, Shaw is a heavy bettor and Simon will be lucky to see that money again. Simon has also supported Henry Thompson with a false alibi over a traffic offence.' Clarissa shook her head, her pretty face miserable. Her dream of a happy marriage with a man she had adored for his dashing ways, lay in tatters. Elizabeth, usually so decisive, was at a loss. She could think of but one recourse to ease Clarissa's life with Simon Drake – an appeal to his father and mother, Sir Robert and Lady Pamela. Perhaps they had some influence over him. She would arrange a visit.

And then, for Toby, the moment of truth, sooner than he expected, for Margaret Fairbairn was shown into the room, a guest for dinner. Had she received the letter? The post could at times be notoriously slow. If she had received it, what would be her response? Was she already spoken for? Had his single-minded drive to establish himself first and provide a house cost him her hand? Was his heart about to be broken through his own dilatory behaviour? There was not her usual beaming smile. Rather, a look of seriousness and sincerity. She walked straight into his arms and they embraced and kissed. He looked at her for an answer but there was none. Perhaps later, he thought, when they were alone. He determined to himself that he would know one way or another before he left Wellington. His heart was beating at 100 miles an hour but he hid his nerves as best he could.

The family was determined not to let the shadow of Simon Drake spoil the occasion. After a sumptuous meal, there was an evening of cards and merriment, enlivened by two songs from Sophie, accompanied by Margaret, and jaunty other numbers with all of them. Then, in the small hours, as much as he was enjoying the conviviality, it was time for Toby to take a horse cab back to Oriental Bay and his mother. He wished he could be taking Margaret Fairbairn back with him as a house guest but she was staying the night at The Elms. There had been no opportunity to talk to her alone at The Elms. Toby could only stew in confusion until their meeting for lunch in a café in Willis Street the next day.

It was a long and restless night. As day dawned, Toby took a long walk along the wharves and lost himself momentarily in all the bustle of the Empire City receiving goods from the rest of the world and sending out its meat, wool, and timber and some of its own manufactured goods. He had to take care as drays could come at him from any direction and the air was full of men's shouts.

At 12 noon he arrived outside The Star Café simultaneously with Margaret and with one word, 'Yes,' from her, and an enveloping embrace, she dispelled all his fears. They clung to each other so long they drew attention from passers-by. Then, tucked into a corner of the café, they spilled out their hearts to each other and shared their dreams for their life together. In bliss they then brought each other up-to-date. For Margaret, that included the news that she had a new adult student learning the pianoforte. Rex Frobisher, a sheep and wool buyer, had never had the opportunity before to learn the pianoforte and he wished to impress a young woman in Bulls he had begun to court. Toby smiled to himself – that had been one needless fear. Then, after a delicious meal of fish and chips, now thankfully out of limbo and snug in each other's company, they arranged another rendezvous at Yarrow's Restaurant in Lambton Quay for the following evening. The rest of the afternoon they dallied downtown, flitting in and out of shops and visiting museums and art galleries, and then strolled the wharves observing the busy sea commerce which reminded them that the good life was based on hard 'yakker'. It was enough then to be together, ensconced in each other's arms.

The next day Toby travelled to Hutt Park to see Norman Kelly. Toby was delighted to see Kelly had a good lot of horses to work with, some of them proven. He raised the subject of Simon Drake and Vernon McCardle.

'Their team's going well,' Kelly said. 'Drake's putting a lot of money into it. He's bought a couple of good ones and culled a couple of also-rans.' Kelly drew deep on his cigarette and looked at Toby with narrowed eyes as he exhaled. 'But there's talk round the tracks that Drake rung in a horse under a false name at a district meeting and he and Eddie Shaw won a packet through a crook bookie. McCardle would have been involved but you've got as much chance of getting anything out of him as opening an oyster with a tram ticket. One thing I'm sure of Toby – you and me are well out of it.'

It was enough talk of Simon Drake. Kelly turned the conversation back on Toby.

'What about yourself now? How are you going up there? Have you got a horse or two in training?'

Toby wished he had. Being at the Hutt Park, immersed in the sights and sounds and smells of a working stable, reminded him of his great love of the thoroughbred and of horse racing. One day perhaps, he thought. The rest of his week flew by in a mix of slow, restful mornings with his mother, afternoon walks in the city with Margaret, and evening social whirls at The Elms. Toby and Margaret decided to keep their commitment to each other secret for now. They each had busy personal lives and a life together would bring massive change. There was much to sort out. They did not welcome a barrage of questions at this time. Except, with Margaret's permission, Toby told his mother and promptly put her in seventh heaven.

Minnie had by now established a warm friendship with Elizabeth McAlistair and accompanied Toby to dinner there one evening. Harry and Sophie took the opportunity to tease Toby about his bachelorhood.

'Now then Toby, surely it's time you had a good woman by your side,' said Harry.

'I have one,' said Toby. 'Mrs Crichton, a rare gem.'

'No no,' said Sophie. 'Don't be such a duffer. A woman who can give you a lot of little Tobys and Tabithas running round the show.'

Toby tried in vain to switch the conversation to them and their own single state but their banter was remorseless and his mother and Elizabeth looked on in helpless laughter as Harry and Sophie told Toby the qualities he must look for in his future wife. At last, they had mercy.

◆ ◆ ◆

One morning, some weeks after Toby had returned north, there was the thrill of looking out from the homestead at a shimmer of green across the flats and hills of Ridgeburn. Within months there was a fine sward of grass for Toby and Lonnie to savour. From September 1905, there were developments abroad as well that had them and the whole country in thrall. The New Zealand footballers – or All Blacks as they were now called – were touring in Great Britain and Ireland and many of Lonnie's old football mates such as Billy Wallace and Fred Roberts were cutting merry capers. Toby and Lonnie devoured the newspaper reports. Then, in 1906, came the great day when they moved in Lincoln sheep, shorthorn cattle and Berkshire pigs and had a productive farm. There was the bonus of a nearby railway line that by now ran deep into the rugged interior, crossing plunging abysses and rushing rivers, nearly to the great high plain at the centre of the North Island.

AN UGLY
CONFRONTATION

I t was not all slog and grind for Toby and Lonnie. There was the hi-jinks one night of the bachelors' ball. For all the frivolity the ball provided, there was a serious side to it. Many farmers and other men of the district were single, as were daughters of the district, and this was a capital chance for lonely hearts to meet. There was an edge in the teasing of Toby over his bachelor status for he was now 34. And Lonnie was 32. Mrs Crichton did her bit to encourage them, even though it might have cost her a job when the woman moved in.

'You boys working dawn to dusk,' she said. 'This poppycock you haven't 'ad time. You'll find time will run out on you and you'll wake up one of these mornings and find yourselves crabbed old men with no one to cuddle. Like some I know.'

In truth, Lonnie as well as Toby was ready for a wife. Toby told Mrs Crichton he had a lovely woman in waiting and, truly, many a night his thoughts drifted to Margaret Fairbairn and he longed for the day he could ask for her hand and bring her into his own house. He reasoned Ridgeburn was all right for him and Lonnie and hardy Mrs Crichton but too raw for Margaret

Fairbairn and, besides, she had her thriving music practice. He comforted himself that the right time would come. But Mrs Crichton said she would believe his ramblings when she met the woman and she had circled the date of the bachelors' ball on the calendar.

To lower the inhibitions of any shy country folk the organisers had made it fancy dress. Lonnie, well-known as a prankster amongst his football mates, considered going as a cabbage tree but Toby suggested that could make him simply a figure of fun and repel the fine lasses. He settled for a soldier and Toby for a jockey and on the great night they mingled with the strangest array of things on two legs ever seen in Mangaweka, including a kangaroo, penguin, wine bottle opener and back scratcher.

How lively was the music from the local quintet! How happy the voices of the revellers! How full of promise the pulsating hall!

At one point Toby heard Lonnie advocating sheep dip as a hair restorer to an aged bachelor farm worker and was disturbed to see the man taking him seriously. Toby nudged Lonnie, reminding him what they were there for.

'I know, don't worry. I'll get on to it. I'm just helping me mate here.'

Toby entered the spirit of it, dancing with several of the ladies and chatting with many more. As the beer and spirits flowed and many became pleasantly tipsy, the noise level rose and the dancing got livelier. Toby noticed one group in a heated discussion. It turned out some were relatives of a widower, 70, and the others of a woman, 20, who were dancing with each other. Her parents were keen on the match but his relatives were accusing her of being a gold digger and talking of taking procedures under the Lunacy Act to prevent the liaison. While debate raged, a fracas erupted in another part of the hall when one man's bid for a dance was rejected. Constable Timothy O'Halloran was on hand to cool things down. As if he didn't have enough to do as clerk of the court, bailiff, inspector of weights and measures, inspector of noxious weeds, registrar of dogs, inspector of licensed houses, trust officer and inspector of slaughter houses, amongst other duties. A bachelor himself, he had fervently hoped to meet someone this evening and was engaged in a promising chat when he had to tend to the fracas. He was in no mood to be crossed.

'Any more of that and I'll stand you on your head in the bowl of trifle,' he said as he assisted the rebuffed man out the door with one hand on his collar and the other on the seat of his trousers. When O'Halloran returned, the woman he had been chatting to was dancing with another. The next offender would have been wise to eject himself.

Lonnie eventually put himself forward but after the lights went out and they were driving back to the homestead, they were still two bachelors not spoken for. They had at least made their presence known and, little did they know it, but under lamplights all over the town and countryside, their names were bandied about by single women and by mothers and fathers anxious for a sound son-in-law. It was clear they were good catches – they had knocked Ridgeburn into shape and were starting to get a return from it. The land itself had at least doubled in value since they had purchased it.

But for Toby, the partnership had run its course. It had been immensely satisfying to develop Ridgeburn from bush and swamp but he could see that Lonnie's heart was more in farming than his. Toby yearned to be back training racehorses. There was something about rising each day to tend to the horses and nurturing the thought that one day there might be a champion. On the days when he dared to dream, he saw himself not only as a trainer but as a breeder and owner. And crucially, it would mean moving to a city, or close by, and having his own house where he could properly provide for Margaret.

Lonnie was not surprised. He had seen the restlessness in Toby since Toby's return from visiting Norman Kelly at Hutt Park. 'We'll work something out fair and square mate,' he said. 'Let's get dad up here and see if I can buy your share of it. Bet he'll loan me the extra money I'll need. He knows a good thing when he sees it.'

When Noel Sparks visited, he did indeed know a good thing when he saw it. Not only had there been a great increase in Ridgeburn's capital value, but its stock were thriving and there was potential for yet more value to be added. He was happy to give his son a generous loan to enable Toby to be paid out, according to the terms of the original purchase. The document had dotted every 'i' and crossed every 't', and the pay-out included the chattels right down to the chamber pots in the bedrooms. When Lonnie drove Toby in the trap to the train, Toby had a substantial payment in his bank account and all his worldly possessions in the trunk by his feet. He farewelled Mrs Crichton with a kiss and embrace and promised to keep in touch. She had a tear in her eye as the trap rattled down the driveway – she knew his grit and resilience but as he disappeared, she couldn't help but pray life's storms would pass him by.

Toby's own emotions were welling up. Ridgeburn had been his life for years and Lonnie and Mrs Crichton his closest companions. Lonnie, too, was affected. They travelled in silence until Ridgeburn was behind them and they were on the main road south. Then they talked of farming, football and horses until the township loomed when they fell silent once more.

'Look after yourself mate,' said Lonnie, grasping Toby's hand. 'Thanks for everything.'

Then both realised a handshake was not enough and embraced.

'Make sure it's not back in scrub when I visit,' Toby said. 'Mrs Crichton promised to keep you up to the mark.' He turned after stepping onto the train. 'And write me a letter.' With a wave of the hand and 'All the best mate', he entered the carriage, bound for Palmerston North and the next stage of his life.

Three years before, in 1903, a fine new racecourse had been opened at Awapuni, in Palmerston North. Toby had been pleased to see the end of the crude old course which had been in a paddock within an easy walk of town, cut out of the bush. The encroachments of the Manawatu River could be thanked for that course's demise. The Manawatu Racing Club had purchased 100 acres on a nearby plateau and established a course one mile in circumference. Seeing its potential as a training centre, the club had also put a trial grass and plough track inside the main track. Toby had been one of the ten thousand at the first meeting. Perhaps it was then, gazing at the fine track with bush and hills beyond and a sliver of lagoon alive with water birds, he first mused about making his home here.

Toby had since followed developments in Palmerston North with interest. The town had grown rapidly and by 1906 its population was over 10,000 and it was the fifth town in the colony with flourishing shops, hotels, schools, churches, newspapers, sports facilities, hospital, telephone exchange and modern gaslight. Even an observatory was in the planning. Most importantly, Palmerston North was superbly located for a racing stable, within easy reach, via the railway, of all the major racetracks in the southern North Island and the ferry at Wellington put Riccarton within range. There was, too, the opportunity of acquiring a property right next to the new racecourse and Toby swooped. Shortly, he was able to telephone Margaret that he was just down the road from her and telephone his mother that he was just up the road from her.

His backer was Mr J. P. Staveley, the timber mill owner whose men had cleared the bush on Ridgeburn. Staveley, in his 50s, large and ruby-faced, had a ramrod spine, a spade beard flecked with grey and the most discerning of eyes. His men were cutting up to 100,000 feet of timber a week throughout the region. No obstacle was too great; his tram lines stretched from ridges right across valley floors. As he felled the native trees, he replanted with the unfashionable radiata pine. Acland down at Mt Peel in South Canterbury swore by it and his own trials with it had been exciting. Extraordinary growth considering the tree was so ordinary at its home on the Monterey Peninsula of California. Soon, radiata pine was putting even more money in his pockets and he decided the time was right to spend some of it on his dream of owning thoroughbred horses. He had been hugely impressed in his dealings with Toby and Lonnie, and when he heard that Toby was selling up to train racehorses, he hastened to quiz him about it.

'Tell me Toby, man to man, am I likely to make money at it?'

'That I cannot tell you, JP. There are many imponderables. I can only say that if you go into it as informed as possible, with good people around you, and are prepared to spend money to get quality horses, you have a fighting chance. And you should have a lot of fun along the way.'

As they talked, and as Toby's experience of horses and training became apparent, J.P. Staveley's mind was made up. He had always liked the stamp of Toby Page. He admired his military record and had seen first-hand his work with horses on the farm and his work ethic.

'Can you help me choose some horses and train them for me?'

'That I can. It would be a pleasure.'

The timing for Toby could not have been better. He had had enough funds to purchase the land, build the stable and get started with a small team but with JP Staveley's backing, there was a good chance of earlier and greater success. As for Staveley, there was the satisfaction of using his 'new' money to compete against the 'old' money of the landed gentry. Orphaned at a young age, raised by a kindly saddler and his wife, educated in a one-roomed school, and gone out into the world at age 12, he was a rough-hewn, self-made man. At social gatherings, he had often felt some of the gentry looked at him sideways, regarding him as not quite acceptable, to be tolerated rather than welcomed into the fold. When the country mourned the death this year of Premier Seddon, of a heart attack returning from Australia, Staveley mourned more than most as he saw Seddon, like himself, as a man of the people.

There were two other key components of the Toby Page stable – Toby's head man, Robbie Paget, and the stable jockey, Rowley O'Neill. Paget, squat, taciturn, clean-shaven and a chain smoker, was a former jockey Toby had known from his time with Norman Kelly. He was a good worker and trustworthy. O'Neill was a natural horseman with a ready smile and intelligent eyes. He came from school looking for work and when Toby put him to mucking out and he took up the pitchfork with a will, it earned him a foot in the door. He was well used to horses having delivered goods around the countryside for his father. He was short and slight in build but strong and when Toby put him on a horse, he demonstrated perfect balance straight away. Shortly afterwards his parents were there, the father European and the mother Maori, of Ngati Raukawa iwi. They approved his conditions of employment – board and five shillings a week – and Rowley O'Neill joined the staff.

Once the stable was running smoothly, Toby took time out to visit his mother and his other family at The Elms. Minnie met him at the Wellington Railway Station and they lunched at the Club Hotel on Lambton Quay. She was still a sparkling presence who could light up a room but as he eyed her over his oysters and glass of beer, he could see her 50 years beginning to show in faint crow's feet round the eyes and greying of the hair. But her zeal for social reform was as sharp as ever. The latest piece of legislation she was championing was The Workers' Dwellings Act.

'There's a crying need for it, Toby. The average urban worker cannot afford to buy a house for his family,' she said. 'With this Act, the workers can now either rent or buy outright. I do have my doubts though. The houses being built under the Act are still too expensive and there are not enough of them.'

'A good cause right enough,' said Toby. 'It's the worker's right to have his own house over his head. There are not so many of us in this country, after all. The day must surely come when there will be a house for everyone's pocket.'

Minnie went on to lament the lack of pensions for invalids and widows. Invalids were still the responsibility of the family, and even the widows with dependent children received no help from the government. Toby looked at her in love and admiration. He had always looked up to her for her battles on behalf of the disadvantaged and for her toughness in seeing things through. He could see that in many ways she had been both mother and father to him.

From the Club Hotel, they took a horse cab to His Majesty's Theatre where Sophie McAlistair was performing at an afternoon concert. At the corner of Willis Street and Lambton Quay, there was the sudden blast of an automobile backfiring and their horse threatened to bolt.

'Damn pestilence!' their driver exploded. 'Could have been the death of us.'

Since businessman William McLean had imported the first two petrol-driven automobiles into Wellington in 1898, automobiles had proliferated and now in 1907 they co-existed uneasily with the horses. Toby had to concede that as much as he loved horses, the automobiles had a great fascination for him and he was looking to buy one himself.

Toby and Minnie met Elizabeth, Harry, and Clarissa in the foyer. With Sophie in the theatre as well, it was all of Toby's family in the one place and he felt a deeply satisfying wholeness. Toby could see the regard Elizabeth and Minnie had for each other and the regard his siblings had for his mother. Harry looked down from his lofty six foot at diminutive Minnie but just the day before he had been looking up at her when she stood on the platform of a hall at the university speaking about the urgent need for changes in the colony. She had shocked him, and others too he could tell, with her examples of the poverty and deprivation in Te Aro and elsewhere in the Empire City, such as a house of five rooms with a family in every room. An example of kindness too – a butcher refusing meat to a family who could no longer pay, but the family still receiving meat as the carter paid the bill.

Joining the people streaming past them into the hall, Elizabeth and Clarissa quizzed Toby about his property in Palmerston North and his horse-training venture. Within minutes, the lights were dimmed and the clear, ringing note of a cornet stilled the chatter. A brass band ensemble followed and then a mandolin and guitar duet, a vocal duet, two pieces by a chamber orchestra, two more by a string quartet, and then the high point of the concert, the acclaimed Sophie McAlistair, soprano, accompanied by Maurice Sutherland at the piano. Sophie at 26 had blossomed into a beauty. There was a striking contrast between the blonde hair tumbling to her shoulders and her dress of black velvet reaching to her ankles. Maurice Sutherland, 28, a tall, slender man with jet-black hair and a trim moustache, took her by the elbow and led her to the centre of the stage. There was a touching gentleness in his manner. As she stood before the audience alone and sightless, she had their hearts even before her first pure notes.

She began with the soprano solo from Mendelssohn's *Lauda Sion* and proceeded with *Et in Carnatus*, *Going To Kildare*, *Leonore*, *I Cannot Say Goodbye* and *God Be With You*. Her voice charmed and delighted and at times touched the heart in a way only exquisite music can. Minnie and Toby could see the benefits of her study under Madame Probert and her perfect understanding with Maurice Sutherland.

'Bravo! Bravo! Bravo!' rang out as Sophie bowed after the final encore, and the applause continued until it was apparent she would sing no more that evening. What a performance! As Toby stood with the others amidst the waves of acclaim, his chest swelled with pride. Backstage, he and Sophie joyously reunited and Sophie introduced her family to Maurice Sutherland. He clearly had a sparkling future himself.

With the weary but elated Sophie in their midst, they hailed a carriage and repaired to The Elms for dinner. Elizabeth had a modest household staff of two – a cook, Ethel, and a housemaid, Katherine. A gardener, Alexander, visited when necessary. Talk over dinner ranged far and wide. One subject discreetly not touched upon was Glenview. Toby observed with alarm how strained Clarissa was at unguarded moments. What a disastrous union it had been. He determined not to add to her stress by telling her of the rumour from the racetrack regarding her husband and the 'rung in' horse. But a knock at the door and moments later a dead hand fell on the evening. Elizabeth, at the head of the table, was first to see the visitor standing by Katherine.

'Simon.'

Silence hung heavy. The atmosphere was now as buoyant as that of a charnel house at dusk. Simon was scowling at all of them. A nerve was twitching in his cheek and the sinews of his neck were like razor blades. Toby was especially the target of his burning blue eyes. But then they settled on Clarissa. Once she had been entranced by those eyes; now she visibly wilted under their glower.

'How much longer are you here?' he demanded. 'My friends are in the house and there is no wife to ensure we have what we need.'

Toby saw the anger flood into Elizabeth. She had confided to Minnie that she worried ceaselessly about Clarissa. Her visit to Sir Robert and Pamela Drake had proved to be of no use. Indeed, it appeared to have exacerbated the situation. Simon had been even more boorish and disrespectful to Clarissa since.

'How dare you storm into my house and confront my daughter in such a manner!' she said. Fled was the atmosphere of calm and goodwill of moments before. Faces were taut and bodies tense with fear and anger. Drunk and furious, how far would Simon go to assert his authority?

'Your daughter, madam is a damned, good-for-nothing vixen,' said Drake. 'She complains about my friends and me every waking hour. And she never heeds what I say about the estate. I will never get acknowledgement while she is in charge.'

'That's a wicked thing to say.' Clarissa had leapt to her feet. Though small and vulnerable, she had too much spirit to be totally cowed by him. 'Before, when you were involved in our discussions, it was your way or no way and finally you flounced off and haven't returned. I have constantly invited you to come back.'

Drake seethed. The blood-shot eyes and ruddy nose revealed the drink in him. The marriage to Clarissa had not been the instant passport to an estate and its associated money and influence he had expected. Instead, he had found himself powerless to make decisions and, even worse, feeling subservient to his wife. Sometimes he even sensed his friends saw him as more of a gelding than a stallion in his own home and were laughing at him for not seizing control and putting her in her place. What was it Arthur Wilson had said recently: 'Woman is a fit helpmate to man but never his equal in either physical or mental power.' Not only was she now defying him, but that damned Toby Page was there to witness it.

'You are to come home with me this instant,' he demanded. 'I have my friends in residence and the damned household staff appear to have vanished.'

Clarissa was not surprised the staff had sought sanctuary somewhere. Simon Drake's companions should have been at home with their wives, not harassing her staff with demands for endless alcohol and food. 'I will return tomorrow as planned,' said Clarissa. 'Before I return, your friends can go back to their own hard-put wives.'

Minnie Page sensed that if he and the others had not been there, Drake would have stalked across the floor, grabbed Clarissa and dragged her to his trap, by her hair if necessary. She was back in an instant to her own incarceration by Adam Gibson and at the mercy of a demented man.

'I will say this just once more,' Drake said, ominously quietly.

'Come with me this instant.'

Minnie could also sense that Toby could barely restrain himself and that any moment there could be mayhem and who knew how that could end? Drake appeared to be unarmed but there were knives aplenty to hand. She prayed for calm and restraint.

Truth to tell, Toby would not have minded coming to physical blows with Drake. He rose to his feet, braced for action, ready to intercept Drake if necessary.

'She has given you your answer,' Toby said.

Drake looked at him with contempt and loathing. 'Page. Nothing but a bloody groom with pretensions to training horses. Son of a wailing bitch who should have been left to rot in the shack.'

Anywhere else, Toby would have had at him. He was restrained either side by Clarissa and Minnie and given the vital seconds to think better of assaulting Drake.

'Do nothing,' urged Minnie.

'I can promise you Page, your time is coming,' hissed Drake. 'Your horses will be shown up for the rubbish they are, fit only to run against station hacks. I will see to it your stable goes belly up.' And then, jeering at Toby, Clarissa, and them all, he turned on his heel.

'You don't deserve her,' Toby said to his departing back.

Word later was that Drake withdrew to the smoky confines of his gentleman's club to cool down, and was subsequently seen in a seedy back street. His threat, though, hung in the air at The Elms for the rest of the night.

THE LURE OF RACING

Over the next few months, into 1907, Toby assisted J.P. Staveley in selecting five horses: a yearling, three two-year-olds and a three-year-old. When another owner transferred two horses to his stable, Toby suddenly had seven. Toby and Robbie Paget already had their hands full and it was apparent more staff would be needed. To Toby's surprise, his mother then expressed interest in owning a horse herself. Her painting was flourishing and she judged the time was right to indulge in her lifelong love of horse racing. Toby accompanied her to a sale and they settled on a handsome young bay colt.

'Could it be another Machine Gun?' she asked coyly.

Toby certainly hoped so. Machine Gun, owned by George Stead and trained by Dick Mason, that had won the Randolph Handicap at Riccarton for the second year on end, carrying 11 stone 5 pounds and speeding over the five furlongs in 58 seconds, a New Zealand record. But Toby knew as well as anyone the vagaries of racing. There could be the gangly thing all bones and legs that became a champion and the beautiful creature begging to be painted that was no good at all. And then there were those who could scarcely raise a gallop but were a great success at stud. There were few certainties in racing. She named it 'Easel'. She knew it was a gamble but surely people could dream.

Rowley O'Neill was helping in the stable as part of his apprenticeship and soon three others lads – Bill Gough, Maurie Wood and Roy Waddell – joined him as the stable expanded. It was a tough and spartan life: up at 3.30am taking the horses for training exercises and gallops, back for stable duties, breakfast, feeding the horses and more stable duties on and on for 12 to 14 hours, all for five shillings a week and board. Being spirited boys, there was the odd spot of mischief such as placing a sack over the chimney of Toby's house, but nothing a stern word couldn't sort. They were fortunate they could bunk in the house and get three meals a day; some boys elsewhere slept in the stable, washed in a kerosene tin and lived off scraps.

The meals were cooked by Toby's loquacious housekeeper, Dot Prendergast. She could have been the sister of Mrs Crichton of Ridgeburn for her similar 'lived-in' face, full of character. Both women were widows and both had the priceless attribute of kindness, though their demeanours were quite different. Where Mrs Crichton was all benevolence and smiles, Dot Prendergast was all snap and crackle and ever ready to take a bite out of any of them, including Toby, for lateness and laxity. (The ruse with the sack on the chimney happened but once!). Dot Prendergast made it clear there would be no breakfast if the bed was not made and that any coins left in the pockets of their clothing for laundry on Mondays, were hers.

'You boys know the meals are on the table at 12,' she would growl if they were a minute late. But her bark helped give the boys backbone, the comfort of order and security, and good work ethic. The boys did not know it but Dot Prendergast often felt numbing tremors of fear on race day and always heaved a sigh of relief when the boys were back round her table at night, safe from the danger of hurtling round the track on half a tonne of rampaging thoroughbred.

Toby had a way with the apprentices and soon all four of them were tending the horses with care and riding them at work according to instructions. Toby believed good hands were made in part, not solely inherited, though the best did have natural gift. He was acutely aware of his responsibilities to the owners who were trusting him with their property, to the boys' parents who were trusting him with their welfare, and to the horses themselves who were dependent on him for everything. Just as Dot Prendergast established boundaries in the house, Toby established boundaries in the stable. He was 'Mr Page' or 'boss'. He loved his new life. He trusted those around him, he could see the horses thriving, and he and his owners had reason to anticipate good results. Like his counterparts, he wore a smart hat at the races, a dark suit and or dark jacket and trousers, looked at the world with a realistic eye, and was close-lipped. He was different from most in being without beard or even full moustache and not smoking cigarette or cigar. His abstinence from smoking was not for reasons of health – indeed some doctors advocated smoking – but simply personal preference. He loved the smell of the grass after a shower of rain and even the aroma of the stable and did not want the smoke to sully it.

When the Manawatu Racing Club's Christmas carnival rolled around, Toby had his team raring to go. As the first streaks of the sun hit the Awapuni race course, the excitement even got to Dot Prendergast and she found she was on her second cup of tea already with one more sugar than usual as she waited for her boys to come to the breakfast table. The stable's routine was a wonderful 'settler'. Somehow, amidst the flurry of connecting with owners, jockeys, officials, Robbie Paget, stable hands, other trainers, friends and well-wishers, Toby found time to see to his horses.

Train after train arrived from north and south and east and west for Cup Day. Thousands streamed to the racecourse, the women in all the colours of the rainbow and more besides, making up for the sober black or grey of most of the men. There was colour as well in the flower beds and borders and colour of a different sort in the bookmakers, 17 in all, shouting their odds so loudly that people wishing to talk had to draw away towards the rail. It was a case of punters beware as a few of the bookies were dodgy and had in the past been 'scalers' – climbers of fences to get away quickly. Despite the bookies' exhortations, most people were lining up at the totalisator. When Lord and Lady Plunket and others of the vice-regal party arrived, all those in the grandstand stood and the Palmerston North Band played *God Save the King*. How Edward VII himself, a devotee of this 'sport of kings', would have revelled in the occasion!

Toby came to the course from meeting his mother and J.P. Staveley in the stable. Just as well he arranged to meet them there, he thought, surveying the packed crowd; he would have struggled to find them otherwise. Minnie's big day was two days away, on Saturday, with Easel in the inaugural Manawatu Sires Produce Stakes of six furlongs for the grand prize of 1,000 sovereigns. It would be the richest two-year-old race in New Zealand. Today was Mr Staveley's big day with his Egmont in the Manawatu Cup. Toby gave them both a chance. Egmont was as good as he'd ever had him; he'd been cleaning out his manger in great fashion. Toby's eye went from the crowd to the track itself. Some of the tracks throughout the country were so narrow and tight it was the inside track or nothing, but the Awapuni track had a noble breadth and easy curves. A dash of rain earlier in the week had taken the hardness out of it but it was still firm and fast, good for all four of their starters. But as Toby passed the saddling yard, his attention was on a horse he knew from his days with Norman Kelly in the McAlistair stable. Tatler, a black gelding, had been a promising two-year-old then; now it was nine and the property of Simon Drake. It was old for a horse and had more than earned its keep but Toby could see it was favouring a leg and was unsound. He drew the attention of a steward to it and followed the subsequent proceedings with interest. The steward summoned the veterinary surgeon who examined the horse and promptly reported back to the steward who then spoke to Simon Drake who was hovering nearby. Toby saw Drake turn crimson and then become agitated and angry. He picked up the drift of the conversation.

'There is no question. Tatler must be withdrawn. If it runs, it will damage itself irreparably.'

There was nothing more Simon Drake could say. It was obvious the horse was unsound. (It transpired that the horse was heavily insured and worth more to him broken down and shot than alive. Drake's ploy was thwarted.) Now, Drake turned and glared at Toby, his face a mask of fury. He had seen Toby speaking to the steward.

Toby had no time to linger or even ponder the matter. He was busyness itself, coming and going between horses, owners, jockeys, and others. The stable was pleased with a second, third and fourth. Then it was Egmont's turn. He was one of those who was docile before he reached the racetrack and then became focused and aggressive. He featured in what the *Manawatu Standard* described as 'the finest race ever witnessed there and amongst the most exciting ever run in New Zealand'. The field of 13 got away well after two false starts. Then one horse tore away spectacularly and tried to bury the field, but it was done by a mile and a bit. When the horses came round the final bend, it looked as though any one of a dozen could win. Then three horses – Tangimoana, Ovation and Egmont – poured on the speed and edged clear. They ran the final 200 yards stride for stride with the crowd in pandemonium. J.P. Staveley could not speak for the excitement of it. In the shadow of the post, Tangimoana got its nostril in front of Ovation with Egmont a neck back third. Much more of that and J.P. Staveley would need to be on sedatives to watch his horses race.

As Toby helped tidy up back at the stalls, he felt a jab in his ribs and turned to see the curdled face of Simon Drake.

'That should be a knife not my finger,' said Drake. 'What d'y mean sticking your damn nose into my business, you interfering scumbag.'

Toby instinctively, from his boxing training, stepped back a pace to give him time to react to a fist or worse. 'That horse would never have finished the race. The most placid thing on four legs and you would have had it shot.'

His knowledge of the horse had helped him pick up the abnormality in its action but it had been arrogant of Drake to think he could get away with running the horse at such a prominent meeting. Drake's breath was heavy with whisky and he was sweating heavily. Toby sensed that Drake would have launched himself at him in another place at another time. Toby was not to know that, already that day, in a quiet spot at the back of the racecourse, Drake had thrashed a jockey who had won against instructions after Drake and Eddie Shaw had placed a heavy bet on the horse of another trainer to win.

'If you know what's good for you, keep your bloody mouth shut about other people's horses.' He added a string of words not heard in polite society.

'I'll speak up if I see a wrong.'

Drake took a step forward. 'Keep to your fecking pigsty of a stable and stay away from what's mine.' His voice had become shrill and along the line of stalls, heads turned to look at them. 'Just remember, Glenview's nothing to do with you and neither is The Elms. Everything there is mine, by entitlement, and you're not to put a foot across the door.'

'We'll see about that,' said Toby. 'The last I heard, Mrs McAlistair was the owner and her daughter had the running of the estate. You'll do better to stick to your horses and take proper care of them.'

Drake was apoplectic but had enough sense to realise that in a fair fight, man to man, Toby Page would better him and anyway, neither the racing club nor the New Zealand Racing Conference would look kindly on one trainer physically attacking another. He clenched a fist, shook it in Toby's face and stalked off.

'You should have biffed him on the boko,' said Robbie Paget, emerging from a horse stall. But he knew Toby had too much restraint for that and the repercussions would have spoilt a good day. The stable was beginning to make a name for itself.

'So much hate in him,' said Toby. 'He nurtures his bitterness.'

A strong field lined up two days later for the Manawatu Sires Produce Stakes. To see her horse parade brought a flush to Minnie's cheeks and caused her heart to skip. Her fingers tightened on the small silver horseshoe in her pocket. Easel, with Rowley O'Neill up, stood quietly at the start. His composure in the sale ring had been one of the attributes drawing Toby to him – the horse had looked him straight in the eye in the saleyard and his blink had seemed like a wink. Rowley O'Neill had ridden him in all his trackwork and the two of them had a bond. Some might have mistaken their calm for casual but their three victories from three runs had shown they liked to win. This test would be tougher, up against some of the best young horses from both islands. Suddenly it was time. The tape went up and they were racing. Minnie strained to see, even on her tip toes, beyond the giants of people around her and the bobbing hats. As if people weren't tall enough, some had to have a foot or more of hat on top! Far better for the feathers to be on the ostrich than on someone's head! At least the hats had shrunk now from the towering creations that had obscured the sun, but they would have to shrink to nothing for Minnie to get a view.

In no time the horses were rounding the turn. She sighted the favourite, Maori King, swinging wide but then straightening and thundering up the straight. Then she glimpsed Easel dropping his head and ripping along after it, uncoiling his power, driving with everything he had and drawing ever closer. A woman close behind started shouting 'Easel! Easel!' and Minnie's heart beat so fast she thought she might faint and she put a hand on the shoulder of the stranger in front to keep from falling. When she next caught a glimpse, the horses were past the post. Whatever the result, she would never forget the race though she scarcely saw any of it. Next time she determined to find a solitary spot that afforded a view, even from a distant knoll. By season's end, the talisman in her pocket would likely be rubbed to a lustrous sheen.

'Maori King too good,' someone behind said. 'Easel second.' Happy for herself and Toby and Rowley, Minnie caressed the silver horseshoe and edged through the crowd towards the birdcage. Easel's 100 sovereigns and 20 percent of the sweepstake would supplement income from brush and palette nicely.

Toby was thrilled for her and pleased for the stable. But as Easel was being led back to the stalls, he was digesting the whisper he'd heard of Simon Drake thrashing his jockey for not giving the horse 'a quiet one'. This was not the first time he'd heard of such sharp practice and of such a beating. An owner had once told him, 'We are not backing this horse today' and Toby had replied, 'Well, if you think he can win, you should.' Another time Toby had been offered big money to shove a sponge up a favourite's nose to make it go slower, and once the opposite – to feed a horse arsenic to make it go faster. He had refused on both occasions and reported the incidents. Once, he had even heard of two horses pulled in a three-horse race. At least he was sure that, in this year of 1908, there was less skulduggery than before.

The whisper of the thrashing of the jockey made him mindful he had been well served by those above him through the years. Frank Wallis, Stanley Goodwin and his father Charles McAlistair had all been true gentlemen. They would never misuse either people or horses. And his mother and nan would always take the side of the disadvantaged.

Six months later the stable needed horses that could run in heavy ground for it was the Winter Meeting of the Wellington

Racing Club at Trentham racecourse and the abundant bright dresses of a sunny December gave way to the scattered few macintoshes and umbrellas of a wet July. After days of rain, the racing club doggedly posted a notice, 'Races at Trentham, wet or fine!' And, as the heavens parted and pools of water gathered, the trainers scratched those no good in the wet and gamblers looked for the mudlarks. Toby put Buccaroon, a horse for all seasons, in the Parliamentary Handicap of one mile and Mexican Bride, as tough as old leather, in the Miramar Handicap of seven furlongs. First Call, his good five-year-old jumper, was entered in the Peninsula Hurdle Race. He had called on the jockey Harry Telford to give him extra schooling and Telford now said he was ready.

It turned out to be a day when the gamblers knew something – the favourites won all seven races. Buccaroon ploughed through the slush for a good third, Mexican Bride hung on doggedly for second and First Call leapt like a deer and splashed to a win for J.P. Staveley.

'I reckon the plaudits of the day should go to the officials,' Toby said to Robbie Paget afterwards. 'That was a shrewd move to strew straw on the lawn and enclosures.'

'It was, fair dinkum,' said Paget, looking down at his own boots. He had scraped the worst of the mud off but wondered if they'd ever be properly clean again.

MERRIMENT
AND MALICE

On the evening after the second day's racing, Toby and Minnie Page attended the Race Ball. The theatre itself was dramatic with its pilasters and decorative motifs. Some of the seating had been removed and some moved to the sides. No need to strew straw on this pristine floor and no need either to dress up the walls or hide the ceiling as in most halls up and down the country where dances were held. The Wellington Racing Club had nevertheless arranged for fifty bouquets embedded in ice to be placed along the sides and there were huge flags above as well as sashes commemorating champion horses which had graced the courses at Hutt Park and Trentham. Mr Percy Montgomery's fine orchestra was on the stage and the cooks in the kitchen were busy preparing a supper ranging from sucking pig to sweets. All was in readiness for one of the capital's social events of the year.

More than 150 couples, including His Excellency the Governor Sir William Plunket and Lady Plunket, circulated in their finery. On the arm of J.P. Staveley, a bachelor, was Minnie Page and on Toby's arm was Margaret Fairbairn. J.P. Staveley enjoyed a social function and he would never pass up the opportunity to rub shoulders with the nation's glitterati. He was well versed in reading people and picked up disdain towards him from a few arrogant, old-money people. He took a perverse pleasure in brushing up against them.

'How are those things of yours going, Stavely?' one might say to him. No 'JP', 'Bender', 'Jinnar', or other friendly nickname, and no confidences about their own horses.

But he also sensed respect from those who valued business acumen. He suspected, too, there were those who reckoned he must have something to be accompanying the redoubtable Minnie Page.

Minnie moved comfortably in all strata of society and would be an interested observer. As for Margaret, it was a bonus to be entertained herself for a change and not to be doing the entertaining. The *Evening Post* reported that Mrs Minnie Page was in an exquisite chiffon frock of mauve, very full and flowing, worn with a wreath of green leaves in the hair, while Miss Margaret Fairbairn wore a beautiful gown of white chiffon satin with shoulder bands embroidered in gold. The men were splendid in their black dress suits. Also present were Elizabeth McAlistair and son Harry, there to support Sophie McAlistair who was contributing to the musical programme with Maurice Sutherland. The air was thick with introductions and JP was in his element. He was, though, disconcerted to discover that one who had greeted him effusively and left a card was a funeral director.

The orchestra struck up with music in bright tempo. After two items, the president of the Wellington Racing Club, Mr J.B. Harcourt, took the stage and welcomed the dignitaries. When he momentarily forgot the surname of one of the worthies, an astute clearing of the throat gave him time to remember it and honour was salvaged. Governor Plunket declared his delight New Zealand was now a dominion and his gratification at its continuing unswerving loyalty to Great Britain. 'Plenty of evidence of that in South Africa,' he said, to a chorus of 'Hear, hear!' Guests launched into the National Anthem with gusto and a Master of Ceremonies then took the stage and introduced the orchestra, and the dancing began.

Toby noticed Sir Robert and Pamela Drake introducing Paul Drake and his wife Dorothy to the Governor and Lady Plunket. He was pleased to see J.P. Staveley and his mother consorting with some of the movers and shakers of the dominion. Some of them had sat for her and their portraits now hung in hallway, boardroom, or national collection. Most, he knew, looked on her with favour but a few with wariness as well for her portraits had revealed arrogance, petulance or subterfuge they would rather have kept concealed.

Sophie McAlistair, the epitome of grace in a gown of black satin with a white shawl round her shoulders, enchanted the gathering with her *Queen of the Night*. Her star had risen. Some were even calling her Madame Sophie. She sang both simple songs and classical pieces with a purity that enchanted. Clarissa was there with Simon Drake. Or rather, on the fringe of Simon Drake for he and his companions were well into the claret and oblivious of most others, even their wives, who were talking to one another or others. When Simon Drake saw Clarissa with her family, Minnie Page, and J.P. Staveley, he stared balefully and then turned back to his cohorts and said something which made them guffaw. Soon afterwards, Arthur Wilson and Eddie Shaw were talking loudly within the hearing of Minnie Page and J.P. Staveley. Both were in the lounge suits, tie, and tie pin, watch and watch chain of gentlemen, but their talk was far from gentlemanly.

On destitute women.

Shaw: 'Why should the man pay maintenance when the woman has contributed to the breakdown of the marriage or the woman has neither the work ethic nor skills to make a living on her own?'

On pensions.

Wilson: 'There is too much charity in this country and not enough encouragement of thrift. Some of the aged are such dottards and wastrels that poisoning might be better than pensioning.'

On equality of the sexes.

Shaw: 'Equality is not according to the laws of nature. It is the woman's role to look to the man for comfort and protection. And if there is to be universal equality, women should be eligible to serve as soldiers, sailors, and constables. Do we want that?'

Wilson: 'Look at the countries that have voted for women – those great metropolises of New Zealand, Iceland, Pitcairn Island and the Isle of Man.'

The sneering comments were so pointed that both Minnie Page and her escort believed they were purposely intended for their ears. And then Arthur Wilson clinched that thought.

'Take Minnie Page. I cannot reckon her common sense. She is impulsive and mentally flighty.'

Some men would have steered the target of the insults safely away into a quiet haven but J.P. Staveley was not of that sort. He had an elderly gentleman's code of honour and he knew unmanly provocation when he heard it. Coves like these two considered themselves his superior but were nothing better than the scum who dwelt in the stews.

Next moment Arthur Wilson had a large, fierce man with a bristling moustache in his face.

'How dare you sir! You are a damned rascal and I am calling you out!' J.P. Staveley's eyes were blazing and a close observer would have noticed the taut sinews in the neck and the body primed for action. 'Your insults are within clear hearing of the lady and are not the words of a gentleman.'

'No JP,' urged Minnie. 'Let the man be. Don't let him goad you.'

But to calm J.P. Staveley, once roused and in defence of a woman, was like trying to douse an inferno with a watering can.

Staveley ripped off a glove and threw it in Wilson's face. 'That sir is my challenge to you. In the street now, man to man.'

Heads were turning – such a to-do at a function with the Governor present. Toby hastened to Minnie's side, also urging restraint.

Arthur Wilson's face flushed and his eyes bulged. He was in a considerable dilemma – not about whether to take part in a street brawl but how best to extricate himself with a modicum of dignity. There was no support from Eddie Shaw who had retreated from his side. Wilson stepped back a pace from the thrusting head, nervously stroked his handlebar moustache and croaked, 'My comments were private and not meant for your ears sir. If I offended, I apologise.'

The bull was partially appeased, which would have surprised some who had known him on his rise to money and power. But Wilson still had some way to go.

'You will apologise unreservedly to Mrs Page,' demanded Staveley, with a vehemence that suggested Wilson might be downed there and then if he did not comply. He was half the man's age but there was a chilling ferocity about the challenge.

Wilson coughed and spluttered, drew himself up, delivered the required apology and slunk back to his companions. Toby Page caught the venomous eye of Simon Drake. J.P. Staveley turned his back on them and drew a deep breath. His face was dangerously flushed. He had been considerably shaken. He was, after all, in his late 50s and had come to the ball to be in the company of vivacious Minnie Page and hobnob with the high and mighty, not to invite a cad to a gutter brawl.

He turned to Minnie Page. 'My apologies for that my dear. Damned unpleasant business. Blighters had no right to be talking like that.'

Minnie patted his arm and murmured her thanks. J.P. then became dizzy and realised he should be resting. His doctor had recently diagnosed a heart flutter and had warned him not to overdo it. He was staying the night at his club in the capital and common sense dictated he repair to its comforts before the evening was much older. Minnie Page was safely in the care of Toby and would be returning with Toby to her home in Oriental Bay. Feeling faint, he reached for a chair to steady himself.

'My dear, I must apologise again. I'm not at my peak and I believe I should put my head down back at the club.' Toby could see he was unsteady on his feet and helped him sit. With the 'breather', his heart soon calmed, his colour returned to normal and before long he was happily chatting once more, the unpleasant incident pushed into the background. Half an hour later, he announced he was on his way to his club, waved away the offers of help, shook hands all round, collected his hat, coat and cane from the cloakroom, and stepped into the night.

The attack came the moment he moved from the lights at the theatre entrance into the shadows between the theatre and the horse cabs. A hefty figure emerged from the blackness and swung a cosh with full force into the back of Staveley's head. With a terrible groan, he fell heavily onto his shoulder and lay shuddering. Another assailant then rushed in from the darkness at the right, putting a mighty kick into his ribs. The second assailant stood there a moment looking with satisfaction at his victim at his feet and was drawing back his boot to sink another one home when a movement made him look left. But too late to take evasive action. Toby's right fist smashed into his face. From his training, Toby used the two knuckles closest to his thumb and they shattered the man's cheekbone and sent him crashing onto the street. The first assailant roared and cursed and came wildly at Toby, his cosh drawn back, prepared to crack Toby's skull. Toby ducked, warded off the blow with his left arm and threw a short, overhand right that travelled barely a foot but had started from the pivot of his feet and exploded with all the power from the twist of his muscled body. The fist crashed into the man's nose and sent him sprawling onto the pavement. This was not what the two thugs had taken cash for. One minute they had had every advantage in the confrontation and were looking forward to earning their pay; the next, they were hurting and in danger of being locked up for their skulduggery. A nearby cabman was shouting and at this rate the constabulary would be there any moment. The two thugs probably considered they had spent enough time in the custody of His Majesty in the past for they had no sooner clambered to their feet and cursed Toby to hell, than they hurried towards the darkness of an alley and disappeared.

Toby thanked God he had gone to the theatre door to see J.P. safely to a horse cab after his earlier offer to accompany him to the club had been rejected. There was no doubt Toby's swift intervention had saved Staveley from yet more severe injury or even death.

J.P. had been raised in a hard school and had been in plenty of scrapes on his rise to wealth and he was not one to bemoan a knock or a bruise to cultivate sympathy. Once he was upright and had shaken himself off, he felt ready to go on to his club. He put a hand on the tender spot on the back of his head.

'Those cowardly devils,' he said. 'Coming out of nowhere. Must have been after my money. I believe I can thank my titfer.' His tit for tat, or hat, had indeed deflected some of the blow. 'And you too my boy.' He embraced Toby in gratitude. Their bond was cemented. 'You better get back to your mother and Margaret.'

And that is what Toby did. Within five minutes he was dancing with Margaret Fairbairn and she was none the wiser he had been brawling in the street and had possibly saved a man's life.

On the other side of the theatre, outside the pub where Simon Drake had hired the two assailants, the 'Hellfire Boys' were skulking in the shadows. They squirmed in frustration at the turn of events. They had observed J.P. Staveley resting and had correctly surmised he would be departing early. Arthur Wilson had particularly relished the blows on the 'bloody old buzzard', but then Toby Page had ruined things. They could only watch with gritted teeth and grudging admiration at Page's boxing skills. Then it struck them that they must return quickly to the theatre to shield themselves from any involvement. As Simon Drake withdrew, he punched the wall of the theatre and scarcely felt the pain in his knuckles. He vowed that Toby Page would never thwart him again.

Toby remained silent to both his mother and Margaret about the attack, not wishing to worry them that evening. He would tell them later. Toby and Margaret retired to separate bedrooms in Minnie's home in Oriental Bay but when the lights went out and the door of Margaret's room opened soon afterwards, she was happy to welcome Toby into her bed and into her arms. They had both long yearned for this. Margaret, passionate and sensitive by nature, devoted to poetry as well as music, had lain alone countless nights, unfulfilled and melancholy. Passions also ran deep for Toby but time and again they had been diverted by trauma and his rigid reserve. Now the barriers of decorum and distance were removed and Toby and Margaret were naked and kissing each other softly and then passionately, and running their hands up and down each other's bodies. They caressed, murmured words of love and pleasured each other over and over until they succumbed to all their pent-up passion and came together as one. It was everything they had desired and imagined. They made love again and again until they fell asleep wrapped in each other's arms. On waking just before dawn, Toby looked at her and longed to make love again, but left her warm bed and crawled between the cold sheets of his own. Yes, his mother was a liberal thinker but he wished, for everyone's sake, to maintain a sense of propriety.

At breakfast Minnie and Margaret shuddered at Toby's account of the attack on J.P. Staveley. He minimised his role as rescuer but both women knew how self-effacing he was and how perilous the situation must have been for both J.P. and Toby. After breakfast, Toby and Margaret got a horse cab to the railway station, Toby bound for Palmerston North and Margaret for Marton. They kissed and embraced on parting and promised to see each other soon. Margaret said a silent prayer for him as she boarded her train.

Meantime, Minnie was on her way to see Elizabeth McAlistair at The Elms. She had decided it was time Elizabeth knew of Toby's parentage. Elizabeth could then tell her children as she wished. As the horse's hooves rattled through the central city to Molesworth Street and past the Houses of Parliament, she felt sure that Charles McAlistair would approve. It was 36 years since she and Charlie had made love, she at 16, he at 17, long before Charles met Elizabeth. She was grateful Charles and Toby had known each other as father and son. Now, it was time for the children to know Toby was their half-brother and for Elizabeth to know she was Toby's step-mother.

Minnie delivered the first shock by telling Elizabeth of the attack on J.P. Staveley just after he had left them the night before, and of Toby coming to his rescue. As Elizabeth recoiled in dismay, Minnie was able to assure her that J.P. was little the worse for it and had returned to his home and business, and that Toby was unharmed. But the shock of that news was nothing compared to the shock of the revelation of Toby's parentage.

'I would have spoken sooner,' said Minnie, 'but then Charles had his accident and the time was not right.'

With each word Minnie spoke, she could see Elizabeth shrink more and more in dismay. This made the telling of it much harder and when she finished, Minnie felt as wrung out as a towel in a mangle. Should she have spoken sooner? They sat in numbed silence until Elizabeth finally spoke.

'You are telling me that Toby is the half-brother of my children and that Charles knew of this for years and Toby has known of it,' said Elizabeth. Deep in her heart, she was hurt on several counts: that her Charlie had made love to another and one she now counted as a dear friend, that he had not confided in her, that she had believed her family was one thing and had found out only now it was quite another, that others had known while she had not.

'I think you had better go,' she said, standing and showing Minnie the door. Sophie entered the room just as Minnie was leaving.

'Minnie,' said Sophie, 'must you go so soon?'

But Minnie could but give a hurried greeting and farewell to Sophie for Elizabeth wanted her out of there that instant. As Minnie vanished into Tinakori Road, Elizabeth's mind was racing. Her world had been turned asunder: Charlie and Minnie making love, an illegitimate child, her children acquiring a brother at this stage of their lives. And then other thoughts – a brother accused of assaulting a sister and that the catalyst for Minnie telling Charles. Charles knowing of Toby's parentage while Elizabeth knew nothing. Elizabeth felt as though she had been living in blind ignorance.

REVELATION AND CONFRONTATION

D ay and night, Elizabeth McAlistair reflected on Minnie Page's revelation until Harry and Sophie asked what was troubling her. At first, she fobbed them off and kept her silence. For one thing, it had been a huge shock to learn that Charles had once loved another and had fathered a child with her. And for another, that the woman concerned had been Minnie Page, someone she saw almost weekly and considered a confidant but was now looking at askance. Then there was the knowledge that Charles and Toby had known but not herself. But day by day, there was a change in her outlook. She saw herself at 16, passionately in love with the son of her family's gardener. She could speak of it to no one, even to the boy himself, for this was a love that could never be requited. For months she had struggled with the agony of it and now she realised, that if she were honest with herself, her passions over him had never abated until she met Charles. There was, too, her responsibility towards her children. They had a right to know they had a brother. True, strictly speaking, a half-brother but she had seen how deeply they were drawn to one another and to them it would be a brother. Elizabeth resolved to tell them.

The perfect opportunity came the next day when Clarissa visited. The children were riveted by the story and by the end of it, their minds were spinning so much the three of them sat in silence. Elizabeth knew she had made the right decision. She saw their initial shock but soon their joy at knowing Toby was their brother. They had always admired and loved him; he had indeed been their quasi-brother even before they knew him as their real brother. Elizabeth could see their father was not diminished in their eyes. By now they had seen and felt enough of life themselves, with all its complications, to understand a straying from the norm when passions were involved – their father and Minnie Page had given way, in their youth, to forces of nature. For herself, it was an almighty relief to have the truth of it off her chest.

Harry was first to speak. 'I knew it. I felt it all along.' They all laughed at his fore-knowledge.

'When will we next see our brother and our step-mother?' asked Sophie.

'Give me more time to think it all through,' Clarissa said. 'I'm looking at father differently.'

Elizabeth embraced her and the others joined them. They felt their lives had all changed, but for the better.

Sophie's desire for a meeting as soon as possible with Toby and Minnie was indeed what Elizabeth herself wanted as soon as possible. She felt bad at her coldness to Minnie Page at the time of the revelation and at her silence towards her since. She felt now an intense need to see Minnie and to envelop the children in the reconciliation.

Later, when Sophie and Harry left the room and Clarissa was alone with her mother, her face grew solemn.

'I believe Simon has another woman. Her name is Becky.'

Elizabeth took in the hollow eyes and long face. Clarissa appeared to age before her eyes whenever the talk was of Simon Drake.

Clarissa made a quick, dismissive gesture. 'I know it's no surprise to hear of another woman but I believe he is seeing this one often. He constantly tells me of it by subtle indications.'

Elizabeth was a practical woman with a hard on running an estate and not given to extravagant displays of emotion, but her heart shrivelled as she looked at her daughter and considered Simon Drake's sordid couplings. Reflecting, she could see how Simon's mother, Lady Pamela, had almost warned her off the marriage. She and Sir Robert had told her privately that they hoped it would be the making of Simon. 'Hoped' now seemed the height of optimism, a frivolous dream, a ridiculous fancy. She had tried to stop her daughter rushing into this. How could she best help her now, in the wreckage of it? A divorce seemed inevitable, with all the public washing of dirty linen that entailed and the inevitable fighting over money and lawyers' fees. Elizabeth was at heart an optimist, but looking ahead she could see nothing but strife and danger. There was no solace, however she contemplated it.

Minnie was delighted to receive a card from Elizabeth inviting her and Toby to dinner. When his mother said she had informed Elizabeth of his parentage, Toby ensured he would be there. On arriving at the door, Minnie and Toby heard a pounding of footsteps and next moment Harry and Sophie were in their arms. Later, when Clarissa arrived, she too embraced them. The McAlistairs, though, were still coming to terms with their modified family. There were many angles to consider. The pecking order for one. Clarissa was now no longer the eldest sibling nor Harry the eldest son. What about Toby's name? His father was Charles McAlistair – should he not take the McAlistair name to make it plain to the world? He said he was content with Page. And, as a McAlistair by blood and the eldest to boot, would he not be a benefiary of the McAlistair estate? Toby raised that issue himself and promptly dismissed the idea, saying he would never make a claim on it. 'My own way or nothing,' he said. And Minnie, from being a valued family friend, was now mother of a part-sibling. What did that make her? 'A semi-step mother, I believe,' quipped Minnie, and they looked forward to introducing her as such at their next occasion.

There would soon be yet another to add to the burgeoning family, for on the following Saturday Toby, 36, and Margaret, 30, decided they had waited long enough. It would not be a long engagement. A short walk later to the vicar of St Stephens Church down the road at Marton, and the wedding was booked for six weeks' time – just time enough time to get the invitations out and the replies and arrange for their attendants, the catering, the photography and the hundred and one other things. For Margaret especially, there was much else to arrange as she would be moving to Palmerston North and starting a new school of pianoforte and dance there. Another teacher would need to be found for her pupils. To her relief, she quickly found one – the wife of a newly appointed teacher at the Marton Technical School. The pupils' tuition would be seamless and Margaret could put the funds from the sale of her cottage and school to the new house which she and Toby planned to build in Palmerston North. A previous teacher at the Marton Technical School, Stephen Bannister, was leaving to live and marry elsewhere.

For Toby, the 26 miles of road between Palmerston North and Marton was much travelled in those six weeks. He took every opportunity to visit and by the lamplight of her cosy cottage, long into the night, they talked of family and friends, wedding and house, school and stable, and then tumbled into bed, touching and kissing and making love before drifting off into deep, serene sleep. The more they saw of each other, the more they realised they were meant to be together. She could understand his passion for the horses. She loved the horses too and it was a great joy to attend the race meetings and see them run. Most thrilling of all, to see the horses run while carrying her two or three shillings to a dividend. In time she would establish her new school but for now, it was all about the wedding and the new house. The final key elements of the wedding were sorted – the best man would be Lonnie Sparks and the chief bridesmaid Sophie McAlistair. When Lonnie confirmed his availability, Toby was delighted to learn Lonnie was himself trotting out a lady, Miss Gladys Jopson, the daughter of a farmer in the Wairarapa.

'She's a good sort,' Lonnie assured Toby, 'and as handy on the end of a shovel as the end of a saucepan.'

'I hope she's got a tongue on her,' Toby said. 'You need someone to keep you in line.'

'She has old son, like you wouldn't believe. No doubt about that. But she's grand fun too.'

They sounded like a good match and Toby promised to do the honours when it was Lonnie's turn.

The house now took up much of the talk. It was the best sort of talk, exhilarating and positive. They had already purchased the one-acre section for it, near the stable. They would retain Toby's house and Dot Prendergast would continue living there with the apprentices. The only difference would be no Toby under its roof. Dot Prendergast had always managed its affairs anyway. There would be seven rooms in the new house (three of them bedrooms), a bathroom with a patent WC, a kitchen, a living-room and a lounge with a bay window. There would be gas throughout with ornamental burners, hot and cold water, a porcelain bath, a scullery, a pantry, a linen press, and a range with a high-pressure boiler in the kitchen. The timber would be jarrah heartwood from South Australia and the ceilings would have ornamental plasterwork. The house would have front, side, and back verandahs. The half-acre section would give ample scope for a wash-house, a green-house and extensive gardens. On one side the house looked towards the stables and on the other towards the Tararua mountain range.

'All in all, a good mix of the functional and the decorative,' Toby said.

Margaret was an avid gardener and she could already see the bright yellows and purples, oranges and pinks, reds and whites of the borders and flower beds and the rose garden, and the white of the jasmine and creamy yellow of the honeysuckle against the fence. There would be a deciduous hedge screening the greenhouse, crazy paving connecting the house and greenhouse, pots of blue asters and orange tagetes near the house and a small orchard at the back.

'I'll bring some of my plantings from Marton to give us a head start,' she said.

The house would be both a retreat and an outlet for any spare energy they might have after their paying work was completed.

The apprentices took an interest when construction of the house started.

'Will you put in a sauna and plunge pool?' one of the more impish ones asked.

'And have all the jockeys of the district visit us to dry out,' said Toby in horror. 'Not likely.'

The McAlistair family followed developments closely, thrilled about the forthcoming marriage. It was quickly decided with Toby and Margaret that Sophie would provide a solo at the wedding.

It was as well there was joy on the Page side of the family for the misery soon deepened even further for Clarissa. She returned from a meeting with Elizabeth and Monty Powell in Marton one afternoon to discover Simon in her bed with Becky Kneebone, his infatuation of the moment. It was not Clarissa's way to run in tears and shrink in lonely silence as some might have done. She grabbed hold of the bed's coverings and in fury flung them to the floor, revealing the two in their nakedness. Becky Kneebone looked no more than startled while Simon smirked. When Clarissa grasped the chamber pot and raised it as if to toss the contents over them, Simon's smirk vanished and he roared in protest. As they shrank back, she looked at them in contempt and put the chamber pot back down. She could not carry out such a crude act, tempting though it was.

'You deserve to wallow in muck!' she shouted as she left the room.

When Clarissa arrived at The Elms, still white-hot with anger and humiliation, Elizabeth resolved to take the matter to Sir Robert Drake and Lady Pamela. Perhaps they still had some influence over their wayward son. She wrote that day to request a meeting. In the meantime, Clarissa would live at The Elms.

The following day, Elizabeth and Monty Powell drove to the estate. As they entered the house they heard Drake's woman – in racing parlance, the off-course substitute – ordering Mary the parlour maid to bring her tea and biscuits. When Elizabeth and Monty entered the sitting room, Rebecca Kneebone, young and blowsy with straggly, brown hair, was lying across Simon Drake's lap, pouting sullenly. It was barely noon but already they were drinking. The visitors stopped in their tracks in the doorway. Powell, a decent man verging on puritanical, flushed red as a boiled beet. Elizabeth's nervousness fled as her anger rushed in. She was so incensed it took all her self-control not to cross the room in three strides, rip Becky Kneebone off him and boot her out the door on her backside.

'Welcome to Glenview,' said Simon Drake, leering at them. 'May

I introduce Rebecca Kneebone. What can we do for you?'

Rebecca Kneebone had picked up enough of the atmosphere to attempt to rise, but Drake restrained her in his lap. Powell grimaced. The man had not even the manners to rise at the entrance of visitors who included a lady, his mother-in-law no less and the owner of the house. What an unmannerly oaf!

Elizabeth's voice started low and icy but her final word cracked like a whip. 'She is to go this instant!' When Elizabeth stepped towards them, her eye fell on the fire poker to her left and if Rebecca Kneebone had not seen the fire in Elizabeth's eye and had enough sense of self-preservation to tear herself from Drake and stand up, Elizabeth might very well have seized it and beaten Drake and her about the body with it. As Rebecca Kneebone rose and sprang aside and Elizabeth stood over him, he was momentarily at a loss.

'What's this? Coming into a man's house uninvited and disrespecting his guest.'

Elizabeth looked down at him in rage and disgust and, in the depths of her heart, in pity as well for her daughter that she had bound herself to him. She took in the dazzling blue eyes, handsome features, and well-formed body. Her Clarissa had been helplessly drawn in, especially when she had been so vulnerable. There was at least the comfort that the estate and house was not his, as much as he might consider it was by reason of marriage and male prerogative.

He gazed at her defiantly but in some confusion, his glass still in hand. He was one of those so hopelessly addicted, that once he started, he never put his glass down. Elizabeth sensed, that for this moment at least, she had the upper hand by reason of surprise and forcefulness.

'Understand Simon, this is my property and unless you reform your filthy ways, you will cease to live here. I have written to your father and Lady Pamela and shall be discussing your future with them. Be assured, you will not continue to treat my daughter with disrespect. Have you no shame that you would sully your marriage in this way?'

Monty Powell had come close behind Elizabeth in support and was nodding vigorously. Mary the parlour maid arrived to the doorway with tea and biscuits as instructed, fluttered there a moment, and then hastily withdrew as she caught the tenor of proceedings.

Elizabeth continued. 'I shall instruct one of the staff to take a trap and remove that woman immediately from the property.' Elizabeth turned and barked at Rebecca Kneebone. 'Get your things and bring them down!'

With no contrary instruction from Simon Drake, the woman stumped out of the room, disappeared upstairs, and was down soon after with her bag. As Elizabeth bustled her out of the house and summoned a staff member to drive her away, Drake sat back down and poured himself another drink. His face was twisted in bitterness and frustration. Humiliating. Still under the thrall of others. A bitch for a mother-in-law and a meeting looming, yet again, with his father. When would he ever be master in his own house? When would he ever be respected in his own right? That morning, he had woken to a complete blackout of the week before, disconcerting in one way but convenient in another.

◆ ◆ ◆

One glance at Elizabeth's tight smile and anxious eyes confirmed for Sir Robert and Lady Pamela that their meeting would be difficult.

'We had fervently wished for better,' said Sir Robert. 'Simon has given us many concerns through the years, and, I must say, not a little distress. I have done my best with him but he has made it deuced difficult.' Sir Robert looked through his window across his estate but his mind appeared to be back in time. 'He promised to be so much more. Plenty of spirit. A good horseman. Would have been a capital polo player if he'd applied himself. He had success at school at football and cricket but stopped those the moment he left.' The knight of the realm looked at them impotently. 'There appears to be an anger in him that won't be cooled.' He thought back to scrapes he had sorted with money and a word. 'Those fellows he consorts with don't help.'

'Women and drink.' Lady Pamela did not hedge her words. 'They have been his curse. We prayed the marriage to Clarissa would prove his salvation.'

Elizabeth writhed in dismay. She felt her daughter had been a sacrificial lamb in the attempted salvation of Simon Drake. Sir Robert promised to have a word with his son but appeared already to regard it as a hopeless cause. Elizabeth left the house laden with the anguish of a mother whose daughter is trapped in a vile marriage to a drunk. She had not realised the extent of his drinking. She had always supported license and seen no-license as a killjoy faction, designed for those excessively religious or moralistic. But when she had watched him fingering his drink that recent hideous morning, she had begun to see the merits of no-license.

◆ ◆ ◆

As Sir Robert Drake drove his automobile to Glenview Estate the following morning, his hands twitched at the wheel and every so often he huffed and grimaced. How often through the years he had been asked to have a word with Simon. Never a problem with Paul, Ralph, or the girls. With each mile, his anger grew so that, on arrival, he parked the automobile sharply, stalked to the house and rapped on the door in a way that demanded attention. Mary was momentarily flummoxed on seeing the stern features of Sir Robert Drake glowering at her. Being the gentleman he was, he noticed her discomfiture and softened his manner.

'Is he in, my dear?'

Without a word, she led him into the sitting room. Simon was smoking a cigar, a gin in his hand, a newspaper in his lap. He remained sitting and looked at his father warily as smoke wreathed between them. Sir Robert had entered full of wrath and bristling but as he looked at his son, he saw his grandfather Ted and his brother Bertie, and the steam went out of him. Sir Robert, confidant of Governors and Prime Ministers, respected the length of the land, stood there defeated. He could see the gloom and edginess in his son. It was the wariness of the boy in the headmaster's office and the young man in the police station. Son looked at father inquisitively. Sir Robert sat and for a minute there was no sound until the triple chime of the grandfather clock on the hour.

'Drunk as a Drake,' Sir Robert said at last, resignedly, in sorrow. He looked his son in the eye. 'There are some who should never drink. We have a long line through the Drake family of drunkards and wastrels, boozers, and good-for-nothings. We must forever guard against liquor. I barely touch the stuff myself because I have seen the effects up close and Paul does the same.' He paused and looked in dismay at the glass still in Simon's hand. 'But you have never learnt and now you and the McAlistairs are paying the price for it.'

Simon stirred and some of the glaze in his eyes cleared. 'You are for Prohibition then?'

'I am not, as a matter of fact. I believe liquor has a place and I have always provided for my guests. But there are some who should never drink and the Drakes are amongst them. You have never listened to me. Perhaps if you had seen what I have seen.' Sir Robert looked reflective, sad, and wearied. 'It is our curse and we must steer clear of it.' He looked at the sprawled figure of his son, already drunk before noon. 'What's to be done then? Your behaviour has been reprehensible. These women you have. Have you no respect for your wife? She's a dear girl.'

'She's a harridan,' he said. He laid his cigar in the ashtray, put the newspaper aside, walked to the window, and gazed out. 'I have nothing here. I married to improve my situation but am no better off than when I was in your house.' He continued to hold his glass of gin and took a sip. 'I am scarcely even the master here. The staff look at me as though I'm an interloper. I feel like a tenant on my own estate.'

'You have an opportunity here. You have always had opportunities.'

Simon turned and looked at his father. 'It was always Paul walking in your footsteps. Paul the head boy, hero at polo, leader of the militia. Never a prank, never a wrong word, never carousing. Not once can I remember Paul sent to his room. But me…'

'You seem to forget your advantages. You never wanted for anything. You had the best of educations. You had everything Paul had.'

'Except your attention.'

Sir Robert accepted he might have had shortcomings as a father. Had he given the lion's share of attention to Paul? Perhaps, for Paul had been the first-born and had always shone at everything. But he felt the blame was not all his. He had seen enough of people to know what havoc jealousy could cause. 'I have always been proud of you for many things – your love for your sisters and mother, your gift for friendship. Proud of you, too, as a horseman. You have a remarkable talent there.' He looked with a shrivelled heart into the watery and bloodshot eyes of his son. 'I have loved you as a father but I have grieved at many of your words and actions. Your treatment of Clarissa has hurt your mother and me terribly.'

Simon slumped once more in his chair and they sat in silence before Sir Robert stood to go. 'To recover your marriage, you must give up the drink. I shall mention your affliction to Dr Armitage. But the treatment will be worthless unless you want it. I beg you, Simon. Let the curse of the Drakes end with you.'

As Simon watched the car disappear down the driveway and its dust settle, he reflected on his father's words, 'Drunk as a Drake'. He liked a drink, he admitted. But no more than others. He could cut back a bit if he had to, to keep the old man happy.

When Elizabeth returned to the estate with Clarissa a week later, the evicted woman was not in residence and Simon was sober and seemed unusually subdued. Clarissa greeted him coldly, repressing the feelings he still stirred in her, and told him she would be returning to live in the house the following week. He nodded, but not in surprise. He knew he still had a hold over her.

VAIN BID FOR GLORY

Minnie Page, like Elizabeth McAlistair, enjoyed the occasional nip of spirits or sip of wine, but had recently been propounding the merits of no-license. In the latter part of 1908, with an election looming, the liquor debate was in the newspapers daily. Every three years since the early 1890s, New Zealanders had been given the opportunity to vote in their own electoral districts for no-license, and some districts had indeed gone 'dry' and with great benefit, it was claimed. Mrs Hill of Ashburton had recently stated that in her no-license town the gaol had been empty for 10 weeks. And just the other day the police had declared a considerable decrease in crime in Southland during the 18 months of no-license there.

The intense debates took Minnie Page back to the battle over the women's suffrage which had culminated in such triumph 15 years before. Since her unfortunate encounter with the crazed Adam Gibson, she had kept a low political profile, preferring to work quietly in the background for social reform. But the propaganda of those with a vested interest in the liquor trade had begun to irk her more than somewhat. When a State goes 'dry', they thundered, the trade goes underground and there is the dangerous illicit still, the faker of liquor, sly grog places, houses of dubious fame, and women resorting to the bottle in the corner cupboard. Why should the majority suffer for the few who abused alcohol? Do you amputate a leg to cure an in-grown toenail? They also pointed out the benefit to the State of duties on legal liquor. On the other side the New Zealand Alliance, representing the many local temperance groups, argued that alcohol was the cause of poverty, ill-health, neglect, and abuse of families. It quoted the remarkable growth of no license in America and authorities such as the King's doctor, who said alcohol was injurious to mankind.

Minnie Page increasingly saw the thundering for license driven mainly by coin. Central to her thinking was the woman and her children dependent on the man with a weakness for liquor. With jobs for women so scarce, and lowly paid at that, the wife could only stand by helplessly while he drank them out of furniture and home. She started to throw her unsubstantial physical weight, but considerable moral weight, behind the no-license cause. As the election in November loomed ever closer, she became more deeply embroiled. One evening in October, driven partly she would have had to concede, by a sense of mischief, she spoke at a political meeting at Marton when one of the speakers was none other than Arthur Wilson, Conservative candidate for Rangitikei, who had goaded her at the race ball. Opposing him was the Liberal candidate, Arthur Remington. Politicians had freedom of choice regarding the liquor question and Wilson was an avowed advocate of license.

'Decent spirit merchants and brewers want to prevent the evils of underground drinking,' he said. 'Properly regulated and well-conducted hotels are necessary in every civilised community. Let us be able to ease life's passage with a glass or two of liquor openly, not in a secretive way. Prohibition districts are hot beds of vice, depravity, and malevolent espionage.'

He drew applause for that and Minnie Page had to admit he had a point. There was an oily largesse about him that she conceded might appeal to some.

She was so diminutive she had been hidden from his sight in the audience and when she took the stage to speak, he was greatly surprised and had to struggle to restrain a cough and splutter. Perhaps a memory stirred of being called out and humiliated. Minnie could not restrain a smile at his obvious discomfort. Then she remembered what she was there for and spoke of families she knew and the troubles drink had caused them.

'The eldest child, a girl of nine, is sent to the pub to encourage her father to return home before he spends all their housekeeping money for the week.' And, 'The breadwinner, body wracked by alcohol and repeating himself in senseless rants, while his wife and children line up outside the office of the Charitable Aid Board.' And, 'The loving father, losing all judgment once he has drink, reaching for a whip to beat his wife and children into submission.'

She drew her share of applause, and some grimaces and groans of dismay from the more susceptible of the audience. The vote for women had helped the women's cause immensely but there was still a considerable way to go. Still no pensions for war widows and no maintenance orders for women against the fathers of their children. If the man walked out, the wives were often left destitute. Another issue, too, had recently come to light that she would not be silent about – the shocking punishments meted out at Te Oranga Home, the Dominion's reformatory for girls, near Christchurch. A woman of 20, could be laid on a bed there face down, clad in a nightdress, and receive 12 blows of a strap on her body. Other punishments included a hair-cut, wearing a 'punishment dress' – a dress strikingly unattractive – and being put on only bread and water. How ironic that 'Te Oranga' in Maori meant well-being. She also spoke against the corporal punishment at the boys' reformatory at Burnham.

There may have been no other Adam Gibson, at least yet, but there was a publican so malicious he arranged for a towering pyramid of empty bottles of beer, of whisky, of gin, of vodka, to be left by her letterbox, as though she were a drunken sot. A regiment of thirsty troopers could scarcely have emptied that lot, even over a week. She promptly arranged for a glass merchant to pick them up and donated the proceeds to the fight for no-license.

In the second week of November, 2008, the Canterbury Spring Carnival was all the talk in horse- racing circles. There had been a huge upheaval in Canterbury racing this year after the collapse of the celebrated owner George Stead from an acute attack of Bright's disease at the Riccarton races and his death two days later. A dispersal sale of his stud and racing team followed. Stead as owner and Dick Mason as trainer had dominated the classic races of New Zealand like no pair before. Another component of their success was also gone, departed for Europe – brilliant jockey Leslie 'Tod' Hewitt, first in Australasia to adopt the short riding style, who had won 85 of his 172 rides for Stead.

'Well Robbie, great sadness for racing with the death of Mr Stead but I have to say, opportunities there for us,' Toby said. Riccarton provided four days of racing for gallopers and high stakes, with some classic races, and Toby had the inestimable gift for a trainer of being able to place his horses in races astutely.

'Too right boss,' said Robbie Paget. 'We could do well with an ounce of luck. There are several cherry-ripe and ready to run. Even Rudolph's worth a go.' Rudolph, a six-year-old bay gelding, was a bit of a plodder with only placings to his name, but a trier through and through.

'J.P.'s making the trip and I want to make it worthwhile for him,' said Toby. 'Egmont's been working like a Trojan and should see out the two miles of the New Zealand Cup. And Easel in the Stewards will give them a run for their money.' Toby became aware only after he had said it, that he had spoken the name of his heroic horse of the veldt. On reflection, it seemed a good omen.

Minnie Page was returning to Christchurch for the first time since her ordeal there at the hands of Adam Gibson and Toby wanted to make it rewarding for her. Both races were on the first day. The cup had the superb prize of 2,000 sovereigns to the winner and the Stewards a handsome 1,000 sovereigns. Also racing on the first day, in the Welcome Stakes of four furlongs for 800 sovereigns, was J.P.'s exciting yearling of the year before, Blink of an Eye. On the third day, Rudolph was in the Canterbury Cup of two and a quarter miles and Mexican Bride in the weight-for-age Electric Plate of four furlongs. On the last day, Joyful Bell would race in the Members' Handicap of seven furlongs and Buccaroon in the one and a quarter mile

G.G. Stead Memorial Gold Cup. Besides Toby, Robbie Paget and Rowley O'Neill would accompany the seven-horse team. Toby could also call on the leading hoop, the Bulls jockey Charlie Jenkins.

Simon Drake was travelling south with six horses including his three best-performed – Jubilee Boy in the New Zealand Cup, Catch the Wind in the Canterbury Cup and Jonty's Pride in the G.G. Stead Memorial Gold Cup. There was no Vernon McCardle with him. McCardle had surprised Drake three weeks before by resigning. The last straw had been Drake's insistence that a horse that had disappointed him be sent to the knacker's yard. McCardle had a soft spot for the good-natured horse and spirited it away to a family in the country for use as a hack. He then resigned. Drake was putting feelers out for another trainer but he had always had a heavy hand in the training anyway and had no qualms about coping in the meantime. In fact, he was relieved in a way to be rid of McCardle who had started to question some of the special concoctions. Untoward practices still occurred in racing, despite increasing surveillance, and sometimes offenders got off ludicrously lightly when found out. One jockey struck another just above the temple with the brass knob on the end of his whip on the run home at Manaia in March, causing two bloody gashes. His penalty – suspension for the rest of the meeting. A man struck the handicapper at a meeting of the Kaikaka Hack Racing Club and was fined just £1. At Avondale one jockey gave another an unmerciful thrashing during the race, injuring him so badly he was unable to ride again at the meeting, and was not at first reported. Stewards eventually called an inquiry, determined to stamp out foul practice. Simon Drake, in his desperation to succeed, was taking an almighty risk with his concoctions.

On arrival, Toby and his team found the country had come to town. The boarding houses and hotels of Christchurch were creaking at the seams and people were even sleeping in corridors and dining rooms. Some of the hotels had a back door for diligent drinkers. Toby was familiar with it all but Robbie and Rowley were wide-eyed. The weather for the first day was perfect and as it was a Saturday as well, folk came in their thousands and by noon, the grandstands, lawn, and paddock were pulsating. Twenty-five bookmakers shouted the odds in the paddock and another 34 in the outside enclosure. Governor Plunket, Lady Plunket, and other dignitaries were hobnobbing and visitors from all parts of the dominion were greeting old friends. The stage was set for the real stars of the day – the horses and their jockeys.

A record field of 21 went to the post for the New Zealand Cup. J.P. Staveley's Egmont, in the hands of Rowley O'Neill, was carrying a hefty nine stone one pound, just eight pounds less than the top weight. Sir Robert Drake's Trident got in with eight stone seven and Simon Drake's Jubilee Boy with only seven stone two pounds. In the stand, J.P. Staveley heard another owner protesting to his wife. 'Too much weight. Why should the good horses get murdered and the others get in with nothing?' He sympathised with him but said nothing to Minnie Page beside him. That was the nature of handicap racing and they were at the mercy of the handicapper.

The horses got away to an excellent start. O'Neill sought the inside rail and found it near the tail of the field. Staveley could see the horse relax. The furlongs flew by. O'Neill pulled Egmont out in the back straight and took him around the field. As they rounded the home turn, Egmont sighted the leader, flattened his ears, and hurled himself forward. In the stand, J.P. Staveley threw up his arms and bellowed with the loudest of them. Up to fourth, then third and second, screaming along. But the post came too soon with the leader half a length clear. Egmont had run gallantly and J.P. Staveley had run every yard of it with him. As Staveley bent forward in the stand to get blood into his head and calm his heart, Minnie Page feared it might have been too much. But to her relief, he straightened and smiled. So nearly a win but consoling to be second. Then both became aware of a commotion in the stand to their right. Simon Drake and Eddie Shaw were whooping with joy. Drake's Jubilee Boy, in the hands of his stable jockey, Lex Jordan, had taken full benefit of his light weight and held on to win. Drake, as the owner as well as the trainer, would collect the 2,000 sovereigns and a cup. He would also collect a hefty bet with the bookmakers and Shaw, too, would have a handsome collect. Sir Robert's Trident finished near the tail of the field.

This was ecstasy, surely, such as Simon Drake had never felt before. The absolute best of it was to bask in the envy of others in the stand. Any one of them would cherish the New Zealand Cup adorning their sideboard. The congratulations of Sir Robert when the horses returned to scale was the sweetest of music to his ears. At the presentation, there was no wife by his side but there was the huge satisfaction of Sir Robert and Paul looking on as well as the Governor, the Prime Minister, and other dignitaries. Jubilee Boy was briefly in the spotlight, receiving the victor's sash, and then was led away head down, drained – under the urgings of Lex Jordan he had given it his all and then some. Indeed, the horse looked weak to the point of collapse.

Easel was up against many seasoned performers in the Stewards but had the advantage of only seven stone three pounds against the top weight's nine stone seven. Away they went, the quickest in the country, scorching the six furlongs, and in no time they were tearing for the post. Minnie had gone to a top corner of the stand where she had an unimpeded view. Where were her colours of pink with a white sash? There, charging for the line with three others. Now it was Minnie's turn to run with them to the finish. They were spread across the track, a line of four. And with a last frantic beat of her heart, they were there and Easel could have been first or fourth for all she knew. It turned out to be third, with a head to second and a nose to first. A pleasing result, considering the top-class field. Last one up was Blink of an Eye in the Welcome Stakes and it came home in such a rush for fourth that J.P. and Toby were excited about its prospects. A good day for the stable but an even better one for Simon Drake.

As the day was winding up, grim news changed everything. Word flashed around the trainers – Jubilee Boy had keeled over and died. Heart attack, it was said. The sheer willpower of the horse had pushed it beyond its capability.

'I am not at all surprised at the death Robbie,' Toby said on hearing the news. 'I have never seen a winning horse look so poorly.' The horse had reminded him of a pitiful foot runner he had once seen who had crawled to the finish.

'A sad thing,' said Robbie Paget. 'To lose a horse just after its greatest triumph.'

The sheer willpower of the horse was indeed a part of it. But the crucial factor in the death of Jubilee Boy was the arsenical solution that Simon Drake had administered as a stimulant that morning. Drake was shocked. He had desperately wanted to win the race for the prestige of it, as well as the heavy bets he and Shaw had placed, but he had never considered the possibility of the horse dying. Jubilee Boy was insured against both accident and untimely death but the insurers and the racing authorities would be asking questions if foul play were suggested. Drake acted rapidly and by the next nightfall the horse had been fed to hounds. Some of them sickened but not sufficiently to cause an inquiry. As Drake continued to celebrate with Eddie Shaw, he rued the loss of Jubilee Boy but at least the horse had gone out in a blaze of glory, forever in the record books as the winner of the New Zealand Cup. And there as well, as owner and trainer, was Simon Drake.

The collapse and death of Jubilee Boy cast a pall over the second day's racing. It was evident to all that racing was dangerous but it was still a shock when a jockey was badly hurt or a horse died or had to be put down. There was even worse to come on the third day. There was no hint of anything untoward when the field lined up for the Canterbury Cup. Both Toby Page and Simon Drake had a horse entered. Toby's placid but doughty stayer, Rudolph, had Rowley O'Neill up and Drake's Catch the Wind was in the hands of his promising apprentice, Baden Jones. The field got away well. In two-and-a-quarter miles a lot could happen and O'Neill's main concern was to guard against getting too far back and leaving the horse too much to do. He wanted an honest pace as Rudolph would never come charging home but might grind the others out of it. O'Neill kept well up with the leaders and took the lead coming into the straight. Now, let them try to pass! One by one they came alongside, caught his horse's blazing eye, and fell away until Rudolph had the last 100 yards to himself. A superb win for Rowley O'Neill and Toby's stable. But the race would not be remembered for Rudolph and Rowley O'Neill but for Catch the Wind and Baden Jones.

Behind Rudolph, coming round the final bend, Catch the Wind had clipped the heel of another horse and gone down. Baden Jones had had no chance. He had plummeted over the horse's head, hit the ground hard and broken his spine between the first and second vertebrae. The 'hangman's break' killed him instantly. Simon Drake had been watching from the paddock. In dread, he had seen Catch the Wind dip, and Jones go down. There was a big bet riding on it but it was not that which caused the blood to rush to his temple and his head to pound. As the other horses raced past, he ran to the fence, clambered over it and began to run up the track towards his fallen jockey. But others were closer and were by the side of Baden Jones long before he got there. Drake could only stand and watch in mounting horror as the jockey was removed to the ambulance room beneath the grandstand. It was there that a battery-operated device was found in his clothing. Jones had not had the opportunity to throw it away to the outside rail where a stable-hand could collect it. Drake had escaped the disgrace of feeding a banned substance to Jubilee Boy, but there was no escaping the use of an illegal device on Baden Jones.

The comments in the inquiry room reflected the comments soon in the jockeys' room and in bars and workplaces and sitting rooms up and down the country.

'Shocking bad sportsmanship.'

'The man should be put in the stocks and then the prison.'

'He used his apprentice for his own evil ends.'

'He dare not show his face at the funeral.'

'What show has the betting man got? Has he done it before?'

'We must stamp this out once and for all.'

Toby Page had heard of much racing skulduggery in his time but he had never heard of the electrical stimulant. It had to be the recourse of only the most desperate. The New Zealand Racing Conference moved quickly and disqualified Simon Drake for life. The New Zealand Cup would forever stand lonely on his sideboard. From being the toast of the national racing world two days before, he was now a pariah.

'Blackballed,' said Sir Robert Drake to son Paul in dismay. They were both deeply upset. They had both harboured hopes for Simon at his marriage. Now any hopes of his success were shattered. And the Drake family itself would be forever tarnished.

The rest of the racing carnival was run under the shadow of the scandal. Toby's Mexican Bride missed the start in the Electric Plate and had no chance to make up the ground, Joyful Bell ran a good third in the Members' Handicap and Buccaroon beat everything but the winner in the G.G. Stead Memorial Gold Cup. With Drake, its trainer, banned, Jonty's Pride was withdrawn from that race. Simon Drake had sunk all his efforts into his High Flight Racing Lodge. Now he had nothing.

LOVE AND HATE

T he wedding of Margaret Fairbairn and Toby Page was widely reported. Margaret was, after all, a well-known teacher of pianoforte and dance and a prominent pianist while Toby was conspicuous in horse-racing circles, a decorated soldier and the son of the artist and social reformer Minnie Page.

The local newspaper, *The Rangitikei Advocate and Manawatu Argus*, conveyed the essential information in a nutshell, with appropriate embellishment regarding dress. 'Margaret Jean Fairbairn, daughter of Mrs Isabel Fairbairn and the late Mr Terence Fairbairn, was united to Toby Charles Page, son of Mr Charles McAlistair and Mrs Willemina Page, at St Stephen's Church, Marton. The Rev. Drinkwater, M.A., officiated. The church was wonderfully decorated by friends of the bride. The bride was given away by her mother. The chief bridesmaid was Miss Sophie McAlistair and the best man was Mr Lonnie Sparks. The bride wore a handsome dress of dove-grey crepoline, trimmed with glossy silk to match and cream silk trimmings, a white picture hat trimmed with ostrich feathers and chiffon, and carried a shower bouquet. The chief bridesmaid was in cream voile with bodice of soft cream silk, trimmed with silk net. The other bridesmaids were Miss Ethel Goodwin and Mabel Goodwin, friends of the bridegroom, who looked enchanting in dainty dresses of white silk and carried the usual baskets and bouquets. The service included the beautiful aria, *Where'er You Walk*, by George Frederic Handel, sung by Miss Sophie McAlistair. After the ceremony about sixty guests sat down to a lavish breakfast that was tastefully laid out. Amid showers of rice and good wishes, the happy couple left by the express train for Wellington and hence to Picton by steamer for cruising in the Sounds. The bride's travelling dress was a navy-blue costume. Gifts included cheques, a biscuit barrel, pillow slips, a cruet, a butter dish, a preserving pan, a toasting fork, and six hens.'

Elizabeth felt this marriage of Toby and Margaret was sanctified while that of Simon and Clarissa, to her profound sadness, was not. At the reception, Minnie Page was delighted to draw a promise from Lonnie Sparks that when he next visited Wellington, he would bring Mrs Crichton with him for her portrait to be painted. Minnie was craving to transfer her face to canvas. Toby Page had been delighted to give the newspaper the name of his father as well as his mother and the report was the talk of the district for weeks.

There were moments in the Sounds, wrapped in each other, with the beauty of the water and the bush all around, when Margaret and Toby could have stayed forever. But, eager to build their new life together, a week later they returned to Palmerston North where Margaret took the first steps in establishing her school of pianoforte and dance and Toby resumed his work with the horses. Two months later, there was the thrill of moving into their new house. How they looked forward to hosting the McAlistair family, and, further down the track, Lonnie Sparks and his sweetheart as well. The McAlistairs were never far from Toby's mind. It was Toby who had telephoned them with the news of the racing scandal.

'What is it?' Clarissa had asked, seeing her mother's drawn face after coming off the telephone.

'Your husband.'

'What's he done?'

'He's got himself banned forever from racing horses.' She explained what had happened.

Clarissa sought for the support of a chair, stunned. She knew the implications of it immediately. The lofty horse-racing fraternity, who prided themselves on conducting the Sport of Kings in decorous fashion, had shunned her husband. Apart from the unsavoury Eddie Shaw, Henry Thompson, and Arthur Wilson, it was the only fraternity he cared about. Without the racing, what would he do? There was something else. She, as his wife, as a Drake, bore part of the shame. Once, the name 'Drake' had stood for honour and decency. Now, it stood for subterfuge and sharp practice. And by her association, she had dragged the McAlistair name into the mire.

'What have I done?' Clarissa asked herself. Elizabeth sat by her and put a comforting arm round her shoulder.

'There was nothing you could have done. It has all been his own doing.'

'He will never leave the house now, except for his boozing and whoring,' Clarissa said.

They sat for a long time in misery until eventually Sophie and then Harry joined them. After many tears from Clarissa and Sophie, and much frank discussion, they agreed the only possible course of action was complete severance from Simon Drake. The New Zealand Racing Conference had achieved it after one meeting and the stroke of a pen. With the holy sanctimony of marriage in 1908, and its legal bindings, it would never be that simple for Clarissa McAlistair and the McAlistair family. Though the house and estate belonged to Elizabeth, Simon Drake was the legal husband of her daughter and Glenview was his home as much as it was hers. Elizabeth could not simply have the police toss him and his baggage out by the ear, as much as she might wish it. There was also the shadowy, universal principle of the primacy of the male, reflected in so many legal documents.

◆ ◆ ◆

Simon Drake no longer had even the consolation of his friends' companionship. For Shaw, Wilson, and Thompson it was more rewarding to be cavorting with the son of a knight than with a man blackballed from the best company. For Shaw, too, there would be no more inside knowledge of racing and for Wilson, ambitious for a life in politics, there would be possible harm from association. And Thompson, desirous of more respect, had no wish to fraternise with a social pariah. In his silence and seclusion, one pang of conscience did gnaw away at Drake – the death of his apprentice. Baden Jones had been reluctant to use the electrical device but Drake had insisted and said he was down the road if he refused. Now, flickering in Drake's gin-soaked brain, was the image of the parents and sister of Baden

Jones weeping outside the ambulance room. Did the charge from the electrical device propel Jubilee Boy onto the hooves of the horse in front, causing it to fall and the jockey to lose his life? As Drake reflected alone in his cavernous house, he wished he could turn back the clock. The rest of the day passed in a blur of alcohol.

The next day he rose in bitterness and anger and set about selling High Flight Racing Lodge and his horses. He also got word to his lawyer, George Patrick, he wanted a meeting as soon as possible. Patrick, in Marton, was also the lawyer of Elizabeth McAlistair. At 2pm that same day, Simon Drake was seated in Patrick's office.

'The long and short of it George, is that I must call in your debt to me.'

George Patrick gazed at Drake in dismay. Patrick was of average height and slight build, with each hair of his head exactly where it should be, his moustache trimmed to perfection and his suit immaculate. At 55 and married with a grown-up family, he presented himself to the world as the very model of order and stability. His financial advice was much valued and many of the community had their investments with him. But, unbeknown to them, one ill-judged bet at horse racing a year before had cost him a packet and started him on the disastrous path of trying to make good his loss with another bet, so that he departed from betting in a disciplined, spare manner and began betting emotively and large. After he had run through his own savings, he had turned to those of his clients and many of those were sucked into the fearsome vortex of his gambling. Then, on the verge of having his embezzlement revealed, he had turned to Simon Drake who had bailed him out. Subsequently, by huge exercise of willpower, Patrick had reined his gambling in and begun to pay monies back into his clients' accounts.

'I am not yet in a position to repay you. Give me another six months.'

The day was cool but there was sweat on his brow. Exposure, he knew, would not only wreck his marriage but put him behind bars. Already, he had handed over the ownership to Drake of a promising young filly he had owned. Fortunately, when Margaret Fairbairn (now Margaret Page) had requested her funds towards the payment of their house, he had managed to scrabble together enough to replace those he had removed.

Drake twiddled with a pen from the desk. He saw the pasty face, the beads of sweat, the desperation in the eyes. He had Patrick at his mercy. 'There is one thing that will postpone repayment,' he said.

'What's that?'

'Show me the contents of the will of Elizabeth McAlistair.'

'You know I can't reveal that. Client privilege.'

'There is, then, no other way. You must repay me or it's the Law Society and the police.'

Patrick slumped. Just that morning he had begun to think he might yet escape from his difficulties.

Drake was well versed enough at poker to read his man. 'You need say nothing. Simply go to your file and leave it open on the desk for me to read. Then you will not have told me but I will know and I will be on my way.'

'You would ask that of me?' If he did as Simon Drake suggested, he would be yet more enslaved to the man, and conspiring against a woman he greatly respected.

'It will benefit both of us. Where is the damage? For God's sake, I am the woman's son-in-law. I have a right to know.'

'She has a right to keep her business private.'

'Do nothing then. Look away while I go to the file.' Drake rose, his blue eyes hard as ice.

In a ghastly kaleidoscope, Patrick saw the fallout from exposure: the despair of his wife, the rage of those he had betrayed, his life of shame in gaol. As Drake stepped towards his files, he reasoned, what is one more compromise? One look and he's gone and nobody need know. Patrick rose, went to the cabinet, removed the McAlistair file and left the will open on his desk for Simon Drake to read. As he sat down and turned away, he knew a part of him had died. It took Drake just a minute to absorb the gist of it. Written after the death of Charles McAlistair, the will stipulated that in the event of Elizabeth's death, the estate would go to Clarissa McAlistair, and, if she should be married, to her husband jointly. He read it twice to confirm the contents and smiled in satisfaction. It was standard for the times and what he had hoped and expected. He turned at the door.

'Be sure to tell me of any change.'

When the door closed, George Patrick felt dizzy and breathed deep until his heart calmed. Then he rose, closed the file, and returned it to the cabinet. The 'compromise' had at least given him more precious time to get the funds in order.

◆ ◆ ◆

As the election heated up, victimisation of Minnie Page continued. Instead of bottles by a letterbox, a cartoon poster of Minnie Page lurching along the street clutching a bottle was pasted on walls and pillars throughout the central city overnight. Police surveillance of Oriental Parade became regular. But as often as police called by to check for bottles or posters, no perpetrator was ever discovered.

'Don't worry yourselves too much,' Minnie told the police sergeant. 'I've had worse.'

In one way, the victimisation was a tribute to her success, not that she wanted it. The shouting and the noise of the liquor debate exceeded even that of the Parliamentary election, with the streets echoing to the verbal blasts and the newspapers full of it. And indeed, there were many hundreds of thousands of pounds involved in the sale of liquor, and many jobs at stake.

'It's not the bottles and posters which bother me,' said the sergeant. 'It's what might happen next. You have an enemy

somewhere out there and I suspect he's not right in the head.'
He pointed a finger at his head with a twirling motion.

Minnie Page shrugged. 'There's no good cause to be won except
by a fight.'

'Well, just you be careful m'lady,' the police sergeant said. 'Mark
my word. There are some rum ones out there.'

Caught up in the spirit of battle, Minnie Page continued to
speak at meetings, fending off the verbal barbs and returning
them with interest. She also cocked a snoot at danger by
purchasing a motor-car. So prolifically had people adopted
them that already there were many second-hand ones, selling
at a fraction of the cost of the new. Minnie Page chose a
10-12 horse-power Clement-Talbot, in bright red, all the better
to be seen by the unwary. Minnie was so small at the wheel
that, when observed head-on going up the slightest rise, the
car appeared to be driving itself and had given many people a
nasty turn. At first, before she had much understanding of the
controls, there were many close shaves with pedestrians and
horses and it got so bad that when neighbours heard her car
start up, they rang one another in warning. Later, she proved
to have a head for speed and one day her name appeared
in the newspaper along with those of burglars, thieves, and
vagabonds, for exceeding the speed limit by driving at 12 miles
per hour through an intersection. Another day she was fined
for leaving her car unattended. The sergeant began to think
she was more dangerous to others than others were to her, but
then he recalled the incensed eyes and hate-filled speech of the
extremists and kept a protective eye on her.

MEN ALONE

Solitary in the sitting room at Glenview, sprawled in the shadows of the lamplight with a bottle of whisky at hand, Simon Drake felt as abandoned as a mariner stranded on an atoll in an ocean. There had always been company: first his sisters and Ralph and then the lads at the boarding school where he had finished up a cock of the walk with a host of acolytes, and then his Hellfire companions and women. Always women. Now, there was no one to jest with, no one to bad mouth with, no one to discuss the horses with, no one to pour a glass. As he lolled back, drink in hand, he became aware of a ripple in the gin and tonic. This way and now that way. It was his right hand, trembling against his will. Delirium tremens, Dr Timothy Armitage would have told him. He put his glass down but the hand still trembled, even when he clasped his right wrist with his left hand. Damn and blast, what curse was this? Minutes later, to his great relief, the hand settled and he was able to pick up the glass again without it trembling. He pondered his options and after two more drinks concluded there was but one way forward – by means of the marriage and estate.

That same night, George Patrick, with the day's events heavy on his mind, was lying in bed unable to sleep. To steal from a client and to betray a client's confidence was one thing, and terrible enough. But to be an accessory to murder was another. In the morning, he reached for the telephone.

'Patrick at Marton, Mrs McAlistair. It is imperative I see you most urgently.'

'What's it about Mr Patrick?'

He had no wish to explain himself on the telephone. One operator with flapping ears could tell the whole district. He himself had heard scuttlebutt that had almost certainly started at the exchange. Most operators were discretion itself but it only takes one...

'I would rather not say. Could we please wait until I am with you.'

His reticence was alarming. She, along with many she knew, had her investments with her lawyer, not her bank. Charles and she had had no other lawyer than George Patrick, and he had always been most satisfactory. Was there a problem? Why else would be ask to meet with her urgently?

'Very well then, if we must.' She invited him to lunch and put the telephone down with a frown.

George Patrick rescheduled his appointments for the day and took the train to Wellington. An extravagant sunrise turned the sky a spectacular orange; he was grateful it was not red for a shepherd's warning. He was so preoccupied with the will, he scarcely noticed when he passed through the busy town centre of Palmerston North and by the quaint cottages of Shannon and of Otaki, and when the train passed Pukerua Bay, he saw nothing of the rolling breakers or misty Kapiti Island beyond. Every clanking, steamy mile of the way he saw Elizabeth McAlistair's will spread out on his desk and Simon Drake devouring its contents and then Drake turning to look at him so slyly and with such malice it chilled his heart. He knew first-hand the man's callousness and love of coin. He had seen him using a crooked deck at poker to screw a 'friend'. The report of the electrical device and the banning had not surprised him in the least. The worse mistake of his life had been to go to Simon Drake for a loan. Several times he opened his small travelling case, re-read a copy of the will, and pondered. By the time the train reached Johnsonville he knew he was doing the right thing, risky though it was.

Elizabeth McAlistair herself answered the door and took the lawyer straight into the study without even the offer of a cup of tea.

'What's this about?' She closed the door.

'I urge you most strongly to change your will.'

'My will?'

But Elizabeth was not entirely taken aback. She had been concerned about her will ever since the marriage of Clarissa and Simon Drake was mooted. Legal custom dictated that wife and husband were one so that property bequeathed to a daughter would, in practice, be bequeathed also to the husband.

'What do you know Mr Patrick?'

He fidgeted and hesitated.

'Sit down, sit down,' she said, gesturing to a chair and taking the one beside it herself.

He fumbled with his case and shakily withdrew a copy of her will. 'You must protect yourself and your daughter, Mrs McAlistair. Without delay.'

'It's Simon Drake isn't it. Is he a danger to me?'

He nodded, and involuntarily gave a small gasp of relief. That was one thing off his conscience though really, he had only replaced one fear with another.

'Should I summon the police?'

'No, no, don't do that. He has done nothing. It is what he might do that concerns me. Should you and Clarissa die, the property is his.'

'You are suggesting murder Mr Patrick.'

He cleared his throat. 'I am suggesting you change your will to remove the threat of danger to you, your daughter or other family.'

She looked at him long and hard and with gratitude.

'Let us get you a cup of tea and something to eat. You have

come a long way with great urgency with my family's interests at heart, and I appreciate it.'

After lunch, they withdrew into the study and began to draw up a new will. Elizabeth also discussed with George Patrick how Clarissa might best proceed with divorce from Simon Drake.

With business concluded and the lawyer departed for Marton, she ordered a taxi cab and called on Monty Powell. George Patrick had been visibly shaken when she had asked for an update on her holdings. He had blustered that she would have it at the first convenience. That had concerned her and she wanted advice on how best to pursue the matter.

Arthur Wilson, along with Eddie Shaw and Henry Thompson, had been devastated by the banning of Simon Drake by the New Zealand Racing Conference. It had cost Drake and their group enormous social cachet and for Arthur Wilson could not have come at a worse time.

'Damn fool,' said Wilson, caressing the end of his waxed moustache. 'The less I have to do with him the better.'

Shaw and Thompson nodded. Simon Drake had been a great disappointment to them lately and they could see that any further contact would only drag them down.

'Not the man we thought he was,' said Eddie Shaw, partner in countless scrapes and ruses.

'Bad form,' said Henry Thompson, beneficiary of several alibis provided by Drake.

Wilson was in the throes of his 1908 election campaign, speaking as a Conservative candidate at tinpot halls all over the Rangitikei district. His opponent was the well-entrenched Liberal candidate, Arthur Remington, but Wilson was not without hope. The Liberal Party had been in power for 17 years and social reform was slowing; workers were getting disenchanted. As well, now that land reform had been achieved, farmers appeared to be drifting to the Conservatives. Wilson had promoted himself as a man of integrity, a battling farmer, intent on improving the lot of the worker both in country and town. He was in fact quite the opposite, son of a well-to-do farmer and with a property of his own, riding round his fences on a large, white horse and chasing away the poachers of his game birds with a gun. As for his declared aim of 'A fair go for all', he had once been a member of the anti-women franchise league. He could scarcely believe his eyes at Marton when Minnie Page popped up. Bad enough to have an opposing view let alone have it stated by a woman. He had twanged his braces so hard he had damaged them and feared his trousers would fall down.

By December the results were in: Remington, Liberal, 2218 and Wilson, Conservative, 1877. Across the nation, the Liberal Party won 50 seats and the Conservatives 26, with Independent 3 seats and the Independent Labour League 1.

Arthur Wilson's supporters gave him a banquet and presented him with a tea and coffee service but he told them he would not contest the next election – he had found the whole thing an almighty travesty and strain. He had a standard reply for opposing views: 'But you must be wrong for I am a logical thinker'. Some, however, had gibed at the insinuation they were not and had even had the effrontery to call him arrogant.

His last word on the subject was, 'If the price of power and influence is to be forced to listen to the drivel of tradesmen, small farmers and women, then politics is not for me.'

◆ ◆ ◆

Minnie Page was pleased with the result of her efforts towards no-licence in Wellington. Both Wellington South and Wellington Suburbs had become no-license districts along with Bruce, Eden, Masterton and Ohinemuri. With the fait accompli, the hot air went out of the debate, at least for another three years, and soon the posters of the drunken, lurching Minnie Page were covered by fresh promotions. She was content to slip back into relative anonymity.

The anonymity did not last long. One Saturday morning shortly afterwards, during rain, Minnie took her Clement-Talbot for a spin around the streets above Oriental Bay. The horse of the milk cart must have been in a very good paddock the day before as its manure was spread copiously along a street Minnie Page was travelling down. Attempting to avoid the manure, Minnie spun the wheel sharply left and put the Clement-Talbot directly on a line towards a roadside tree. Seconds later, with the tree looming ever larger, she pushed her brake to the floor. But the horse's manure was not finished with her yet. Wet and clogging, it turned the car's tyres into skates and the motor-car slowed not a whit. It crashed with a fearful bang and crunch into the tree and became a story in Monday morning's newspaper.

Fortunately, the story was only a brief on page five, not an eye-catcher on page one. Minnie Page, by great fortune and the crumpling rather than disintegration of the motor vehicle, stepped from the wreckage of the Clement-Talbot unscathed. No skulduggery had occurred and even the publican who had arranged for the bottles and posters was pleased to hear Minnie Page was unhurt.

DEATH COMES STALKING

Events proceeded quickly after Elizabeth McAlistair's visit to Monty Powell. A broader inquiry began. That, in turn, led to the involvement of the police and charges being brought against George Patrick for embezzlement. Many had been aware of his punting but had no idea of the extent of it. Two who knew better were Simon Drake and his crooked bookmaker friend Scobie King ('King of the Ring' as he called himself). Patrick was heavily in debt to them both and when Patrick's bankruptcy and larceny became public knowledge, they decided it was time to pay him a visit.

Patrick was, as always now, alone in his office – he had laid his assistant off a month before. He could not afford to pay her and, anyway, he preferred the silence and solitude of the office, away as well from the weeping and distress in his home. It was late in the day when the two men arrived and no one was around. The office was suddenly cramped for Simon Drake had become decidedly fleshy since his disgrace and Scobie King, though only average in height, was as wide as he was tall. King's great bulk filled the doorway until George Patrick invited them to sit. Drake chose to remain standing. Patrick could not help but notice how ragged Drake appeared – his moustache was untidy, his hair unkempt and his clothing slovenly. His breath reeked of alcohol. King, by comparison, was pristine – his silver moustache neat, the fringe round the great bald dome of his head trimmed and his suit well-tailored. There was no alcohol on his breath for he had realised long before that bookmaking and alcohol do not mix. George Patrick was slight as a twig alongside their great trunks.

'Where's our money then?' said Drake.

'You know there is no money,' Patrick said.

Drake clenched his hands. 'How will you repay us?'

Patrick looked up at him with a blank face and empty eyes. He had reckoned the public exposure to be the greatest punishment he could face. It had devastated his wife and, he was certain, had destroyed his marriage. There was, though, something else. For the first time for years, he looked at Simon Drake without feeling under his power. Now, the whole world knew of his financial difficulties and Drake was simply one of many creditors.

'I have no idea,' said Patrick.

'You better get an idea, quick as you can.'

Then George Patrick remembered there was something he must tell Drake, something he had meant to tell him ever since he had returned from the meeting with Elizabeth McAlistair in Wellington. He had been waiting for the chance to tell him but just after his return the storm had broken and his life had unravelled. Now, he remembered his obligation.

'There is something you must know. Elizabeth McAlistair, of course, has now dropped me as her lawyer. But when we spoke in Wellington, she indicated she would be changing her will.'

Drake clenched his fist and took a step towards George Patrick so that he was towering right over him. 'You told her I had seen the will!' he roared. 'You tipped her off. Why else would you travel to see her?'

Patrick did not flinch. He felt past that. His fear had flown out the door. 'She has funds with me we needed to discuss.'

'What's the new will?'

'I don't know. She was talking about it, that was all. I never saw it.'

Drake took one more step forward and put his hands around Patrick's throat. 'Don't take me for a fool! You travelled to Wellington and advised her to change her will.'

'I advised her as lawyer to client, that is all.'

Drake called George Patrick names that should never be in print and with each word, tightened his grip around Patrick's slender neck. Patrick leant back in his chair and grasped Drake's arms but he had no strength to pull them apart. As he gasped for breath under the relentless grip, his eyes began to bulge and his face went red. Scobie King rose out of his chair as if he might come to the lawyer's assistance, but he took not a step. He stood and watched, transfixed, as Drake squeezed harder and harder, twisting Patrick's neck as if wringing the neck of a chicken, until the lawyer's arms were flopping uselessly, his lips were blue and, with one final wrench, his last breath was choked out of him. With a grunt and a final curse, Drake lifted the lifeless body and tossed it back into the chair like so much rubbish. Drake was breathing heavily, gasping. Then he began to curse until he ran out of words. He and King stood in silence for some time until King spoke.

'Well, here's a thing.'

'It was suicide. He was brought low by his business failings,' Drake said. Drake appeared to be emerging from a spell, shaking his hands as if to exonerate them from what they had done through fury and frustration.

Drake and King searched the office for a suitable site for a hanging. They found it above a doorway. The room had the standard high ceiling and just an inch or two from the top was a hook from which a heavy painting was suspended. Fossicking in a cupboard, Drake found a cord. Drake tied the cord around the corpse's throat in such a way that it might very well have caused the bruising there. Then, positioning the table and climbing on top of it with the aid of a chair, he removed the painting, tied the cord to the hook, and, with the help of King, hung the body from the hook. Back on the ground, he pulled away the table, placing it on its side, and let the body swing.

'Overcome by the shame,' said Drake, 'he climbed onto the chair and then the table, put the cord on the hook and round his miserable fecking neck, and then kicked the table away. Good riddance.'

◆ ◆ ◆

To the relief of Elizabeth and Clarissa McAlistair, when they next met with Monty Powell at Glenview, Simon Drake was alone, lolling in his chair, with no woman and no louche companions. To their consternation, though, he already had a glass of spirits in his hand and it was not yet 10 am. Clarissa became aware for the first time, on seeing him, there was no quickening of her heart nor craving in her limbs. The magnetic blue eyes were almost hidden behind folds of fat, his jowls hung heavy, his gut drooped and his clothing was shabby and dishevelled. He appeared to have lost all respect for himself. Elizabeth and Clarissa looked at each other in dismay that he could be Clarissa's husband. If Charles McAlistair could see them now!

'You've deigned to visit me then,' Simon Drake said. 'Are you sure I'm good enough for you?'

Monty Powell turned his back on him and moved through to the study, leaving Elizabeth and Clarissa to talk with Drake.

'There is nothing we can say to you until you stop your drinking,' Elizabeth said. 'How can we talk about your future at Glenview when your brain is swimming with alcohol?'

'My future at Glenview.' Drake looked from one to the other, sneering. 'I can assure you, my future at Glenview is very rosy. Very rosy indeed.' He slurred his words. 'No bitch of a mother-in-law and no bitch of a wife meddling in what is rightfully mine.'

Clarissa tossed her head and gestured at Elizabeth for her to join Monty Powell in the study. Elizabeth left Clarissa and Drake alone.

'It's finished,' Clarissa said. 'I can take no more. We are guests of Toby and Margaret Page at their house in Palmerston North from tomorrow. When we return in three days' time, I will begin proceedings for divorce. Just mind how you treat Mary and the other staff while I'm gone.'

'You'll not get out of that Scot-free,' he said. 'Just remember my entitlements.'

 'I just want you gone from my life. You deserve nothing from me.'

'We'll see about that.'

❖ ❖ ❖

Simon Drake had never had trouble finding people to do his bidding. He knew that every society has scum who will do the most heinous work for coin. At Marton he had removed the problem of George Patrick himself but emotion had got the better of him. Now, he would revert to keeping his distance. But he would have to be swift to take advantage of the opportunity to remove all the obstacles in his way as well as interfering, fecking Toby Page.

If drowning were the New Zealand death, fire was next, what with open fireplaces, clothing catching alight, lamps with oil and candles with naked flames, gas liable to explode and use of cigarettes and tobacco so prevalent. Every week, at least one fire was reported. Indeed, one recent day there were fires from Invercargill to New Plymouth and another day 13 businesses were destroyed by fire in Hastings. Just as there would be little surprise a crooked lawyer had committed suicide on being exposed, Drake reasoned, there would be little surprise at the destruction of a house by fire and the tragic loss of the people within it. He knew two Wellington men tailormade for the job. They specialised in fires of commercial premises. On the files of the Fire Brigade and the insurance company, the fires were suspicious but origin unknown. Perhaps Ernie Hood and Francis Lindt saw their arsons as a natural extension of their job as coal and firewood merchants. Drake downed the last of his drink, readied his trap, and set off for Wellington. He told the staff he would be back the next day. They were pleased to see the back of him for a night.

It was such joy for Elizabeth, Clarissa, Harry, and Sophie to visit Toby and Margaret at their new house at Palmerston North. It was their first meeting since the wedding and there was much to talk about. Margaret quizzed Sophie about her singing. She had heard with her own ears how the ebullient but demanding Madame Probert had developed the range of Sophie's voice and brought out its natural richness. The skilled and sympathetic accompaniment of Maurice Sutherland had also been a help. Seeing Sophie light up at mention of his name,

Margaret probed further and became certain another wedding was on the horizon. Clarissa wanted to hear about the horses. What did Toby have in the stable? What champions were in the making? She had always followed her father's horses closely. All the visitors were agog about the modern appliances in the house – the 'Perfection' oil stove, the high-pressure boiler, the Banner Rotary washing machine (at £3. 10s and under twopence per wash, their very presence meant economy). Sophie admired the upright grand piano by Allison and Co, London.

Elizabeth outlined the trouble at Glenview for Toby and Margaret, and then put it aside for the rest of their stay and sat back and basked in the warmth of the company. They talked late into the night and all of them except Toby, who rose compulsively at 3.30 am to tend to his horses, slept well into the morning. That day they explored and picnicked in the spectacular Manawatu Gorge and by the time they returned to the house, they were ready for an early night. All the lights were out by 10pm and the Page house slumbered.

At 1am, Ernie Hood and Francis Lindt slunk from their hotel, not far away in Main Street, Palmerston North, and drove swiftly in Lindt's horse and trap to a point just south of their target in Awapuni. There, they took the trap off the road and hitched the horse to a fence. Their baggage was slight – just paper, a bundle of kindling, a half-tin of kerosene and a box of matches. The kerosene was only to be used as a last resort as it could complicate the insurance payout. Hood was short and thin as a whip with the face of a weasel, while Lindt was a tall man and fleshy from the copious amount of beer and meat pies he consumed. Both were moustachioed and wore caps. The sliver of moon cast only the slightest of lights as they crossed the adjoining paddock. They had no difficulty identifying the house to be torched. They had scouted the place out during the day, confirmed it as the dwelling of horse trainer Toby Page and his wife and seen no one in or around it. They had been told no one would be in the house that night and that the owner of the house was hungry for the insurance money and a party to its destruction. Sure enough, the owners must be away. There would be no prying eyes of neighbours to see them come and go – the house stood alone, with nothing but a low fence between them and its timber cladding.

Now, as they stepped over the fence, Hood murmured.

'Money for jam.'

Lindt put his finger to his lips. They were experienced arsonists and prided themselves on their thorough preparation and execution. Silence was a crucial component of that. They stepped lightly to the side of the house on the blind side of neighbours in the far distance and no one saw them place their paper against the cladding of the house, some 10 yards apart, and pile their kindling against it. They had been paid half the fee of £50 already.

On the other side of the cladding, Sophie McAlistair lay sleeping. The two days and nights with Toby and Margaret, her mother, Clarissa, and Harry had been profoundly satisfying. Time with one she had loved before as a friend and now loved as a brother, and with one she had loved as her accompanist and now loved as a sister-in-law. She had cherished participating in their wedding. There had been the new house to celebrate as well. Before retiring to bed that evening, they had gathered round the piano and Margaret had accompanied them in a general sing-song. Then Sophie had sung *The Last Rose of Summer* and *Queen of the Night*. Now, with the rest of her beloved family, she slept in peace.

It was time for the flame. Hood and Lindt, at a signal, struck their matches, the paper flared and the kindling started to burn fiercely. Flames leapt onto the cladding. It began to smoulder and wisps of smoke rose. But to the arsonists' dismay, the fire did not properly take hold and they had nearly used up their paper and kindling. On the other side of the cladding, Sophie McAlistair began to stir. She had smelt smoke. She lay in the darkness, trying to make sense of it. It was a summer's evening and not unduly cold. There had been no fire in the hearth and the heaters had not been on. Was the smoke from the kitchen? She rose and carefully made her way through the house. Night was no different to her than day and she had mentally noted already the placement of furniture. Nothing burning in the kitchen. She returned to her bedroom. Still the smell of smoke. Reluctantly, she went to Toby and Margaret's room and woke Toby. He came to her bedroom, smelt a faint whiff of smoke, looked out into the blackness and thought he detected a movement. Hurrying through the sitting room, he grabbed the fire poker and opened the back door.

In the still of the night, Hood and Lindt heard the opening of the door as clearly as if church bells had started up. Hood had been reluctant to use the kerosene but it had been necessary to use a tiny amount to set the blaze going. With the sound of the door, he panicked. He grabbed the tin, flung the remainder of the kerosene on, and prepared to run. But the fire ran right up the stream of kerosene, engulfed the can in flames and then leapt on to his clothing. As Toby appeared round the corner of the house, shouting, Hood was burning like a candle while Lindt was vanishing into the night. Toby launched himself at the flaming, screaming man feet-first and shouted for blankets. Sophie ripped them from a bed and hurried them out to him. Toby threw one over the man and trampled down its edges to smother the flames. The man's screams of agony and Toby's shouts brought the rest of the household running and set the dog in the faraway house barking. In moments Margaret was on the telephone to the fire service, ambulance, and police.

The kerosene had caused the flames on the cladding to flare but Toby thanked God the flames had not whooshed up in a fireball. He also thanked God the timber was jarrah and highly resistant to fire. He grabbed a spare blanket from the pile Sophie had brought and used it to smother the burning on the cladding. The timber was no more than charred, despite the kerosene. He had no doubt, though, that without Sophie's warning, the house would have gone up in cinders – the arsonist would have found something outside that burned and God knows there was plenty inside that would burn, including his family. Harry had brought a lamp and as they assisted the groaning arsonist by easing the burning with blankets and water, Toby voiced all their thoughts.

'This could have been us.'

The smell of the man's burnt flesh filled the air.

'Thank God I smelled the smoke,' Sophie said.

'Sophie saved us,' Elizabeth said. And that was true – if Sophie had not been blind, her sense of smell might not have been as acute.

Elizabeth and Clarissa remembered Simon Drake back at Glenview and exchanged a wordless look.

The fire service arrived first followed soon after by the ambulance and then the police. The police had been slightly delayed by the arrest of a man fleeing the scene.

FINALE

That evening Simon Drake instructed the kitchen staff at Glenview to prepare a sumptuous meal by way of celebration. When it was served – enough for two gourmands – he instructed them to leave him for the night. This triumph would be savoured alone. He had temporarily lost his acolytes but he had no doubt Shaw, Thompson and Wilson would be back and their usual sycophantic selves when he was master of Glenview and running a stable. The racing officials could not keep him out forever. There had not been a proper inquiry into the use of the electrical stimulant and he was confident he could defer blame on to bookmaking interests. As he sat alone at the dining room's long table with his food and liquor at hand, he visualised his hirelings going about their work that could begin his return to polite society. For an instant he imagined the flames crisping skin and roasting flesh and winced, but then he consoled his conscience that they would be dead already from the smoke inhaled, smothered during sleep. Fires were so prevalent. In just the last week, people had died in house fires in Nelson, Rangiora, and Dunedin. The death of six more in Palmerston North would cause a sad shaking of heads and spur a call for greater safety but would soon be forgotten. When he finished the meal, he drank the last of a bottle of Bordeaux, uncorked another and replenished his glass. An hour later he was sprawled on a couch asleep in the adjoining sitting room.

Hours later, a thunderous knock at the door in the dark of the night stirred him from his drunken sleep. Despite his addled state, he knew instantly it was the police, to tell him of the tragic deaths. Drake opened the door just before the sergeant's fist struck it for the fourth time. By the dim light of the moon, four burly policemen looked back at him.

'Mr Drake?' queried the sergeant, though he had little doubt.

And then, to Drake's surprise, a hand clamped on his shoulder.

By dawn, others were bustling in and out. From their interview of Mary, other staff, and the McAlistairs, the police got abundant information on Simon Drake's indulgent lifestyle but scant else of interest. From their interviews of Hood and Lindt, however, they got plenty for the trial two months later in Wellington. Nine years before, it had been Toby Page in the dock and Simon Drake a witness. Now, it was Simon Drake in the dock and Toby Page and Margaret Fairbairn spectators. The courtroom was as crammed as back then. Elizabeth and Clarissa, too filled with disgust and horror, chose not to attend.

As Toby looked at Drake and his two accomplices, Hood and Lindt, he felt a satisfying sense of retribution but also a disturbing and confusing wave of other emotions. Was he reliving his own ghastly time in the dock? Was he imagining a different outcome – charred bones and ashes? Had the agony of his mother's kidnapping and incarceration resurfaced? Was it the glimpse once more of the extent of rage and bitterness that could engulf a man? Drake, unusually, was now stone cold sober. His face was pale, his moustache untidy and there was stubble on his chin. He had looked once around the courtroom, seen no friend or family, and hadn't looked again. Toby put an arm round Margaret and drew her closer.

Ernie Hood, still bandaged, and Francis Lindt, gazed on resignedly. They had pleaded guilty to attempted incendiarism. In their defence, their counsel said they had understood the house was empty.

Judge Davidson looked at them coldly. 'In your favour, you pleaded guilty, named the man who paid you for the arson and confessed to previous arsons. Seven years' imprisonment.'

Lindt, especially, would do it hard with no beer and few pies.

Simon Drake had pleaded not guilty to procuring others to commit culpable homicide.

'Guilty,' said the jury foreman.

'Ten years' imprisonment with hard labour,' said Judge Davidson. 'I wish it could be more but that is the maximum I am permitted to impose.'

The judge then addressed all three as one. 'But for your own incompetence and the swift response of those you would have killed, there would likely be convictions for murder and probable hanging by the neck until dead.'

Drake, already looking shrunken, followed the others down the stairs out of sight. From there they would be transported to The Terrace Gaol, towering over the suburb of Te Aro, where they would be weighed and measured, don prison dress, and be put in their cells with hammock, blankets, pillow, dish, pannikin, knife, spoon, and piss-pot. Next morning Drake would be marched to Mt Cook to make bricks all day.

Clarissa McAlistair, to her surprise, felt shaken and unsettled as well as relieved. She had known immediately after marriage it had been a mistake. Day by day, he had become more truculent and tyrannical and she had felt as though she were on a chain, tugged every which way he wished. Finally, she had had to admit to herself he cared nothing for her; it was all about the estate. She wondered how she had never seen his abiding bitterness and selfishness long before. Now, she could readily obtain a divorce and part from him for ever.

That night, Elizabeth and Clarissa decided to move back into Glenview. Within the week, Sophie had news for them.

'Maurice has proposed and we will marry in three months.' They gazed on a spectacular engagement ring of glittering diamonds set in a sea of turquoise. Maurice and his delighted mother had described it to her so exactly, Sophie could see it in her mind's eye. She and Maurice would remain in Wellington. They were looking to buy in Kelburn. Sophie had another surprise for them, regarding Harry. 'Possibly another bird soon flying from the nest. Harry's been escorting my dear friend Matilda around town and from what I hear, they are besotted with each other.'

A grilling of Sophie revealed that Matilda was a gifted mezzo soprano whom Sophie had known for years.

'At this rate we will be able to open up our family sing-alongs to the public and charge,' Clarissa said to Elizabeth. 'Margaret and Maurice accompanists, Sophie and Matilda soloists or a duet, Harry a pleasing baritone and you and me the gas bag and wind instrument in the corner.'

'Get away with you,' laughed Elizabeth. 'Though you could have a point.'

That month another gathering took place around the table at Glenview, hosted by Elizabeth and Clarissa. The meal and wine were fine and the company free and easy. Toby and Margaret were there, along with Harry and Matilda, Sophie and Maurice, and Minnie and Walter de Vere, a wealthy widower, a kind man, and Minnie's current escort around town. She was still dear friends with J.P. Staveley but thrived on variety. The evening flew. At one point Elizabeth looked at the happy faces at the table, and the happy face of the parlour maid serving them, and felt the presence of Charles. She was sure he would have approved of the gathering. As for Toby, for the first time for as long as he could remember, he was at peace.

HISTORICAL EVENTS

R eal dates and events in New Zealand in the period of this novel

1891   The Liberal Party is elected.

From this year, Acts are passed that facilitate the State purchase of large estates.

1893   Richard John Seddon becomes leader of the Liberal Party

Universal suffrage is introduced for women aged over 21.

A liquor licensing poll is introduced.

The Government's Criminal Code includes punishments of flogging, whipping and hard labour

for homosexual acts.

1894   Compulsory arbitration of industrial disputes and reformed employment laws including

registration and inspection of factories.

1896   A census measures the national population as 743,214.

The National Council of Women is founded.

1897   Bob Fitzsimmons wins the World Heavyweight Boxing Championship, defeating Jim Corbett.

1898   The pension is introduced for the 'deserving poor'

The first cars are imported.

1899   New Zealand sends troops to the South African War.

1900   The Public Health Act is passed setting up a Department of Public Health in 1901

The Workers Compensation for Accidents Act is passed.

1901   Queen Victoria dies. Edward VII succeeds her.

Royal Tour: The Duke and Duchess of York and Cornwall, the future King George V

and Queen Mary, visit New Zealand.

1903   The first race meeting is held on the new course at Awapuni, Palmerston North.

1905-6   The New Zealand representative football team (The All Blacks) tour Great Britain, Ireland, and France, winning 34 matches and losing one.

1906   The first race meeting is held on the new course at Trentham, Wellington.

1907   New Zealand changes from colony to dominion.

Last-known huia sighted and then shot.

1908   The widow's pension is introduced.

The Auckland to Wellington main trunk railway line opens.

The population reaches one million.

ACKNOWLEDGEMENTS

Thanks

once again to my wife Dale for her cheerful support.

to Sean Monaghan of the Palmerston North City Library for his well-informed advice on publishing, so willingly given.

to the National Library of New Zealand for their wonderful Papers Past which opens a window on the country's history.

to Amazon.com

BOOKS BY THIS AUTHOR

The Rugby Quiz Book (With Craig Mcfarlane

Fancy That!

Black Jersey Silver Fern Tom Ellison

New Zealand On Foot

New Zealand Adventures By Rail

The Good Citizen

Group Tours Unveiled

Billy Wallace

The Walking Frame War

www.ingramcontent.com/pod-product-compliance
Lightning Source LLC
Chambersburg PA
CBHWC22017240626
47154CB00007B/2150